"That was a hot kiss. I'll grant you that."

It had set Darcy on fire, and she was still uncomfortably aroused. "But it doesn't mean I'm going to sleep with you."

Patrick's eyes went all heavy-lidded again. "You want to."

"Doesn't matter. This can't go anywhere. You're going back to Detroit in a few weeks." Her heart thudded heavily as he held her gaze. If he kept looking at her like that, they'd be in her bedroom in minutes.

"It would be a fun few weeks," he said, his voice a low rasp.

Yeah, it would. But it was the kind of fun she couldn't afford to have. "I'm not interested in flings."

He shifted his feet, as if he was uncomfortable. "I didn't think you were, but it was worth a try." His mouth curved into a smile as he watched her. "And I'm not giving up."

Her breath caught. "I'm pretty good at saying no."

"I'll do my best to change your mind."

Dear Reader,

Have you ever wanted to run away from something in your past? Change parts of your life? Yeah, me too. I'm sure all of us have been there. What happens, though, when you're *forced* to run away? When you have to change *everything* about yourself, from your name to the way you look to your job? And what if you've committed a crime while doing it?

Meet Darcy Gordon, who had to flee an abusive ex-husband to save her life. Although she regrets all the lies and is sorry about the crimes she's committed, Darcy knows she had no choice. Then she meets Patrick Devereux. An FBI agent. A man who can bring her world crashing down.

I loved bringing these two people together—the fugitive and the cop. How do you tell someone who you really are when it could be the most dangerous thing you've ever done? Trust is such a fragile thing. Yet it's vital when two people fall in love.

I hope you enjoy Darcy and Patrick's journey to trust and love. I really enjoyed writing it. And I love to hear from readers! You can contact me through my website, www.margaretwatson.com, or at margaret@margaretwatson.com.

Yours,

Margaret Watson

The Woman He Knows

MARGARET WATSON

HARLEQUIN®

entertain, enrich, inspire™

Recycling programs
for this product may
not exist in your area.

ISBN-13: 978-0-373-71804-7

THE WOMAN HE KNOWS

Copyright © 2012 by Margaret Watson

ABOUT THE AUTHOR

Margaret Watson has always made up stories in her head. When she started actually writing them down, she realized she'd found exactly what she wanted to do with the rest of her life. Almost twenty years after staring at that first blank page, she's an award-winning, two time RITA® Award finalist, who was recently honored by Harlequin for her twenty-fifth book. When she's not writing or spending time with her family, she practices veterinary medicine. Although she enjoys that job, writing is her passion. Margaret lives in a Chicago suburb with her husband and three daughters and a menagerie of pets.

Books by Margaret Watson

HARLEQUIN SUPERROMANCE

1205—TWO ON THE RUN
1258—HOMETOWN GIRL
1288—IN HER DEFENSE
1337—FAMILY FIRST
1371—SMALL-TOWN SECRETS
1420—SMALL-TOWN FAMILY
1508—A PLACE CALLED HOME*
1531—NO PLACE LIKE HOME*
1554—HOME AT LAST*
1608—AN UNLIKELY SETUP
1638—CAN'T STAND THE HEAT?
1673—LIFE REWRITTEN
1696—FOR BABY AND ME
1768—A SAFE PLACE

*The McInnes Triplets

Other titles by this author available in ebook format.

For Chelsea,
my wise, charming and brilliant daughter.
You are an amazing woman and
I am so very, very proud of you.

CHAPTER ONE

DARCY STEPPED ONTO the small patio of Mama's Place and stood in the shadows for a moment, watching. The dark could hide many things.

The restaurant was closed, and the waitresses and cooks were doing their final cleanup. As she began to pick up the table settings, the night air was fragrant with the sharp scent of chrysanthemums and the first hint of wood burning in fireplaces. She could take a deep breath for the moment.

But she had to be alert, as well.

She slid another ketchup bottle and four more sets of cutlery onto the large tray, and found a tip stuck beneath the salt shaker. Four singles. She made a mental note to give it to Phyllis.

"How are you doing out here, Darce?"

Nathan. "I'm good," she answered without bothering to turn around. No matter how many times she told him she didn't need help, Nathan would do what he did every night—he'd put the chairs on top of the tables, fold and put away the umbrellas. The restaurant owner didn't want his waitresses lifting the heavy, awkward furnishings.

"It was a good night," he said with satisfaction.

"I got a lot of compliments on Marco's specials."

"My brother's pretty amazing."

"You sound surprised." Darcy smiled. "He's all grown up now, and he's a fabulous chef."

"I have to stop thinking of him as that irritating fifteen-year-old." Nathan grunted as he lifted an umbrella from its base. "Too bad you don't have any siblings, Darcy. You don't know what you missed."

She laughed. "I have siblings, Nate. You and Marco. My favorite brothers."

Nathan grinned as he set the umbrella inside the door. "And you're my second favorite sister. First, sometimes, when Frankie's a pain in the ass."

Darcy suppressed a tiny stab of envy. The Devereux siblings were a close-knit group. Their love for one another was obvious.

Maybe, if she'd had a sibling, things would have been different. Maybe she wouldn't have been so desperate for a family that she allowed Tim to talk her into marriage.

"How's Patrick?" she asked casually. The fourth Devereux was an FBI agent in Detroit. She'd met him only once, but the feelings he'd roused hadn't been sisterly. He'd come to Chicago several weeks ago for Frankie's engagement party, but instead of paying attention to his sister, he'd watched Darcy all evening. Her skin still prickled when she thought about his blue eyes focused on her like a spotlight.

She would take a few days off when he came back for Frankie's wedding.

FBI attention. She shuddered. Her worst nightmare.

No. Her second worst nightmare.

"He's good," Nathan said, struggling with the corner umbrella. "Too busy to visit."

Thank God. She helped free the base of the umbrella for him.

As she stood, a car drove past, slowing when it reached the restaurant. For a moment, the headlights illuminated her. Then the vehicle sped up, and Darcy watched its taillights disappear. Illinois license plate. Probably checking to see if Mama's Place was open.

At eleven o'clock, the street was almost deserted in this small business district nestled in a residential neighborhood on the northwest side of Chicago. That's why Darcy had settled here. Big city, small-town feel. The restaurant was on the corner of a busy street close to the train tracks. The last commuter train of the evening had already been through, and now only the occasional car passed by. In Wildwood, this time of night, the darkness hid her well.

A low roar grew louder as another car accelerated down the street. She turned to help Nathan carry the umbrella inside but he dropped it and shouted, "Darcy! Move!"

She stared at him, puzzled, then he shoved her toward the open door. As she went flying into the restaurant she heard a sickening thud.

Scrambling to her feet, she saw that the flimsy fence around the seating area was crushed, and Nathan lay beneath an overturned table. His left leg was bent at an unnatural angle and blood pooled beneath it. As she ran to him, a dark car swerved back onto the street and drove off, the sound of its engine swallowed by the night.

MAMA'S PLACE had reopened three days ago. It had been closed for two days. On the first, everyone had been at the hospital with Nathan. The second day, they'd cleaned up the patio and figured out how to manage without him for six weeks... or longer.

Now it seemed as if everyone in Wildwood wanted to eat at Mama's. There was an hour-long wait for a table tonight, and Darcy had called two extra waitresses in to work.

Glancing at Theresa Smith, sitting at her usual table at the window, Darcy seated a couple, then hurried to the kitchen to pick up the order for the four top in the corner. No way was she going to hurry Theresa along. The woman needed the respite that her evenings at Mama's provided.

No one seemed in a particular rush tonight, anyway. All the customers wanted to know what had happened to Nate, and she had the answers down pat.

"The police think it was a drunk driver." "Nathan will be in the hospital for a while, but he's going to be fine." "Broke his left leg in three places and his left arm in two." "No, the police haven't caught the driver yet."

She knew everyone was worried about Nathan. The Devereux roots ran deep in Wildwood—the siblings had been born there, and the restaurant was a neighborhood institution. Of course people wanted to know what had happened.

But every time someone asked about the accident, it ratcheted up her guilt a little more. If Nathan hadn't stopped to push her out of the way, he wouldn't have gotten hurt. He wouldn't be lying in a hospital bed, rods and bolts sticking out of his leg and arm, immobilized by a complicated, traction-like device above his bed.

The fear was even more insidious. What if the driver of that car hadn't been a random drunk? What if he'd known exactly what he was doing? What if he'd hit the wrong person?

He would be back.

Her instincts were screaming for her to run. To pack her meager belongings and leave Chicago far behind.

She had to ignore them.

Nathan had been injured trying to protect her. She couldn't abandon his family when they needed her help.

Not to mention Theresa Smith. Darcy could help the woman, if only Theresa would give her a chance.

Darcy stopped by her table. "How are you doing, Theresa?" she asked quietly.

"I'm fine." The middle-aged woman, her dark hair carefully coifed, didn't look at Darcy. Instead, she sipped her martini and continued to gaze out the window.

Darcy saw the healing bruise, half-hidden beneath the cuff of Theresa's blouse.

Anger burning, she glanced toward the bar. The man who always accompanied Theresa sat on a stool, a glass of amber liquid in front of him as he watched a baseball game on television.

"Let me know if you need anything," she said, touching the woman's shoulder lightly.

"I will." She finally looked at Darcy and her carefully blank expression relaxed a little. "Thank you."

"Anytime. You know that, right? You memorized my phone number?"

Her nod was a barely perceptible movement.

Theresa came to Mama's two or three times a week, had two martinis, picked at the food she ordered. The same beefy guy escorted her every night. When she'd asked Theresa if it was her husband, she had shaken her head. "My...protection. My husband is very concerned about my safety."

Theresa never used a credit card, and it had taken her six months to tell Darcy her last name. Judging by her reluctance to meet Darcy's eyes when she did it, it was probably false, anyway.

A few weeks ago, Darcy had followed her into the restroom. Knowing the signs well, she had asked the older woman if she was being abused. Theresa had shaken her head. But her eyes glittered with tears as she'd locked herself in a stall.

Darcy couldn't abandon her.

The waitresses and Marco had been struggling to keep Mama's Place going since the accident. Patrick and Frankie had been at the hospital with Nathan. In a few days, when he was more stable, Frankie was going to take over managing the restaurant.

At least it wouldn't be Patrick. Having him around all the time would be too stressful. Too...distracting. She hadn't forgotten the way he'd watched her at Frankie's engagement party.

Hadn't forgotten the way she'd watched him back. Or the awareness of him that she had felt all night.

When Frankie took over, she'd need Darcy's help. She had no choice but to stay.

If the driver of that car *had* been a random drunk, she was as safe as she'd been before.

If not, she'd just have to be more careful. More watchful. One of the things she liked about Wildwood was that everyone knew their neighbors. If a stranger was looking for Darcy, she'd hear about it.

A very thin safety net, but it was all she had.

THE NEXT AFTERNOON, in the quiet before the restaurant opened at five, Darcy closed her eyes as she tasted Marco's butternut-squash ravioli with brown butter sage sauce. "Your brother is not paying you enough money, dude."

Marco grinned and bumped fists with her. "I think I'm in love. Marry me, Darce."

"Let me think." She took another bite and the flavors exploded on her tongue. "Food like this? I'd marry you in a second." She pointed her fork at him. "Oh, wait. I can get this food by coming to work every day. Never mind."

"You're breaking my heart."

"That's life." She swabbed the last ravioli through the sauce and sighed as she finished it. "I hope you made plenty. We're going to run out of this."

Phyllis and Ashley agreed. The fourth waitress, Carol, squinched her face. "People like regular ravioli," she said.

Everyone sitting around the large table in the corner shrugged. Carol never liked any of Marco's specials. She never liked much of anything. All of them had learned to ignore her.

The waitresses usually arrived an hour early to set up, then taste Marco's daily specials. It had been six days since Nathan's accident, and Carol's complaints meant things were getting back to normal.

Nathan was the only one missing.

"What's the update?" Phyllis asked.

"He's good." Marco dished out small plates of the seafood pasta. "Antsy as hell, though. Asking about the restaurant, insisting he needs to come home. They think it will be a few more days. He'll be in bed for a while, then in a wheelchair, but Patrick and Frankie are going to take turns staying with him. Home health care will fill in the gaps."

"Patrick doesn't have to get back to Detroit?" Darcy asked, keeping her voice casual.

"He took a leave of absence, so he'll be around for a while." Marco tasted the pasta. "Said he needed to be here for us."

The shrimp in Darcy's mouth was suddenly tasteless. So

was Marco's spicy sauce. "I thought he only had a few days. How long is 'a while'?"

"As long as we need him, he said." Marco ate a scallop. "My guess? Not that long. He'll go into withdrawal if he's not catching bad guys."

"Sounds like he takes his job pretty seriously."

"That's Paddy. Serious to the bone. Mr. Black and White."

"He doesn't sound like a lot of fun," Phyllis said with a wink. The waitress was closer to fifty than forty, with bright red hair and a perpetual smile. She definitely enjoyed life.

"Hey, Paddy can be a lot of fun," Marco said. He winked back at Phyllis. "As long as you're not a criminal."

Her hand trembling, Darcy picked up her dirty dishes and carried them into the kitchen. As she deposited them by the dishwasher, the back door opened and a tall figure with dark hair walked in.

Patrick.

Her heart raced and her hands got clammy. Avoiding his gaze, she headed toward the dining room. "Darcy?" Patrick called. "Hold on a minute."

As he got closer, his bright blue eyes scanned her, as if he were committing her face to memory. "I'm Patrick. We met at Frankie's engagement party."

"Right. Hi, Patrick." She wiped her hands on her apron. "How's Nathan doing today?"

"Cranky. Always a good sign."

She managed to smile, although her face felt as if it would crack. "It is."

His gaze lingered on her short, layered hair, and she smoothed it back self-consciously. Were her blond roots showing? "Let's go in the other room where it isn't so noisy," he said. "I need to talk to you."

She froze for a moment as he held the swinging door open, then forced her legs to move. Her heart racing, her palms sweating, she wondered what he wanted. Why he wanted to talk to *her*.

"Hey, Marco," Patrick said with a wave as he followed her.

He poured himself a cup of coffee and offered her one. When she shook her head, he led the way to a table in the corner opposite the one where the other waitresses and Marco still sat.

"Nathan told me you're organized and smart, and you pay attention to everything. I'm throwing myself on your mercy, because I'm going to need your help."

"With what?" The end of the red-checked tablecloth lay on her lap, and she pleated it with fingers that shook.

"Running Mama's Place. I worked here years ago, but I was just a kid. All I had to do was clear tables and wash dishes. I didn't have to actually think about the business."

"You're running the restaurant?" Darcy swallowed. "Marco said Frankie was doing it."

"She offered, but Frankie has her plate full right now. She's expanding her teen center, some kid she knows is about to have a baby, and she and Cal are planning their wedding." He shook his head. "Those two could be a commercial for the Lifetime channel, and I don't have the stomach to watch it."

"How…romantic." As soon as the words were out of her mouth, Darcy closed her fist around the tablecloth. Had she really said that?

She was too used to joking around with Nathan and Marco.

One side of his mouth curled up. "Nathan said you had a mouth on you." He studied her assessingly. "You have something going with him?"

"With Nathan? Nah! He's like a brother. Marco, too." Heat crept up her face and she cleared her throat. "Why?"

"I like to connect all the dots. Put the pieces together, see how they fit." He shrugged.

"I work for your brothers. It would be stupid to get involved with either of them."

"Lot of stupidity going around."

"Not here. Not me." When she'd started at Mama's Place, she'd been too on edge to pay attention to anyone. By the time she'd relaxed a little, been able to take a deep breath, Nathan and Marco were the guys she worked for. Joked around with. Friends. They'd never be more.

"Focused on your job?" He raised one eyebrow.

"Yep."

"Good. Then you won't mind helping me out. Nathan said you've been working four nights a week. Would you be able to take on a fifth?"

She volunteered at the women's shelter on her nights off. "Maybe. I'll check."

"We really need you, Darcy."

She knew that. But the women needed her, too. "I'll let you know."

His gaze sharpened. "You have another job?"

"No, other commitments." She should tell him what she was doing, but keeping secrets had become second nature.

"Okay. Can you run me through a typical night? Tell me what Nathan does?"

TWO HOURS LATER, Patrick stood at the podium by the door, watching a smiling Darcy chat with a table of two couples. There were several people waiting to be seated, the bartender was mixing drinks as fast as he could and was still behind, and the busboy was moving too slowly.

Finally a table was ready, and Patrick called the next name on the waiting list. He smiled as he seated the group of four and told them their waitress would be right over.

On the way back to the podium, he helped the busboy clear another table, then seated the next group on the list.

Patrick had a million other things to think about tonight. But he found himself looking for Darcy again. Just like he'd done too many times this evening.

Which was stupid. But he'd thought about her, off and on, since Frankie's engagement party. He hadn't been able to stop watching her that night, either.

She was short and slender, but she had curves in all the right places. That dark red hair of hers had glowed as she glided from table to table, and her low laugh had made him shiver. She'd made everyone feel included. Welcome. He'd watched her and wanted what she had.

Nathan had noticed him watching.

After getting in a couple of older-brother digs, Nathan had warned him to back off. To forget about Darcy. He'd told Patrick exactly how he'd kick his baby brother's ass if said brother hit on his best waitress. No way was Patrick going back to Detroit, leaving Nathan to deal with the fallout.

Patrick had backed off. But he hadn't forgotten about Darcy.

Now he was watching her again. And wondering.

Darcy joked with the customers, teased Marco, laughed with the other waitresses. She even spoke enough Spanish to make the cooks and dishwashers smile.

She was friendly and warm with everyone.

Except him.

After pausing for a moment at another table, she hurried past the podium and didn't meet his gaze.

With him, she was cautious. Careful. She'd made the joke about him not being romantic, but she'd immediately reined herself in.

Why did Darcy treat him differently than everyone else?

CHAPTER TWO

PATRICK TURNED THE lock as the last guest left, then took a deep breath. He'd had no idea how hard Nathan worked every night.

And they weren't done. Now they had to clean.

Marco was in the kitchen, helping to scrub it down. Two waitresses grabbed trays and began to pick up the dishes of freshly grated Parmesan cheese on each table. The other two wiped down the salt and pepper shakers. They worked methodically, chatting with each other as they moved from one table to the next.

It was a well-oiled machine, and Patrick wasn't part of it. He shifted from one foot to the other, his gaze going first to the kitchen, then to the waitresses.

Out of the corner of his eye, he saw Darcy head for the patio. Carol had set up the tables before he could stop her, but no one had been seated out there. The staff needed a little distance from the accident before that happened. Now the table settings had to be collected.

Darcy carried a silver bus tray, and it wobbled a little as she opened the door.

He hurried after her. She stood in the doorway, drawing a deep breath, her shoulders stiffening.

"Darcy, why don't you clean the front room tonight?"

When she glanced back at him, her eyes were dilated. Almost completely black. "I'm fine," she said, her voice barely above a whisper.

"I can see that." He tugged the tray out of her hands, and she resisted for a moment. Finally she let it go.

"What are you trying to prove?" he asked.

"Nothing. I'm doing my job."

"Tonight, your job is in a different part of the restaurant." He held tightly to the tray as she tried to take it. "I've got the patio."

Her eyes narrowed. "You think I'm afraid to go out there?"

Yes. "You saw Nathan get hit by a car. Anyone would be shaken up." But shaken up was different than afraid.

She stared at the dark cluster of tables, faintly illuminated by the lanterns strung above them. "He pushed me out of the way," she said, so softly Patrick barely heard her. "That's why he was hit."

"You think he should have stood there and watched you get pancaked?"

"He wouldn't have gotten hurt. He wouldn't be in the hospital right now."

"How long have you been working here?"

Most people wouldn't have noticed her sudden tension. She swallowed once, staring into the darkness. "Three years."

"So you know Nathan pretty well. You know that's who he is—the guy who saves babies and kittens." *The guy who sacrificed his future to keep his family together. The guy who hadn't blamed his brother for killing his parents.* "And women who work for him."

She let go of the tray. "Fine. You can clean it." She hurried past, being careful not to touch him. He watched her veer toward a corner of the front room and grab another tray. Her movements were jerky as she picked up the salt and pepper shakers and a stray ketchup bottle. They nearly slid off as she moved to the next table.

He made Darcy nervous.

He wondered why.

As Patrick was tucking the cash into the bank bag, Marco grabbed a bottle of wine from beneath the bar. He headed toward the family table, where a couple of the line cooks and most of the waitresses were sitting. The cooks had a beer, Ash-

ley had a soda. Someone laughed as Marco twisted the cork-
screw. Phyllis set five wineglasses on the table.

It looked like they'd done this before.

"One for you, Paddy?" Marco called.

"Sure." Wine would be good.

His back hurt, his legs were cramping and his head ached
from everything he had to remember. How the hell was he
going to handle this for six weeks?

His face burned with shame as he tucked the money bag
into the small safe beneath the bar. Nathan had been doing
this since he was twenty-two years old. Along with raising
Patrick, Frankie and Marco. And Patrick was complaining
about six lousy weeks.

He had cases pending in Detroit. Obligations. A life of his
own. A life he wanted to get back to.

Nathan had given up his dreams when he took over Mama's,
and starting tonight, Patrick would suck it up and do the best
job he could.

When he finally went back to his life in Detroit, he'd know
he'd paid a small part of the debt he owed his brother.

He walked over to the table and picked up one of the two
unclaimed glasses of wine. As he took a sip, he didn't realize
he was looking for her until he saw she wasn't there.

"Darcy already gone?" he asked casually.

"She's putting away the cheese," Phyllis said.

"She always sticks around," Marco added. He took a drink
of his wine, then stuck his head into the kitchen. "Your wine's
getting cold, Darce."

"Thanks, Marco, but I'm not staying tonight," she called.

"Okay. Be right there." Marco returned to the table, set his
glass down and headed toward the kitchen.

Patrick must have look puzzled, because one of the waitresses explained, "Marco or Nathan always walk Darcy to
her car."

Without thinking, Patrick stood up. "Hey, Marco. I'll walk
her out tonight."

His brother was halfway through the kitchen door, but he stopped. "You sure?"

"Yeah. Go sit down."

Darcy stood waiting at the back door. When she saw him, she fumbled it open. "Good night, Patrick. I'll see you tomorrow."

"Hold on. I'll walk you out."

She flashed a strained smile as she reached into her purse. "Thanks, but I'm fine."

He caught the door before it closed, propped it open and followed her into the dark parking area behind the restaurant. No wonder Nate or Marco accompanied her out. They needed to get some security lights out here. Motion sensitive, maybe. And they should trim those bushes.

He sighed. It was hard to turn off the cop in his head. He caught up with Darcy, who was hurrying toward a small group of cars.

"What's the rush?" he said as he reached her.

"I don't want to keep you. It's been a long night."

"Marco said you usually stay for wine afterward."

"Not tonight." She pulled her hand out of her bag, and her keys were clenched in her fist, the ends pointing out between her fingers. A technique taught in every self-defense class.

Wildwood was safe. Boring. Low crime rate.

So why did Darcy need an escort? She might still be on edge about Nathan's accident, but Marco had said they always walked her to her car. Why not all the women?

She dropped a small cylinder into her bag, and his eyebrows rose. He was almost certain it was pepper spray.

"How come you're running off?" he asked.

"Is socializing part of my job description?"

"Of course not. But why rush off tonight?"

"I have things to do." She inserted her key into the lock of an older model foreign compact. "Thank you, Patrick. I'll see you tomorrow night."

She tugged the door, and he let it go. It slammed with a solid thunk, and she backed out of the parking lot. He watched her taillights disappear down the street.

PATRICK WAS AN FBI agent. Protective. That's why he'd walked her out instead of Marco.

Everyone was still on edge after the accident.

Darcy tossed her purse onto a kitchen chair, where it landed with a thud. She gripped the pepper spray as Cat twined around her ankles, asking for his dinner. "In a minute," she murmured

She waited until her hands were steady again, then searched all four rooms in the small apartment. She looked under the bed, in the closets, behind the shower curtain. Finally sure she was alone, she double-checked the lock on the door and all the windows. Only then did she open a can of food and scrape it into Cat's bowl.

She toed off her shoes and sank wearily onto a chair. "What am I going to do?" she asked. The cat moved one ear and continued eating. "Every time I looked at him, he was watching me." Shivering, she wrapped her arms around herself.

She pushed to her feet, headed into the living room and twitched the curtain to one side. She recognized most of the cars parked on the street. Three dark sedans were unfamiliar.

She studied them until she was sure they were empty, then went back to the kitchen.

Nothing in her alley had looked out of place. She'd checked.

Lately, she'd paced her apartment during the night. Peered out the window too many times. She'd been jumpy ever since Nathan was injured.

By a drunken driver. Hit-and-run. That's all.

But she remembered the way a car had illuminated her minutes before the accident. The way it had slowed for a moment, then sped up again.

Had that car come back for her?

She sank into a chair and watched Cat eat. When he finished, he cleaned his face, then jumped into her lap. He draped himself over her legs, purring, and she stroked him with trembling fingers as she stared out the window into the darkness.

A smart woman would have packed her stuff and disappeared the night Nathan was hit. A smart woman wouldn't have hung around, wondering if Tim had found her.

But the women's shelter counted on her. And Theresa was beginning to trust her. Sooner or later, she'd let Darcy take her to that shelter.

Her fingers tightened in Cat's fur, and he yowled and jumped to the floor.

"Sorry, guy," she crooned, bending to pet him. "It was an accident." Just like what happened to Nathan.

Cat gave her a suspicious look as he groomed himself. Finally he wandered away. Darcy slung her purse over her shoulder and headed for her bedroom. She stopped in the bathroom to brush her teeth, then set the purse next to her bed, pulled out her gun and put it on the night table, undressed and climbed beneath the sheets.

She dreamed of a dark sedan racing toward her. This time, though, she saw the driver clearly.

This time, Nathan wasn't around to save her.

DARCY WAS HALFWAY through her five-mile run the next morning when she heard footsteps behind her. Another runner, coming up on her right.

The footsteps weren't alarming. A lot of people in this neighborhood ran in the morning. After three years, she recognized most of them. Usually exchanged a nod or a "morning" as she let them pass her.

Today, as she slowed, so did the person behind her. She glanced over her shoulder, but couldn't see him clearly. The man ran on the other side of the street, in the deep shade of the trees that lined the parkway. He wore a ball cap and his head was bent as he fiddled with the iPod on his arm.

He was tall. Lean but muscular, if the six-pack abs outlined by his sweaty gray T-shirt were any indication. He ran smoothly and apparently effortlessly, as if he could go for miles.

She stumbled on a small pothole and turned her attention back to where she was going. Her heart pumped harder, her lungs ached as she pulled in more air. The man behind her fell into the same rhythm, neither drawing closer nor falling behind.

She slowed a little more. So did he.

Her heart began to race. The spurt of adrenaline made her muscles coil tightly, her legs move more quickly.

She looked left, then right. At seven in the morning, most of the houses had lights on. But no one was walking to the train or backing out of their driveway.

Her heartbeat echoing in her ears, she turned right at the next corner. Toward downtown Wildwood, where there would be more people. More activity.

Farther from her apartment.

As she rounded the corner, she let herself look at him again. The visor of his cap was pulled low. Golden light filtered through the trees, with their orange and yellow leaves, and reflected off his barely visible sunglasses. He was too far away for her to recognize him, but she stared anyway. To let him know she was watching.

The copper taste of fear flooded her mouth, but she didn't reach for the water bottle strapped to her waist. Instead, she gripped the pepper spray in her fist and ran faster. Two more blocks until she reached busy Devon Avenue and relative safety.

Behind her, his shoes slapped harder against the pavement. Faster. She wasn't going to make it to Devon. After adjusting the pepper spray to point out, she slowed to let him pass.

His footsteps sounded louder as he came up behind her. "Darcy?"

Patrick. Only one word, and she recognized his voice.

She stumbled again, then fell into a walk, scowling at him. "You scared the crap out of me."

"How did I do that?"

"You followed me for a long time. Then all of a sudden, you caught up."

"When you turned the corner, I recognized you." He pulled out his earbuds and let them dangle from his hand. "Cut me some slack, Darcy. I'm barely awake. I didn't mean to scare you."

"You sped up and slowed down when I did." Damn it, he wasn't going to make her feel guilty because she'd been alert.

"Just falling into a rhythm. Easier not to think about what I'm doing if I've got another runner in front of me." He whipped off his sunglasses and stuck them on top of his cap. Dark circles shadowed his eyes, as if he'd barely slept.

Maybe she'd overreacted. "A woman has to be careful, running alone," she said. She slipped the pepper spray into the tiny pocket inside the waistband of her shorts. Patrick noted the action.

Let him watch.

"Yeah, I get that. Sorry I snapped your head off." He wiped sweat off his face and sighed. "I'm not a morning person."

She glanced at him again. "There's a news flash."

He grinned. "Sounds like you'd rather be home in bed, too."

A whisper of suggestion hovered in the air and made her already flushed face hotter.

She turned abruptly and began running again. He fell in beside her.

"I got a phone call early this morning," he said. "That's why my cheerful self is out here. What's your excuse?"

"Was it about Nathan? Is he okay?" Concerned about her boss, she began to reach for Patrick, then snatched her hand back. Again, his gaze followed the movement.

After a too-long pause, he said, "Nathan's fine, far as I know. This was from my office. About a case I'm working."

"Do you have to go back?" She tried not to sound too hopeful, but when he gave her a sharp glance, figured she hadn't succeeded.

"I wouldn't do that to Nate. Or Marco and Frankie," he said quietly. "I'm here as long as they need me."

Damn it. But she wasn't surprised. She felt him studying her face and sucked in a deep breath.

As she started to run harder, he said, "So why are *you* out here so early?"

"I always run early in the morning." It was the best time to check out the neighborhood. Notice anything unusual.

She started to turn down a side street, and he nodded in the opposite direction. "Don't you take the underpass?"

There was a pedestrian walkway beneath the railroad tracks, connecting the two parts of the neighborhood. She avoided it at all costs. Ugly surprises could wait at the ends of tunnels. "No, I live on this side. No reason to."

"Not even for fun?" He glanced toward the tracks, but his feet kept up a steady beat with hers instead of veering off. "I like it—the ramps down and up, the way the tunnel echoes, the weird green lighting."

"Have at it, then."

"I'll stick with your equally cheerful self this morning."

"Get lost, Patrick. I run by myself."

"Then I'll run by myself, too."

He continued beside her. No matter how fast or slow she went, Patrick kept pace. Her chest tightened and her skin tingled. After a few minutes, he said, "So. This is your neighborhood?"

"I live a mile or so from the restaurant."

"Grow up here in Wildwood?"

She ran a little faster. "Moved here."

"Where from?"

A yellow school bus rumbled past, and she edged closer to the shoulder. He did, too. His arm was almost brushing hers as they ran. "I thought you weren't one of those chatty morning people. What's with the third degree?"

"Just being social."

"Too early for that." Time to lose him. "See you at work, Patrick."

She began to sprint away from him. He kept up for a minute, then let her pull ahead. She turned a corner, then another, and lost sight of him.

She wasn't fooling herself, though. She wasn't running away from him. He was letting her go.

PATRICK WATCHED Darcy streak away from him, her legs pumping steadily. They were sleek and surprisingly long for a woman who couldn't be more than a few inches over five feet tall.

Her dark red hair was damp with sweat, and so was the T-shirt she wore. It clung to her chest and the sports bra beneath it. The slight bounce of her breasts as she ran burned into his brain.

The air had quivered with tension as they ran, and it wasn't all coming from him. She'd felt the sizzle, too. Her face had flushed, and not just from exertion. She'd breathed harder. Her eyes had dilated.

It didn't matter.

He wasn't here to get involved with a woman, especially one who worked for Nathan. He was here to help his brother until Nate was back on his feet. He had enough to worry about.

Even if Darcy was willing to have a fling, that's all it would ever be. He wasn't getting involved in a long-distance relationship. They never worked out.

Once burned, twice shy.

He had to go back to Nathan's house and work on one of his cases, a bank robbery gone bad. A teller and a customer had died, and one of the other agents had received a tip this morning. It was beginning to sound like an inside job, and Patrick had offered to work through the bank's accounts. See if anything was off.

He clenched his teeth as he began running again. He needed to be in Detroit, interviewing the tellers and managers, looking for that tell.

Instead he was here in Chicago, running a restaurant.

He headed for the underpass to return to the other side of the tracks, bracing himself for a long day. He organized a list in his head—how to start the search through the bank's records, when he needed to go into Mama's.

In spite of all he had to do today, all he needed to think about, the picture of Darcy, running in the opposite direction, stuck in his head.

CHAPTER THREE

Two and a half weeks later, Patrick walked in the back door of Nathan's house, dropped his gym bag on a kitchen chair and used the towel draped over his shoulders to wipe the sweat from his face. The faint sound of Nathan's voice came from the other room. His brother must be on the phone.

When Nate stopped talking, Patrick stepped out of the kitchen. "Hey, Nate. How's it going?"

"Good. I'm good," Nathan said. He gripped the joystick control of his wheelchair and lurched forward. The footrest caught beneath the coffee table, and with a vicious curse, Nathan tried to work it loose. The motor groaned as it started and stopped. Started and stopped.

Patrick laughed and hurried over to help.

Nathan scowled at him. "Laughing at the cripple. Nice, Paddy. You want a few puppies to kick?"

Patrick separated the table from the wheelchair, then stood, still smiling. "No, thanks. You provide more than enough entertainment."

His brother held up a one-finger salute. "So glad I can make your day brighter. Loser."

"Moron."

"Tool."

Bumping fists, they grinned at each other. Nathan's smile faded as he studied his brother. "You at the gym?"

"Yeah. Sparred a little with one of the instructors." He rubbed the spot beneath his right eye that still hurt. He'd let down his guard for a moment and the guy had nailed him.

"Looks like you're going to have a shiner," Nathan said with a hint of a smile.

"Wouldn't be the first time," he said, understanding his brother's satisfaction. He knew it was hard for Nate, stuck in a wheelchair, watching his brother out running every morning and going to the gym to box.

If Patrick was a sensitive, caring guy, he'd exercise more discreetly. Make sure he changed his sweaty gym clothes before Nathan saw them. But he was too busy to be tactful.

"You're gonna scare the customers," Nathan said, scowling at him. "I need to get back to work."

Nathan had spent a week in the hospital, and when he'd first come home he'd been doped up on painkillers, spending most of his time sleeping in the hospital bed in the den. Finally, this week, the hardware in his limbs had been exchanged for cumbersome casts. He spent his waking hours in the wheelchair, an electric one because he could only use his right hand. His left leg was extended in front of him, his left arm bent at an awkward angle.

He'd been fidgety this week. Impatient with the awkward casts and his inability to function by himself.

At least Nate could laugh at himself again. That had to be a good sign. "You know you can't do that," he said, knowing exactly how Nathan was feeling. Patrick missed his own work just as much. "You need to take it easy."

"You want to know what I need?" Nathan leveled his gaze on his brother. "I need a knife in my hand, need to feel the oven blasting heat when we're really busy and I have to help in the kitchen. I need to have a glass of wine after we close. That's what I want. Not you and Frankie waiting on me."

"Sorry, pal. You're stuck with us for four more weeks, until those casts come off."

"You think I don't know that?" Nathan's phone was facedown in his lap, and he jerked the lever that ran the wheelchair back and forth a few times. "I've got to get back to the restaurant. I have things to do there." He used his good leg to kick the coffee table out of his way, and the computer slid toward the edge. "God! Can't you get me out of this house?"

Patrick's gaze rested on the phone. Had his brother gotten a call that upset him? "You know we can't do that. That was the deal. Minimal movement until the casts come off."

"I know that. I just don't like it."

"You'll be back in a few weeks." He stared at the phone. Who had Nate been talking to? And what had made his brother suddenly so frantic?

"Not soon enough. I'm responsible for Mama's. I appreciate what you're doing, Paddy, but I should be there."

"I'm handling it, Nate."

"Yeah, I know." He jiggled the control of his wheelchair again. "But I also know you want to get back to your life. Your job. We appreciate how you're helping out."

"'Helping?'" Patrick sank into one of the leather chairs by the window. "I'm part of this family, too. This is as much my job as it is yours. So why would I go back to Detroit and leave the rest of you in the lurch?"

"Your life isn't in Chicago. You had to rearrange everything to stay here. Marco and Frankie are just adjusting a little."

"Not a problem."

And it wasn't. He was glad he could help. But he still felt like an outsider.

His sister and two brothers were tight. Interwoven in each other's lives like the three strands of a braid. He'd been separate from them since the day their parents had died in a car accident while he was driving. Guilt put the distance between them initially. Living five hours away widened the gulf.

All these years later and he still didn't do well with the family dynamics.

This time, he couldn't run back to Detroit.

"You wouldn't be worrying about the restaurant so much if you'd made some contingency plans," he said.

"Like I knew I was going to be hit by a car?" Nathan spun the wheelchair around and steered it into the kitchen. In a moment, Patrick heard ice dropping into a glass, followed by the sound of water splashing. When Nathan returned to the living room, a glass of water sat in the cup holder attached to the chair.

"So what's Marco cooking today?" Nathan asked.

"How the hell should I know?" He leaned closer to his brother. "Why don't you want to talk about contingency plans?"

"Back off, Paddy. I don't need plans."

"Shit happens, Nate. You can't control everything. You need a backup plan."

"Fine. I'll work on one."

"You should hire a manager."

"I *am* the manager."

"Exactly. And you don't have a life. You need to take some time away from the restaurant."

"Have you been talking to Frankie?"

"About this? No. Why?"

Nathan rolled his eyes. "I told her I needed some time away from Mama's. That I wanted to do some other stuff." He stared at the cast on his leg. "I've got 'time away' now, and I hate it."

"It's not a bad idea. You've been doing this for a long time. You raised the rest of us." Patrick tried to smile. "Not me, of course. I was a perfect kid. But you spent a lot of time with Marco and Frankie."

"And I wouldn't change a thing about what I did with those years," Nathan said.

"Maybe you were right. Maybe you need to get away after you're out of the chair."

"Not happening. Not now."

"Maybe you should hire a manager."

"No one knows that place better than I do."

"Agreed, but you could teach someone."

"Who? Some stranger who knows nothing about Mama's?"

"What about Darcy?" The waitress was never far from Patrick's mind, but this was actually a good idea. "She'd do a great job."

"Frankie suggested that a while ago. Darcy wouldn't take it on."

"Have you asked her?"

"No," his brother said, not meeting his gaze. "I don't have to. I know what her answer would be."

"Really?" Patrick studied his brother, but Nathan didn't look at him. "She's bright. Capable. Works hard. Why wouldn't she want a promotion and a raise?"

"Leave it alone, Paddy," Nathan said.

"I'm going to ask her tonight," he replied. "Perfect solution. I'll stick around until you're on your feet, of course, but she can work with me in the meantime. Start getting ready."

"No. Don't ask."

"Why the hell not? Is there something I don't know about her? Some deep, dark secret that would prevent her from being the manager?"

"Don't be an ass." Nathan shifted in the chair. "I know her better than you," he said. "She doesn't want to manage Mama's."

"How do you know if you haven't asked?"

"Drop it, Paddy," Nathan said. "Tell me how Marco's doing handling all of the cooking."

Patrick stared at Nathan. He wasn't ready to abandon the discussion about Darcy. It was a perfect solution. "Tell me about Darcy."

"There's nothing to tell. For God's sake, Patrick. I know Mama's. I know the people who work there, what needs to be done, how it needs to be done. You don't. Why would you? You don't come home."

Familiar irritation and guilt shot through him. Patrick stood and paced the small room. "How come, no matter what we talk about, we always come back to the fact that I don't live in Chicago? That I have a job in another city?"

"We don't have a big family," Nathan said quietly. "Only the four of us. We'd like you to be here, too."

He hadn't felt like part of a family for a long time. "It doesn't

work that way. In the Bureau, you go where they send you."
But Patrick couldn't look at his brother. He'd had an opportunity to transfer to Chicago. He'd refused. If he lived here, spent time around his siblings, he would be a constant reminder of the parents they'd lost. And why.

He wouldn't do that to them. Or to himself.

"You haven't even asked, have you?"

"Nathan. My job is not up for discussion."

Nathan held his gaze. "Fine. Then neither is mine."

That was fair, Patrick conceded reluctantly. But it didn't mean he had to like it.

He studied his brother more carefully. Yeah, this was hard for Nathan. Forced inactivity was a bitch. But the anxiety in Nathan's eyes was more than frustration.

He leaned closer. "You're worried about something."

"I'm stuck in this goddamned house!" Nathan spun the wheelchair around. "I'm not at my restaurant. Of course I'm worried."

His brother's back was tense, and he leaned forward, staring out the front window. "Is something wrong at Mama's?" Patrick asked. "You're acting like it'll be the end of the world if you don't get back there."

Nathan's knuckles whitened on the wheelchair joystick but he didn't move. "Nothing's wrong. You're doing a great job, Paddy. Everyone says so. But you don't know the place like I do. You can't do everything."

"Tell me what I'm missing."

"Nuances," he said after a long pause. "Things you get after running a place for a long time."

"Like what?" Patrick edged closer to his brother. Frowned. Nathan was trying to distract him.

"Get out of my face! Don't give me those cop's eyes. I'm your brother. Your *older* brother. Not some criminal you're interrogating."

Patrick leaned even closer. "Why would I interrogate you? I'm just asking."

"I need to be there. Okay? It's my job." The fingers barely showing at the end of Nathan's cast curled around the plaster.

"Not going to happen, and you know it." Patrick shifted on the chair, his antennae twitching. This was about more than Nathan being stuck at home.

Nathan's immobilized hand tensed and released. Tensed and released. "Let me do the bookkeeping, then," he said. "Bring home the money every night. I'll do the ledger and get the bank deposit ready."

"That's the easy part for me," Patrick said. "For God's sake! I do forensic accounting for the Bureau."

"I know." Nathan glanced at him then, a hint of desperation in his eyes. "But it's the one thing I can do from here. Count the money. Enter it in the ledger. Get the deposit ready. God, Paddy. Let me do *something*."

Patrick had never seen his calm, steady brother so worked up about the restaurant. Nathan was the cool one. Why was he losing it now?

If he'd been around more, maybe Nathan would be more open. More willing to talk to him.

Guilt swirled through him. He'd stayed away from Chicago because the memories were too painful.

He should have made more of an effort.

"Talk to me, Nate," he said quietly. "I'm your brother. Tell me what's going on."

For a moment, Nathan's haunted eyes clung to his. Then he stared out the window again. "I need something to do. That's what's wrong."

"Fine," Patrick said. "I'll bring the money home tonight. I'll bring a flash drive with the updated accounts on it. You can take it over."

Nathan's shoulders sagged. "Thanks, Paddy. You're saving my life."

For just a moment, it sounded as if he meant that literally.

Darcy stepped outside her door, turned to lock the dead bolt and froze.

The scraggly tomato plant clinging to life in the big pot directly below her kitchen window had been bent. Several of the smaller branches were broken and hanging askew. Dirt had spilled onto the porch.

It hadn't been that way last night when she got home.

She scanned the small wooden porch for signs of an intruder. It was clean. No footprints, no scratches, no dropped papers or cigarette butts. Nothing to make her think someone had been up here, looking in her window.

She stood at the railing and studied the backyard below her. The apartment was on the second floor of an older house in the neighborhood, remodeled into a separate unit. Wooden stairs ran up the back of the house, widening to a deck outside the first floor's kitchen and a smaller porch outside Darcy's. Her landlord was an older man who loved to garden. None of his plants looked disturbed.

The pungent tomato smell of the broken stems swirled around her. It could have been Princess, Mrs. Barnetti's cat from across the alley. Darcy had caught Princess standing in the pot once, staring in the window. Tormenting Cat.

A person could have broken the stems, too.

She slid her hand into her bag and started down the stairs.

As she approached the alley, she heard a soft crunch of gravel. Fumbling for the handle of her gun, she wrapped her fist around it. Held it there, inside her bag.

Mrs. Barnetti's overweight cat strolled out of the alley, the gravel shifting under her weight. She wound around Darcy's ankles, and Darcy let go of the gun. "You don't need any treats from me, honey," she said as she petted Princess. "If you weighed any more, you'd fall over and not be able to get up."

Princess purred loudly, and Darcy straightened. She pressed the button of the garage door opener she kept in her purse, and waited as the door rumbled open. "Beat it, Princess. I'm backing out."

The cat stared at her, then walked away, tail twitching, as if she understood.

Darcy sat in her car for a few moments, taking deep breaths.

She was going to make herself crazy if she saw bogeymen behind every tree. The accident had been three weeks ago, and nothing suspicious had happened since.

Before this morning and her broken tomato plant.

She started the car and backed out, waiting until the door closed completely before she drove away. Maybe one day she'd accept the fact that she'd escaped. That Tim had no idea where she was. That she was safe.

Right now that day was a long way off.

BY THE TIME she reached Mama's, Darcy had managed to compose herself. It would be a good day at work, she promised herself. She'd see Theresa. Have another chance to talk to her. Sooner or later, the older woman would agree to leave her partner. To go to the shelter.

Theresa usually came to Mama's on Wednesdays, and now that the curiosity seekers had gotten their fill of Nathan's story, the restaurant wasn't as busy. Darcy would have more time to linger at her table. See how she was doing.

She parked beneath the streetlamp that illuminated the parking lot at night, then punched in and got to work. She always came a little early, but Patrick was already there, working on the bookkeeping. He looked up from the ledger entries and nodded as she walked past him.

She stopped, her stomach churning. "What happened to your face?"

He touched the shiner beneath his right eye. "I was sparring and lost concentration for a moment. Took a glove to the face."

"You box?"

"Yeah. It's great exercise. Keeps my reflexes fast." He smiled. "Good way to work off frustrations."

She'd never understood how anyone could allow another person to hit them. Beat them. Boxing was violent and ugly.

Patrick enjoyed it.

"Is this where I'm supposed to ask how the other guy looked? Sorry. I don't want to know."

Patrick's smile faded. "You don't like boxing?"

"No. I don't." She hurried away before he could say anything else.

She'd managed to keep her composure at the restaurant and interact with Patrick calmly and professionally. So far, she was pretty sure she'd been able to fly under the radar with him.

She didn't want to spoil three weeks of effort by arguing about boxing. She wouldn't be able to stay calm and cool. And she didn't want to do anything that drew Patrick's attention. As long as she didn't make any stupid mistakes, there was no reason to fear him.

He watched her, though. She always knew. When it felt as if fingers were brushing her neck, she'd turn and he'd be there.

She was setting out the saucers of grated Parmesan when she heard him behind her. "Hey, Patrick."

"Darcy." His gaze lingered on her face for a moment. "When you're done with that, we need to talk."

Her heart stuttered and began racing. "About…?"

"Finish with the cheese."

He turned and walked away. Oh, God. He'd been working on the ledger entries. Payroll, probably. Had he checked on her credentials? Found out that her social security number wasn't really hers? That her identity was one that had been stolen three years ago?

She pressed a fist to her stomach to stop the churning. She hadn't stayed alert enough. That's why he'd blindsided her.

She'd practiced for this, she reminded herself. She could handle it.

Her hands shook as she set the rest of the cheese containers on the tables, then replaced the bus tray and washed the grated cheese from her hands. Approaching Patrick, she took a deep breath to steady herself.

As she slid into a chair he looked up.

"Hey, you look like you're heading to the executioner. Relax." He grimaced. "I'm not very good at managing people, I guess, if I made you think something was wrong."

"So what's up?" She forced herself to smile.

He leaned closer, his bright blue eyes lasering into her. They were so much like his siblings' eyes that she had to remind herself this wasn't Nathan or Marco. This was Patrick. Patrick, who was dangerous to her.

"Two things. First, I really need you to work that extra day every week."

She relaxed into the chair and exhaled slowly. "I rearranged my schedule, so that's fine."

"Great. I need some more help. I suggested that Nathan make you a manager, but he said you wouldn't be interested."

She'd never told Nathan about her past, but he seemed to understand she didn't want ties or permanence. "I like waitressing."

"You'd get more money as a manager."

More responsibility, too. "I don't think Nate wants anyone else managing the place."

"He's not thinking clearly yet," Patrick said carefully. "But he needs a life beyond Mama's. Until he has someone to help him here, that's not going to happen."

Darcy was touched. Clearly, Patrick was worried about his brother.

"It's very sweet that you want to help him," she said.

Patrick scowled. "I am *not* sweet."

She bit her lip to keep from grinning. "Thoughtful, then. And you're right. Nathan spends all his time here, and a manager would be a good idea. But that's Nathan's decision. Not yours."

Even if she wanted to manage Mama's, she couldn't do it. She had to be free to leave at a moment's notice.

It was easy to find another waitress.

Replacing a manager was a different story.

She owed Nathan and Marco more than that.

He leaned closer, invading her space, even from across the table. "We'll start with the extra day of waitressing, then."

She wanted to back away. Put more space between them. But she refused to let him intimidate her. "We can finish with that, too. What Nathan does about a manager is his business."

He moved closer, and the scent of the coffee he'd been drinking washed over her, mixed with a subtle, spicy aroma. It must be soap—she'd smelled it on Nathan, too.

"Maybe not, but I'm going to be straight with you, Darcy. I need help. I have a complicated case in Detroit that requires my attention. I may have to go back there a couple times in the next three weeks. I'm not going to trust someone I don't know to look after Mama's. I know you will, because you care about it."

He raised his eyebrows expectantly. "Can I count on you?"

CHAPTER FOUR

No, HE COULDN'T count on her. She wasn't going to commit to managing Mama's Place, even temporarily.

But if she refused, he might be suspicious. If Nathan had asked, she would have agreed immediately.

"Sure, you can count on me," she said easily. "If you have to go back to Detroit, I can handle things for a few nights."

"But not permanently when Nathan comes back to work?"

"Why does it matter to you? You won't be here."

"I thought you liked responsibility, Darcy." He watched her as if he was trying to put together a puzzle, and she slid her hands beneath her thighs. "I've seen the way you take charge when things get hectic around here. How the other waitresses look to you for help. This would just be the next step."

"I'll think about it."

She stood up to escape, but he raised his eyebrows. "Two things, remember?"

"Right." She eased back into the chair, anxiety churning in her stomach. Was he suspicious? Was the whole "help me out here" a setup for what he really wanted? Get her mind off the main subject, focus on something insignificant, then pounce?

It was a well-known cop tactic. Tim had used it on her all the time.

She swallowed. "So what was the other thing?"

"Is there a problem here that I don't know about?"

She barely managed not to gasp. *Had* he been checking on her? "What kind of problem?" she asked cautiously. "And what do you mean by *here?*"

"I mean at Mama's," he said sharply. She watched him struggle for composure. Finally he said, "Nathan seems really worried about the business. Almost desperate to get back here. I figured if anyone would know, it would be you. Like I said, you're observant."

The pressure building in her chest eased. He wasn't talking about her personally.

"I don't think so," she said.

"Think about it for a moment. Anything change in the last several months? Anyone acting different?"

She shook her head slowly. "Not that I've noticed. The only thing that's different is Theresa Smith."

Patrick didn't move, but she saw him snap to attention. "Who's Theresa Smith?"

"A customer who comes in several times a week. I'm pretty sure she lives in the neighborhood. She sits at a table for a few hours, drinking martinis and not eating much of her food." She moved the napkin-wrapped silverware an inch to the right. "I think she's an abuse victim." She paused to take a deep breath. "Theresa hasn't said anything. But I'm hoping she will eventually."

"Does she talk to anyone while she's here?"

"Only me. And she doesn't say much beyond ordering her drinks and food."

Patrick shook his head. "I doubt it's her, but point her out to me next time she comes in. I'll keep an eye on her."

"No!" Before she could think, she grabbed his wrist. "Don't treat her any differently than the other customers. If you spook her, she might not come back. Promise me, Patrick. Promise you'll stay away from Theresa."

His skin was warm beneath her fingers, his arm hard and muscular. His gaze heated as he stared at her hand, and she became too aware of the feel of him beneath her fingers. She wanted to slide her palm up his arm, feel the brush of his hair against her skin. She snatched her hand away.

"I just said I'll watch her."

"Like you did to me at Frankie's party? Believe me, I knew you were watching."

"Is that right?"

His gaze had suddenly turned heated, and her skin prickled in response. She needed to look away. Change the subject. But she couldn't speak. Couldn't move.

"It was unnerving," she finally managed to say, although her voice was throaty. "Theresa would be unnerved, too."

"I wouldn't be watching her for the same reason," Patrick said. His voice was huskier than usual.

She would *not* ask him to explain. She wasn't about to flirt with Patrick. "The reason doesn't matter. Don't do anything that would make her uncomfortable."

"Did I make you uncomfortable?"

Yes. "I wondered if I had something stuck in my teeth. Or if I'd spilled red wine on myself."

Amusement glinted in his eyes. "I see."

She was afraid that he *did* see. That she'd given away far too much. Grabbing for her composure, she said, "Just don't do anything to scare Theresa away. It was months before she would tell me her name. She has a 'bodyguard' who comes with her. Every time. He sits at the bar and drinks, but always where he can see her."

"Have you called the police?"

"They won't do anything." She buried the bitter memories deep, keeping her voice flat. "I've asked her if she needs help, and she says no. But she keeps coming in. Sooner or later, I'll be able to help her. But only if you leave her alone."

She could see the wheels turning behind his steady gaze. Finally he said, "All right, I won't pay any extra attention to her. But if Nathan has a problem here, I want to know what it is."

"What has Marco said?"

To her surprise, he rolled a pen back and forth on the table instead of looking at her. "Marco spends most of his time in the kitchen. I started with you because you're all over the restaurant. I figured there was a better chance you'd noticed if something was off."

"You're asking the wrong person," she said, pushing away from the table. "Marco is your brother. I just work here."

"Wait a minute, Darcy. I have more questions."

She'd had enough of his questions. "They'll have to wait. We're opening in less than a half hour. I have things to do."

Her hands were shaking as she walked away from the table. She'd told him about Theresa. She hadn't even told Nathan that much about their customer. But she'd been unnerved by Patrick's threat to watch the woman.

And then she'd let him know she was aware of him. Stupid.

Patrick was an FBI agent. Careful. Observant. And he'd gotten past her guard with disturbing ease.

She'd been the charge nurse in a hospital emergency room. She knew how to keep her head when everything was crashing. And she'd let an FBI agent rattle her into revealing too much.

After three years of constant watchfulness, no one should be able to do that to her.

Patrick was going to be here for at least three more weeks. What other secrets would he finesse her into confiding?

PATRICK WATCHED Darcy walk away. She was so guarded. About everything. Until she'd reacted without thinking and let her defenses slip. Her hazel eyes had sparked as she'd told him to leave Theresa alone.

And she said she'd noticed him watching *her*.

He hadn't imagined that moment of awareness between them. Hadn't imagined her reaction.

There'd been nothing guarded about her then. Nothing restrained.

She'd been equally passionate in her efforts to protect the woman she thought was an abuse victim.

Had a friend of hers been abused?

Had Darcy?

It was hard to imagine strong, take-charge Darcy as a victim. But he knew too well that any woman could fall into that trap.

The Darcy who had practically leaped across the table at him wasn't the one who kept him at arm's length.

Which was the real Darcy? The careful woman? Or the hot-blooded one?

He was betting on the latter. Heat settled low in his gut as he watched her set up the tables. Silverware dropped messily on to the tabletop and she spent too much time straightening each piece.

He replayed the memory of her anger. The fire in her gaze. The hard grip of her fingers when she'd grabbed his arm.

If Darcy was trying to hide who she really was, she'd made a strategic mistake.

She might try to go back to the woman she'd been a half hour ago, but it was too late. Just like it was too late for the too-big white shirt she wore with the slightly baggy black pants.

He vividly remembered her curvy, toned body from the time he'd seen her out jogging a couple of weeks ago.

If she accentuated her beauty, it might bring more tips. But maybe she didn't want to use her attractiveness to make money. That was completely understandable. Honorable.

But he wondered. She was hiding something else behind that controlled, deliberately bland exterior.

He wanted to know what it was.

She walked past his table without looking at him and disappeared into the kitchen. Patrick waited for a moment, but she didn't reappear, so he tried to focus on the laptop. Nathan had arranged his list of suppliers in a spreadsheet, but it was just a bunch of names to Patrick.

He identified at least one liquor wholesaler. But did Nathan use the same people for all his alcohol? Or did he order beer from one, wine from another?

Impatient with a job he didn't want to do, he shoved the computer away. Work was piling up back in Detroit, and it was making him antsy. Yeah, he was on a leave of absence. But the perps he was trying to catch didn't let up. Other agents were picking up the slack, but Patrick knew all the details of his cases. It was taking the other agents too long to get up to speed.

He needed to be back there.

Darcy emerged from the kitchen with a tray full of oil cruets and began setting them on each table. She'd just positioned the first one when a piercing scream came from the back of the restaurant.

Her tray crashed to the floor and she ran for the kitchen. By the time Patrick shoved through the door, she was half supporting, half carrying one of the cooks toward the dishwashing sink. He held one arm stiffly, and it was bright red. Burned, it looked like.

He leaped to help her. Wrapping his arm around the guy's waist, he yelled at the nearest cook, "You. Turn on the cold water."

Darcy glanced at him. Nodded once. Then she called, "Not that hard, Luis," as water gushed out of the faucet. "That's good."

Aside from the injured man's sobs, the kitchen was silent.

Patrick supported the man's weight, while Darcy lifted his arm into the water.

"Ay! Dios Mío" the guy sobbed.

"¿Qué paso, Javier?" Darcy asked as she held his arm beneath the cooling stream.

"Drenaje de la pasta...deslizo," he said, his teeth chattering.

Darcy looked at Patrick. "You speak Spanish?"

"Not much."

"He said he was draining the pasta and he slipped."

"Scalded."

"Yeah." Their eyes met for a moment. She was doing the same thing he was—running down the treatment. Figuring the next step.

"Keep your arm in the water, Javier," she said soothingly. "We need to cool it down."

Javier's skin was blistering already. Her eyes met Patrick's again. "Second-degree burn," she said quietly.

"Yeah." He looked for his brother. "Marco. Call an ambulance."

"Francisco, get some towels," Darcy called.

"Phyllis, Carol, get back in the dining room and finish the setup," Patrick said.

Everyone began moving. Marco had already dialed 911 and was speaking into the phone.

"Luis, get me some scissors," Darcy said.

One of the cooks handed her a pair with orange handles. She glanced at Patrick. "Can you hold his arm, too, for a moment?"

"Yeah. Get that sleeve off."

She picked up the white cotton of Javier's shirt and snipped. Holding the material away from his skin, she cut around the arm hole and tossed the short sleeve away. It landed on the edge of a trash bin, half in and half out.

The redness extended from Javier's forearm almost to his shoulder. The blisters were worsening.

"Francisco," Darcy called. "Where are those towels? Luis, get me a cardboard box."

Darcy took Javier's arm again to hold beneath the cold water. As she leaned toward the shivering man, she pressed against Patrick's side. One of her breasts flattened against him, and she snaked an arm under his to get a better grip on Javier.

He tensed at the contact. Ordered his body to ignore her softness. Wondered at her lack of reaction.

It was an intensely intimate position, but she gave no indication that she realized how closely they were twined. Instead, she rocked Javier's arm back and forth beneath the faucet, rubbing her breast against Patrick in the process.

He knew she was aware of him. He'd seen her eyes dilate when they touched. But right now, he could have been a mannequin.

Who the hell was Darcy Gordon?

She leaned closer to Javier, and Patrick closed his eyes as her body molded to his. "Does it feel any better?" she asked softly.

Hell, yes.

"Sí," Javier said, his voice shaking. "A little."

Patrick opened his eyes to find Javier gray-faced and sweating. Against him, Darcy's muscles were quivering with the effort of holding Javier's arm extended.

"We need to lay him down," Patrick said.

Darcy glanced at Javier's face and nodded. "Yeah."

The scent of simmering tomato sauce drifted over Patrick, as well as the smell of meat burning on the grill. The back door stood open, and cool air shivered over his wet arm.

The smell of Javier's fear hung in the kitchen like a dark cloud.

Darcy smelled like citrus and summer flowers.

"Someone shut the back door!" he shouted.

Marco was on the phone, still talking to the 911 dispatcher. Javier began to crumple, snapping Patrick's attention back to him. Darcy staggered but stayed upright, kept his arm in the water.

"On three," Patrick said. "One, two…"

They moved perfectly in unison as they laid Javier on the wet floor. "I need towels, damn it!" she called. "And where's that box?"

Luis shoved a cardboard box with a picture of a cow at her, and Francisco crouched beside her with a stack of towels.

Patrick took Javier's arm with one hand and lifted the cook's legs with the other. Darcy fumbled the box beneath his calves. As Patrick held his arm steady, Darcy snatched towels off the stack and covered him. Patrick caught her eye and nodded at the water on the floor. "I'll lift."

As he raised the beefy cook inches off the floor, Darcy shoved towels beneath him. When they had him covered, except for his arm, Patrick said, "Plastic wrap."

"I'm on it."

She dashed for the box of wrap on the next counter and

tore off a sheet. Then she squatted next to him and wrapped the plastic around Javier's lower arm. As if they were reading each other's mind, she switched to support the cook's arm as Patrick wrapped the plastic around the upper part. When he'd finished, together they laid Javier's arm across his chest.

Still squatting next to him, Darcy called, "How long on the ambulance, Marco?"

He closed his cell phone. "I hear them now. Meet them at the door."

The whine of an ambulance siren drew closer, then stopped. Patrick ran to the front of the restaurant to wait for the EMTs. "Back here," he said as an older man and a young woman burst through the front door with a gurney and what looked like a huge tackle box.

As they lowered the gurney next to Javier and studied his plastic-wrapped arm, the older guy nodded approvingly. "Nice job. Who did this?"

"We did," he and Darcy said together. She gave him a half smile and bumped his hip with hers.

His gaze held hers and he smiled back. Nodded. *A team.*

Darcy turned to the paramedics. "It's a scald. We cooled it down with cold water first. Elevated his legs because he was getting shocky."

"Good work." The EMT nodded at his partner. "Get an IV going while I check his vitals, then we'll get him to the hospital."

Darcy looked at Marco. "You going to call his wife?"

"Yeah." Marco grabbed a list from the wall and punched a number into his cell phone. *"Hola, Marisol,"* he began in a soothing voice.

Patrick heard a woman wail through the phone as Marco held it away from his ear. Then Marco spoke again. Closed his phone.

"She's on her way to the hospital."

Patrick's hands shook as the adrenaline rush faded. He glanced at Darcy. She was shaking, too.

He had taken extensive first aid classes as part of his training. Practiced every imaginable scenario, over and over. He had muscle memory of the things that needed to be done in an emergency.

Darcy had more than muscle memory. She'd treated burn victims before. Often.

The way they'd worked together, like two people with one brain, had been spooky. He'd never connected like that with any of his partners or fellow agents.

Not with his family, either, for that matter.

Darcy still hadn't looked at him. Now, as the EMTs wheeled Javier out of the kitchen, she put her hand on the man's shoulder and said something in Spanish. Javier nodded and closed his eyes. Moments later, they were gone.

There was a beat of silence. Then Patrick said, "What the hell happened?"

Marco shoved his phone into his pocket. "Apparently, someone jostled him from behind while he was dumping boiling water into the sink. It splashed up on his arm."

Luis's face was as white as the jacket he wore. "It was me, boss. But it was an accident, I swear. The floor was slippery. I tripped and fell into him."

Patrick opened his mouth, but Darcy put her hand on the stricken man's arm. "It's okay, Luis. We know it was an accident. And Javier is going to be fine."

"I never heard nobody scream like that," he said, wiping his hands down the black-and-white herringbone slacks all the cooks wore.

"Come sit down." She guided him out of the kitchen and into the dining room. As the door swung closed, Patrick heard her say, "I'll get you a soda. What do you want?"

There was silence for a moment, then Marco said, "Francisco, clean that grease off the floor so no one else gets hurt. Then we need to get busy. We open in fifteen."

Patrick wiped up the water that had spilled while they were treating Javier's arm, then put the wet towels into the laundry bin. When he was finished, he pushed through the door into the dining room.

Luis sat at a table, sipping cola. The waitresses huddled around him, talking and peppering him with questions. Darcy was finishing the setup.

"You okay, Luis?" he asked.

The cook nodded and pushed the remainder of his drink away. "I'm good. I need to get back there. It's going to be a lot of work without Javier." He stood up and hurried into the kitchen.

Patrick watched as Darcy lit the candles on each table. Her hand shook, making the flame on the match jump as she extended it toward the glass jar.

He walked up behind her. "You were impressive in there," he said.

"Back at you." She moved to the next table, lit another candle. The flame on that one quivered, too.

"You knew what you were doing."

She shrugged as she wiped her hands on her apron, then picked at a loose thread on the pocket. She didn't meet his eyes. "Basic first aid."

"A lot more than basic. You took charge. Got everyone else moving." He edged closer, intrigued by the longing and fear in her expression. "You've done that before." He stepped closer. "What were you before you were a waitress, Darcy?"

At that she looked at him. "Unemployed." Her back was rigid, her mouth a thin line. She held his gaze until he glanced away. Then she pushed past him and went into the kitchen.

When he sat down at the table, staring at the computer screen without really seeing it, Phyllis raised her eyebrows. "Pretty impressive, huh?"

"Yeah." He couldn't remember the last time someone had made him look away first.

"You think that was good? You should have seen her when Francisco nearly cut his finger off last year. All the cooks were standing there, watching the blood spurt. Marco was turning green. Nathan had a towel over Cisco's hand, and it was soaked with blood after about ten seconds. Darcy grabbed the belt out of Francisco's pants and tied a tourniquet around his arm. Then she did the same thing you guys did to Javier—made Francisco lie down, put his legs up, got someone to call an ambulance."

"She's good," Patrick said. "It looks like she stays calm when everything's going to hell."

"Most controlled person I ever met." Phyllis positioned a rolled set of cutlery at each place. "She's scary sometimes."

"Glad we have someone who keeps her head in a crisis." It had been instructive to see her in action.

Clearly, Darcy Gordon had hidden depths.

"You watch her."

He froze. "She's working for me. For my brothers, anyway. Of course I watch her. I watch all of you."

"Not like that, honey." Phyllis grinned. "You got good taste. But don't waste your time. Darcy shuts everyone down."

"Who's everyone?" He frowned as a little zing of jealousy buzzed through him.

The waitress shrugged. "You name it—customers, the UPS guy, Jesse the bartender. The beat cop for this neighborhood. Even the garbage collectors. She'll laugh and joke with them, but if they put a move on her, bam. That's it. Of course, they keep coming back for more. Guys can't resist that mystery thing."

Patrick stared toward the kitchen. Darcy hadn't emerged yet. Was she going to avoid him because he'd asked her where she learned her skills?

He turned back to Phyllis. "I'm not interested in Darcy that way. I'm only here for a few more weeks."

The woman patted his arm. "You keep telling yourself that, hon. Maybe you'll convince yourself it's true."

CHAPTER FIVE

DARCY STOOD NEXT to the pizza counter, trying to suck air into her frozen lungs. She hadn't thought about what Patrick would see when she hurried to help Javier. She'd just reacted.

Now he would wonder. How had she known what to do? Reacted so quickly. Taken charge so easily.

She'd be a puzzle to him. And cops were good at solving puzzles.

She couldn't give him any more clues. She'd stick to her first-aid-class story. She *had* taken one of those. So what if it was in Girl Scouts when she was fourteen? A lifetime ago. Long before the day her whole life became a lie.

She grabbed a towel from the stack near the sink and blotted some of the water from her pants. When they dried, they'd be hopelessly wrinkled.

She had bigger problems than wrinkled pants. Patrick was an FBI agent. Once his questions started, he'd be relentless.

She had to stay off his radar for the rest of the night.

Instead of exiting the kitchen through the door into the dining room, she headed into the bar. A few of the regulars were there, watching the White Sox on television.

She forced a smile. "Why are you losers watching the Sox when there's a Cubs game on?"

"Who wants to watch a bunch of scrubs when there's a real baseball team playing?" one of the guys retorted.

"Anyone who appreciates the nuances of the game," she shot back.

As the guys hooted and booed, she waved and headed for the back room of the dining area. Where Patrick wasn't.

He was at the podium, and she felt him turn toward her. The hair on the back of her neck lifted. He was wondering about her. She didn't have to see his face to know that.

Behind her, she heard Jesse duck out of the bar. "Hey, Darce," he said.

She turned and smiled, relieved for the distraction. "Hey, Jesse. What do you need?"

His eyes lingered on her mouth, but she ignored it. She and Jesse had had a come-to-Jesus meeting a couple of months ago. He knew she wasn't interested.

"I heard about what happened with Javier. Is he going to be okay?"

"Yeah, poor guy. It's a bad burn, but I think he'll be fine."

His gaze lingered on her and he stood a little too close. "I heard how you handled it. But I don't see your cape. You know, the Superwoman one."

She edged away and struggled to smile. Jesse was teasing. Trying to loosen things up. It was better than hitting on her, but she didn't have the energy to deal with him right now. "It's in the wash," she said. "Got all wet saving Javier."

"No spare?" His strained smile told her he was reaching, too.

"You kidding?" She slid to the waitress station and reached for the basket of rolled silverware. "They only issue one per superhero."

"Jesse." Patrick stepped between her and the bartender. "Time to get back to work."

He stood close enough to block her view of Jesse. Close enough for the fine blue stripes on his dress shirt to look larger than they were. The crisp shirt was snug on his wide shoulders and tapered down to his waist. His body heat washed over her, and she swayed toward him, inhaling his subtle, spicy scent.

For a long moment, no one moved. Then she stepped away, far enough to see Jesse's gaze shift from Patrick to her and back. Finally Jesse shrugged. "Sure, boss. Got a lot to do anyway."

Patrick turned to her and she retreated another step. "He a problem?"

"Jesse? Nah." She cleared her throat. "We were just talking." So much for flying below Patrick's radar. Now that he wondered what was going on between her and Jesse, he'd be watching more closely.

"I don't like guys who won't take no for an answer."

"Then there's no problem. Jesse wasn't asking any questions." She didn't want Patrick to get involved. To *think* about her. But in spite of herself, she warmed a little inside. It had been a very long time since someone tried to protect her. "Patrick. The whole 'watch out for my employees' thing is sweet. But do *not* worry about Jesse. There's nothing there."

"Good. Because no one is going to harass my waitresses."

Time to lighten this up. "Wow. You really are Mr. Serve and Protect, aren't you?"

"Yes. I am." He held her gaze. No smile.

When he finally walked away, she swallowed. Okay. In spite of that little flash of heat, she had another reason to stay as far away from Patrick as possible. He was as straight as they came. Someone who believed in right and wrong. Black and white.

She was all about the gray.

TWO NIGHTS LATER, as Darcy set the first martini down in front of Theresa, she clenched her teeth to keep from exploding. Theresa wore more makeup than usual, but even a heavy layer of foundation couldn't quite hide the swollen bruise on the left side of her face.

"Can I get you something to eat?" Darcy asked quietly.

Theresa shook her head. "I'm not hungry," she said, her voice barely above a whisper.

Darcy couldn't tear her gaze away from Theresa's bruise. What was the woman hiding beneath her long-sleeved, turtleneck shirt? "I can help you," she said, her voice barely above a whisper.

Theresa took a sip of her drink and stared out the window. "No. You can't."

"Theresa…"

"He's watching," the woman said. "Pretend you're taking my order."

Darcy fumbled her notepad out of her pocket, her hand shaking.

As she tried to frame a question about Theresa's injuries, the woman glanced over her shoulder. Darcy followed her gaze and saw that, instead of watching the baseball game, the man who always accompanied Theresa was staring at Darcy, his eyes as hard as chips of stone.

Darcy touched Theresa's shoulder. "I'll put your order in," she said, loud enough for the guy to hear her.

As she stood at the computer terminal nearest to Theresa's table, she felt the bodyguard's gaze on her back. She ordered a cup of soup—she had to deliver something, and soup was easy to eat.

The first time Darcy got a break, she confronted Patrick, who was standing at the host's podium. "We need to talk."

His head snapped up. "What's wrong?"

"Privately."

He nodded once and drew Darcy toward the front patio. It was too cold now to seat people outside so they wouldn't be overheard.

The air was crisp and cool, and a few faint stars twinkled in the indigo sky. The spicy scent of the mums in the planters by the door tickled her nose.

"What's up?" Patrick asked.

Darcy held on to the railing behind her as she stared up at Patrick. In the late twilight darkness, his eyes looked navy blue. "Did you see her? Theresa, the woman I told you about?" Her voice rose, and she gripped the railing until the edges cut into her palms. "She's got a bruise on the side of her face."

Patrick stilled. "No, I didn't notice," he finally said. "She came in at the same time as a big group. I was setting tables up for them."

"She covered it with makeup, but it's too much to hide. I want to call the police."

Patrick reached for her, but dropped his hand at the last moment. "Did you ask her what happened?"

"I told her I could help her."

"What did she say?"

Darcy closed her eyes. Pictured Theresa's face—her fear. Her desolation. "She said I couldn't."

"If you call the police, she'll give them one of the stock answers—she walked into a door. Tripped. Lost her balance." A hint of anger rumbled through his voice. "That won't help her, Darcy."

"If I get her license plate number, can you look her up? Find out where she lives?"

"Why? So you can kick her husband's ass?"

"Don't I wish." Darcy tightened her grip on the railing. "No, I'm not going to confront her husband. I know not to poke a stick at a poisonous snake. I just want to be able to keep an eye on her."

"Darcy, even if I could do that, which I can't, no way would I tell you where she lived. You showing up at her door would make things worse for that poor woman."

"Don't you think I know that? But do you have any idea how hard it is to watch her come in here, beaten to hell, and do nothing about it?"

"Until she asks for help, there's nothing you can do." His voice softened and he put his hand on her shoulder. "It's a hard thing to accept. But you can't force her to change."

She knew that far too well. She just hated that it was true.

The weight of his hand was warm. Comforting. The pressure of his fingers seeped through her thin blouse, heating her skin. "Someone needs to help her." All of Darcy's neighbors had ignored the shouting, the screams from her house. She wanted to think that if someone had tried to help, she would have let them.

"You're doing all you can."

"All I want is her address."

"Sorry, Darcy. No can do."

"You can't make an exception? Just this once?"

"No. Not even once." He took his hand off her shoulder, and she shivered. Patrick watched her for a moment longer, then headed back into the restaurant.

As the door closed behind him with a whoosh, she kicked at one of the chairs. It scraped across the concrete sidewalk with a screech, reminding her of the night Nathan was injured. Abruptly, she hurried back into the building.

As she passed the podium, Patrick returned to his post after seating a group of four. Her fingers closed around the order tablet in her apron pocket. She wanted to throw it at his head.

She uncurled her hand from the paper as the realization hit. She *had* learned something valuable. She hurried to the podium. "Patrick," she began.

He turned to her, annoyed. "The answer is no."

"I want to get this straight. You won't step over the line and look up information about someone, even if you're suspicious of them?"

"That's right. I won't. Not without a solid reason."

"Even if you have a feeling something is wrong?"

"I need facts. Information. Not feelings."

Relief coursed through her. So he wouldn't look up Darcy Gordon. As long as she didn't give him a reason to do so.

"Okay. I wanted to be clear."

"And are you?"

"Crystal."

He studied her for a long moment. "You don't strike me as the type who gives up. FYI, you wouldn't be the first relentless person to come after me."

"Good to know you're consistent." She hoped he'd be just as consistent if he ever became suspicious of her.

THE DINNER RUSH had slowed, and Patrick walked through the dining rooms, studying every table that still held customers. In the past few weeks, he'd learned that managing a restaurant was a little like being a cop. You had to be able to read people, be aware of subtle signals, sense when a situation was going to hell.

The two toddlers at the table in the corner were throwing crayons at each other, their mouths trembling. All signs pointed toward an imminent meltdown. He smiled as he approached the harried-looking young couple. "Enjoying your dinner?" he asked. "Anything you need?"

The guy shook his head. "We're good. Thanks."

The wife gave him a strained smile. "Could you have our waitress bring some take-out containers and the check? I think our kids are getting tired."

"Will do," Patrick said. "Thanks for coming to Mama's tonight."

The woman's shoulders relaxed. "It's our favorite restaurant."

"I'll tell my brothers." Patrick made a mental note to have Phyllis comp the couple a dessert to take home.

He swerved toward the bar, studying the man sitting on the end stool. This must be the guy who always came with Darcy's customer.

The guy was bulked up. Locker meat. A hint of acne on the back of his neck—a juicer, maybe. His dark hair was military-short, and his jacket stretched unevenly over his chest.

As he watched, the bodyguard shoved an empty glass toward Jesse. The bartender pulled a bottle of scotch off the top shelf, filled the glass and placed it in front of the guy, who picked it up and took a gulp. A little amber liquid sloshed out of his glass as he set it on the bar.

How many had the guy had? Patrick might have to take away his keys. He walked to the other end of the counter and motioned to the bartender. "That guy in the corner?" he said quietly. "Let me see his tab."

Jesse gave him a puzzled look. "There is no tab."

"What do you mean?"

"Chuck doesn't pay for his drinks." Jesse looked up from the glass he was washing. "Didn't Nathan tell you?"

"No, he didn't. What's he drinking?"

"Macallan. The Eighteen."

Their most expensive scotch. "How many?"

"Four or five."

Patrick studied the guy. His broad shoulders and thick neck signaled bodybuilder. Why was Nathan letting this goon drink Macallan for free? "What do we charge for that stuff?"

"Twenty-one bucks a pop."

His gaze shot back to the bartender. "He's drinking almost a hundred bucks of scotch two, three times a week? On our tab?"

Jesse shrugged. "Has been for a while."

"And Nathan's good with this?"

"Must be. He okayed it."

"It's not okay anymore. I don't know what Nathan's deal is, but from now on, if Chuck wants to drink for free, he drinks the cheap stuff. Give him the well scotch."

Jesse glanced over his shoulder at Chuck. "He won't like that."

"Too damn bad. I'm running the place now, and we're not giving that stuff away. If he has any complaints, he can take it up with me."

Jesse set the clean glass carefully in one of the racks. "Look forward to seeing that."

Ten minutes later, Patrick heard the sound of raised voices from the bar. When he walked in, Chuck was red-faced and yelling at Jesse. "Is there a problem here?" Patrick asked.

"Yeah." Chuck swiveled on the bar stool. "This guy tells me I can't have another scotch."

Patrick nodded to Jesse, who headed toward the far end of the bar. "I don't know what your arrangement is with my brother," he said, leaning closer to Chuck. "But anyone drinking on the house tab gets the well brand. Starting tonight."

"I don't drink that crap," Chuck said, but he leaned away from Patrick.

"Sorry to hear that. You can have beer or wine if you'd prefer. House brands."

The guy's narrow eyes became even smaller. His expression bristled like the stubble on his head, and his right hand drifted toward the lapel of his jacket.

Patrick watched as the guy flexed his fingers. *Goddamn it. The asshole was carrying.*

Chuck let his hand drop. "You might want to check with your brother on that."

"I intend to." He nodded. "Have a good evening."

As Patrick walked away, he ran through his list of contacts in the Chicago police department. Danny Kopecki still worked this district, as far as he knew. Maybe he'd give the guy a call. Suggest they have a beer and catch up.

Minutes later, Chuck stormed through the dining room, grabbed Theresa's arm and towed her along as he left the restaurant. When the door slammed behind them, Darcy rushed toward the patio. Patrick heard the throaty growl of a big car roaring out of their parking lot.

As the noise died away, she hurried back inside, scowling. "What happened?"

"Apparently, Chuck doesn't like our new bar policy."

"Which is?"

"If you drink free, you don't drink the good scotch."

She frowned. "That guy doesn't pay for his drinks? How come?"

"A question I'll be asking Nathan."

"We should be charging him double," she muttered. "From what Jesse says, he's a pain in the ass."

"He's gone, so we'll worry about it tomorrow."

"He won't be back tomorrow. Theresa rarely comes two days in a row."

"Good. That'll give him time to cool off."

Darcy glanced out the window again, then studied his face for a moment. "I hope this doesn't make it harder on Theresa."

"Shouldn't have anything to do with her."

Her gaze lingered for a long moment. "I hope not."

As the evening wound down and Marco was beginning the kitchen clean up, Patrick drew him off to the side. "There was a guy in the bar tonight, drinking our Macallan Eighteen, on the house. A lot of it. He said Nate okayed it. What's going on?"

Marco hunched his shoulders and concentrated on scraping off the grill, drawing a flat piece of steel over the blackened surface in even, regular lines. "Got no idea what you're talking about, Paddy."

'You don't know about that goon Chuck drinking for free?"

"I run the kitchen. Nate runs the rest of the place." He let the charred crumbs drop into the well at the edge of the grill and began again.

"Marco! Stop."

His brother scraped one more line, then slapped the blade on the grill. "What?" He frowned at Patrick. "I need to clean the kitchen. I want to get out of here sometime tonight."

He reached for the blade again, and Patrick slapped a hand on it. "I'm worried there's a problem here. Nate is jumpy and secretive. He insisted on doing the books and handling the money. That goon gulps our best scotch like it's water and doesn't pay a dime. I want to know what's going on."

"No problems, bro. Other than Nate being gone. Once he's back here, we'll be good."

Patrick stared at Marco, wondering why his brother's words hit like a blow even though he was right. Patrick didn't belong here. He belonged back in Detroit. Nathan was the one in charge of Mama's.

"You think I want to be here?" He glared at Marco. "I have a job in Detroit. Cases I should be working. A life. But I thought this was what families did. Help each other out. Do what needs to be done." He took a step toward Marco and satisfaction ripped through him when his brother reared back. "I know everyone here misses Nathan. That he knows what he's doing, and I don't. But I'm all you have right now. You can shut me out, but if there's something wrong at Mama's, I'm going to find out what it is."

CHAPTER SIX

As SHE FINISHED the cleanup in the dining room, Darcy heard Patrick's voice in the kitchen. Then Marco's.

Both men were shouting.

Yesterday, she would have tried to settle them down. Tonight, she didn't care what they were fighting about. She needed to get out of here.

Patrick had watched her all night. Wherever she went, whatever she was doing, she'd felt his gaze.

Every time she'd stepped into the dining room, Patrick had tracked her. She'd spilled a cup of coffee on the floor, almost dropped tiramisu into a customer's lap. Worry about Patrick and what he'd seen bled into worry about Theresa.

She had to *do* something.

She had to get Theresa to safety. Then, when Nathan came back to work, she could disappear again. Start over somewhere else.

She should be relieved. Escape was only a few weeks away.

Instead, her throat swelled and her chest hurt. She'd miss Mama's.

She'd miss the people.

She pushed through the kitchen door, grabbed her purse out of her locker and headed toward the back door just as the kitchen phone rang. Marco and Patrick were having a staredown, so she grabbed it.

"*Hola,* Marisol," she said when she heard Javier's wife's voice. Marisol's voice rose as she spoke rapidly in Spanish, and Darcy held the phone away from her ear.

She murmured a few comforting words until Marisol calmed

down, then asked a couple of questions. After assuring the woman that Javier's job would be waiting for him when he returned to Mama's, she hung up the phone.

"Marco, that was Marisol," she said. "Javier is doing okay, but you should probably look for a temporary cook. Sounds as if it'll be a couple of weeks before he's back."

"Damn it!" Marco picked up the tool he used to clean the grill and hurled it across the room, barely missing Luis's head. "He's been here for two months and just gotten to the point of working on his own. Now I have to train someone new?"

Darcy looked from Marco to a white-faced Luis to the blade on the floor. The perfect topper for a crappy night. "What are you, Marco, some kind of diva chef now? You been watching too much Food Channel?" She picked up the blade and pointed it at him. "Trust me, dude. You're not all that."

Marco scowled as he grabbed the tool from her, and an uneasy murmur slid through the room. Darcy slung her purse over her shoulder, feeling the reassuring weight of her gun settle against her hip, and headed for the back door. As she hurried past Patrick, he held out his fist for a bump. She ignored it. She didn't know what they'd been arguing about, but they were both idiots.

As she threw open the door, Patrick said, "Hold on, Darcy. I'll walk you out."

"Not necessary," she said. His footsteps speeded up behind her, but she didn't turn around. She slid into her car, slammed the door and took off.

THE HOUSE WAS DARK by the time Patrick arrived home that evening. Nathan had left the kitchen light on, but he was sprawled, asleep, on the hospital bed in the den. In the dim light, his hair was disheveled, as if he'd shoved his hands through it repeatedly before he fell asleep. The streetlamp in front of the house cast shadows over the bed and made his white casts gleam in the darkness.

Patrick wanted to wake his brother and demand answers

about Chuck and the free drinks. Tell Nathan to stop shutting him out. Instead, he tightened his grip on the bank bag and the flash drive that held a copy of the ledger. The accountant in him made him open the bag and count the cash. Nathan had been desperate to get his hands on both the ledger and cash. Did they have something to do with whatever was going on at Mama's?

He headed into the kitchen. After his confrontation with Marco, he needed a damn beer.

No one had stayed for wine tonight. After Darcy had stormed out, clearly pissed off at both him and his brother, the other employees had scattered, as well.

Patrick smiled faintly at the memory of Darcy chewing out Marco. Nathan had been right—the woman had a mouth on her.

His smile faded as he gulped the beer. He'd been spending too much time thinking about her mouth. Her ass. Her breasts, bouncing in her running bra.

He hadn't seen her running again, although he'd looked. Had she been going out at a different time? Trying to avoid him?

She cut him off whenever he asked her a personal question, and it had almost been fun to watch her attempts to keep him at a distance. She could dance with the best of them. But he hadn't forgotten what he'd seen two nights ago—the way she'd tended to Javier. The way she'd been desperate to help Theresa tonight.

Darcy was an interesting mystery, one he'd like to solve while he was here. He wasn't looking for anything serious— not long-distance—but maybe he'd come back to visit her once in a while.

His fight with Marco had reminded him that he didn't belong here. This wasn't his home anymore. After Nate was back at work, he'd return to Detroit.

His home. His life. A place with no messy, emotional family complications.

But before he left, he'd do his best to help his brothers if they needed it. They knew how to run a restaurant. He knew how to solve a problem.

Patrick leaned against the den doorway and watched Nathan sleep.

What have you gotten yourself into, Nate?

THE NEXT MORNING, Patrick waited until his brother was eating breakfast, then asked him about Chuck. Pressed him about what was going on at Mama's. Why he'd been so agitated the day before.

Nathan stared him down, his eyes hard, his expression carefully blank. "Butt out, Paddy."

"If you're in some kind of trouble, let me help."

"Run the restaurant for me. That's all the help I need."

The plates rattled as Patrick shoved away from the kitchen table. "I'm good enough to do the work, but not good enough to help you?"

If anything, his brother's expression got harder. "I repeat. Not your business. Not anyone's business but mine."

"If it affects Mama's, it's my business. Marco's and Frankie's, as well." He slid his hands across the table and stared at Nathan. "We own the place, too, buddy."

"You're a silent partner. And you're getting your share of the profits, *buddy*. So back off."

Patrick held his brother's gaze for a long moment, and when Nathan didn't look away, he dropped back into his chair. Nathan was right. He'd never wanted to be involved with Mama's. So why should his brother think anything had changed?

He watched as Nathan stabbed a fork into a crust of wheat toast, swirled it through the yellow smears of yolk on his plate and shoved it into his mouth. Then, holding Patrick's gaze a moment, he swung the wheelchair around and rolled out of the kitchen.

Hell.

Patrick got up and followed Nathan into the living room. His brother had already opened his laptop and inserted the flash drive into one of the USB ports. He ignored Patrick as he typed.

Patrick lowered himself to the couch. "Shouldn't have

jumped on you." He had more finesse than that. He'd been interrogating people for years.

"Don't worry about it." Nathan spoke without looking up, his fingers flying over the keyboard.

"I *am* going to worry about it," he said softly, resting his elbows on his knee as he slid to the edge of the worn plaid couch. "You're my brother. I'm not letting this go. I'm going to keep digging."

"Dig away. You won't find a thing." Computer keys clicked furiously.

"Is that a dare, Nate?" Patrick peered at the laptop, trying to see what was on the screen. "I like dares. You should know that by now."

Nathan slammed the computer closed. "Get the hell out of my face. Go for a run. Go hit somebody at the gym. Come back here all sweaty and tired and rub it in my face that I'm stuck in this chair. Just leave me the hell alone."

Patrick flinched. "Nate, I'm sorry. I'm not trying to rub it in."

"That's what it looks like," Nathan said. He opened the computer screen, closed it, opened it again. "Look. I appreciate you bringing this stuff home. I need to get some work done, to feel like I'm doing something worthwhile. So go away and let me do it."

Patrick stared at his brother, at a loss for words. Before he could figure out what to say, the doorbell rang.

When he opened it, a Chicago police officer stood there. "I need to talk to Nathan. May I come in?"

BRIGHT SUNLIGHT streamed through the trees, dappling the ground with golden light. Sweating, chest heaving, Darcy stumbled to a halt at the top of the pedestrian tunnel beneath the railroad tracks that separated Wildwood from Edgebrook. She'd run down almost every street in her own neighborhood, but anxiety still gnawed at her. Patrick. Theresa. The persistent itch at the back of her neck, as if someone was watching her.

Maybe she should stop by the shelter and talk to Kelly, the woman who ran it. Maybe she would have some suggestions for helping Theresa.

Maybe she'd have some advice for Darcy.

She stared at the ramp to the tunnel. She could do this. It was broad daylight. There were people around. She heard children's voices, laughing and shouting, on the playground at the other end.

Stupid to be afraid. And inconvenient. She could either go through the tunnel, or run an extra six blocks around it.

She took a step onto the ramp. Then another. During the day, the green lights weren't creepy, she told herself. They were only spots of color on the wall. She wiped her hands on her shorts, took another step. Scanned the shadows. Nothing.

Tim wasn't waiting on the other side to grab her.

Damn it, she thought she'd banished this kind of fear from her life. She ran as fast as she could, down the ramp, into the shaded tunnel, up the other side. She staggered as she reached the top and bent over near the playground, hands on her knees, her breath sawing in and out.

As her breathing slowed, she straightened. Three children soared through the air on swings, their legs pumping, huge grins on their faces. A woman she assumed was their mother watched them from a bench, a book in her hand. In another lifetime Darcy had been one of those free, joyful kids, savoring something as simple as a ride on a swing.

The woman smiled at Darcy. Managing an answering smile, Darcy headed for the water fountain near the monkey bars.

Now she was an adult, and joy hadn't been part of her life for a very long time.

She drank the cold water, then lifted her shirt to wipe the sweat from her face. With one last look at the family, she began running again.

She'd needed the reminder that there was still innocence and joy in the world.

Five minutes later, she stood outside the shelter house, which was enclosed by a tall fence. She pressed the buzzer, and after a moment, Kelly's voice answered.

"Who is it, please?"

"Darcy. Do you have a minute to talk?"

The gate unlocked with a click and Darcy pushed through, shutting it firmly behind her. When she reached the front door, it opened wide. The tiny brunette embraced her as she walked in.

"Darcy. What's up?"

Darcy nodded toward the office. "I need to ask you something."

"Sure. Hold on a second." Kelly turned to a tall blonde woman standing behind her. "Are Mary and her girls settled in?"

"No, but she told me to get lost. She's having second thoughts. I'm afraid she's going to leave."

Kelly glanced up the stairs. "I'll do my best to convince her to stay."

"I know. And I'll come back tomorrow to talk to her some more."

"A familiar face will be good." Kelly stepped back. "Emma, this is Darcy Gordon, one of our volunteers. Darce, this is Emma Sloan. She works for the Department of Children and Family Services."

They shook hands, exchanged greetings, then Emma slipped out the door. Once it was closed, Kelly said, "Mary and her two daughters are clients Emma's been working with. Took her a long time to convince the woman to leave." Kelly walked into her office, waited for Darcy to follow, then closed the door. "Hope to God Mary's still here the next time you're working."

"Me, too," Darcy murmured. She looked at the photos Kelly kept on a corkboard above her desk—women and children who'd come through her shelter, who'd successfully escaped from their abusers. She didn't know Mary yet, but she wanted to see her picture on that board. If Mary went back to her husband, the violence would be worse. She might not get a second chance to leave. "Do you want me to talk to her?"

"Not now. Give her a chance to settle." Kelly threw herself into her chair and leaned back. "What can I do for you, Darce?"

Darcy explained about Theresa and her fear that the abuse was escalating. "Any ideas? Suggestions? This is the first time I've seen such a large bruise on her face."

Her rickety chair squeaked as Kelly sat upright. "You know there's nothing more you can do." She held Darcy's gaze. "Don't you, Darcy?"

"Yes." Darcy closed her eyes, remembering Theresa's bruise. Her dead eyes. Her whisper. Had her husband tried to choke her, as well? "That doesn't mean I can't try."

"You're doing everything you can. Keep showing up at work, keep talking to her. And pray that eventually she listens to you."

Darcy thought about the car that had hit Nathan and come so close to hitting her. About Patrick and the questions he asked. The speculation in his eyes. About the itch at the back of her neck that wouldn't go away.

Run? Or save Theresa?

She didn't really have a choice—getting Theresa away from her abuser might save her life. But she needed to act quickly.

She stood up. "I'll be here on Thursday for my regular shift," she said. "If Mary's still here, I'll talk to her then."

"It helps them," Kelly said, standing as well. "Hearing how you escaped. How you got your life back."

She hadn't gotten her life back. Maybe never would. But she was alive. That was something.

And if she stayed in Wildwood, kept working at Mama's, kept volunteering at the shelter, maybe she could keep some other women alive, as well.

CHAPTER SEVEN

"What's this about?"

Patrick's question made the cop frown. "What the hell do you think it's about?"

"I have no idea. That's why I'm asking." Patrick held eye contact with the cop. No local uniform was going to intimidate him.

The cop studied Patrick for a long moment. "You must be the brother. The Fibbie."

"That would be me."

"My business is with Nathan. Not you."

Even the locals were shutting him out. "Let me get him."

Patrick heard the whirring of Nathan's wheelchair. "Paddy, let Marino in," Nathan said behind him.

Patrick spun around to face his brother. "You know this guy?"

"Of course I do. He's the one investigating the accident."

Feeling like an idiot, Patrick stepped to the side. When Marino was in the house, Patrick shut the door, then planted himself on the couch.

"You want some coffee, Marino?" Nathan asked.

"That'd be great," the cop replied.

Nathan glanced at Patrick, who raised his eyebrows. "Paddy, would you mind?" he said through clenched teeth.

"That's why I'm here, right? To serve and protect?" He pushed off the couch, started the coffee, then leaned against the wall in the dining room as it brewed. Nathan and the cop were making neighborhood small talk, and Marino glanced at Patrick. Nodded once.

Satisfied that the cop would wait for Patrick to return before having his conversation with Nathan, he returned to the kitchen and poured two mugs.

Marino called, "Black is fine."

Patrick scowled.

The two men continued talking, their voices a low rumble, as Patrick carried the coffee into the living room. He set one mug on the table next to Marino and put the other in Nathan's cup holder. Then he sat down again.

Nathan narrowed his eyes. Patrick gave him a "go to hell" stare. He hadn't come to Chicago to be dismissed like a friggin' servant when a cop came to talk to his brother.

Marino took a drink then set his coffee down. "So, Nate, good news. We found the person who hit you."

Patrick was watching his brother and it was hard to miss the way Nate went still. Turned a little pale and braced himself. "Yeah? Who did it turn out to be?"

Marino pulled out his notebook and studied it, frowning. Nathan's knuckles whitened on the arm rests. "Bridie Sullivan. Eighty-seven years old. Isn't supposed to drive at night, but she sneaked out when her daughter wasn't home. She knew she'd hit the railing at Mama's, but she'd forgotten to turn her headlights on and didn't realize she'd hit you."

"An old lady?" The relief on Nathan's face was impossible to mistake. "Shut up. No way."

Marino laughed and snapped the notebook closed. "She took the car to a body shop a few miles away, and they called us. She feels horrible. Asked me if she could make you some cookies."

"Cookies? No." Nathan rubbed one finger over the arm in the cast. "So what happens to her?"

"She's been charged with leaving the scene of an accident, failure to report an accident and a bunch of other stuff. I have her insurance info for you." He took a piece of paper out of the pocket of his jacket and handed it to Nathan. "Sounds as if her daughter is taking away her license and getting rid of her car."

"So that's it?" The tension in Nathan's shoulders eased and he exhaled.

"Case closed," Marino said. He narrowed his gaze and glanced over at Patrick. "Unless there's something else you'd like to talk about."

Time to get rid of this guy. Patrick stood up. "You have any brothers, Officer?"

Marino grimaced. "Four of them. Each a bigger pain in the ass than the next. They worry."

"I do, too." Patrick opened the door. "You got the blow-back. Sorry."

"Right." He glanced over his shoulder at Nathan. "Glad you're doing okay."

"Thanks."

Patrick closed the door behind Marino and waited until he drove away. Then he turned to Nathan, who looked like he'd gotten a last-minute pardon from the electric chair.

"You were shocked as hell when he said it was an old lady. Which means you thought you knew who it was."

"I figured it was some drunk," Nathan muttered. He took a deep breath. "You've been a stand-up guy, and I've been an ass. Let's drop this."

"You think you can distract me with a lame apology?" Patrick said scornfully. "Not a chance. I've had pros shining me on. Who did you think hit you, Nate?"

"I had no idea." Nathan jerked on his wheelchair control and spun around to face the window. "I'd have told the police if I did."

Like hell you would. "Come on, Nate, who would run you down? And why?"

"You gotta trust me, Paddy. Have a little faith."

"Pretty hard to do when *you* don't trust *me*." He threw himself into the chair closest to the wheelchair and leaned forward, elbows on his knees. "You don't think this is any of my business. I get that. But I can't stand by and do nothing if my brother is in trouble. Please talk to me. Hell, talk to all of us. Four heads are better than one."

"No, they're not. Drop it, Patrick. It's all good."

Patrick stared at his brother and Nathan held his gaze. Finally he stood. "Fine. Keep your secrets. If you can."

PATRICK SLAMMED through the back door of Mama's an hour late. His office in Detroit had called to remind him he needed to be in court in three weeks to testify about one of his cases. He'd been trying to figure out how to juggle his court date with his responsibilities here, and he'd lost track of the time.

When he hurried into the dining room, the waitresses and cooks were sitting around the big table, tasting Marco's specials of the day—salad with pears and blue cheese and a linguine with roasted vegetables.

Marco nodded at him. "Hungry?"

"Don't have time." They'd had a liquor delivery this morning he hadn't been able to supervise, and he had to make sure the receipt and the actual delivery matched. Then he had to find out what food needed to be ordered for tomorrow.

"Still have to taste them, Paddy. Customers want recommendations."

Patrick dropped his briefcase. "Fine. Set me up."

Just as well. He had to tell everyone the news, anyway. He slid into the open chair at the table and glanced at Darcy. She was carefully avoiding his gaze, eating the linguine as if she were the food critic for the *Herald Times*.

"It's good," she finally told Marco. "A bit bland, though."

Marco frowned. "Really?" He pushed away from the table. "I'll go play with it a little more."

"Hold on, Marco," Patrick said. "I have some news."

His brother sat down. "Yeah? About what?" He tapped his fingers on the table in a jittery rhythm.

"The police stopped by today," Patrick said, watching Marco's face. No reaction. "They found the person who hit Nathan."

Darcy stilled, fork in the air.

Marco's face tightened. "Who was it? Do they have him?"

Phyllis and Jesse shot questions at him at the same time, their words sounding jumbled.

"We need deets, Patrick," Jesse said. "Spill."

Darcy set her fork on the plate. It rattled a little, as if her hand shook. "Yes, Patrick. Who was it?"

She was bone-white, and it looked as if she held her breath. Watching her, glancing at Marco, he said, "The police sent out a bulletin about a dark sedan with front-end damage. A mechanic at a body shop a few miles from here called them."

"Was it some drunk, like we thought?" Phyllis asked.

Patrick smiled. "Bridie Sullivan. Eighty-seven years old." He gave them the rest of the information, still watching Darcy and Marco.

"No way," Marco said, shoulders relaxing.

Darcy slumped against the back of her chair as if someone had cut her strings. "An old woman?"

"Yeah. When the police confronted her, she folded like a cheap lawn chair."

The muscles in her throat rippled as she swallowed once. Again. "Thank God they found her," she said with a forced smile. "Nathan must be happy." She gulped water, coughed, cleared her throat.

More and more interesting. Marco was as relieved as Nathan had been. Darcy was shocked. Which meant all three thought they knew who the driver was.

Darcy *was* involved with what was going on at Mama's. She knew Nathan's secret.

The thought of Nathan and her bound together that way was disturbing, but he ignored the reaction. Focused on the fact that Nathan and Marco wouldn't tell him anything. Their brother.

Pressure built in his chest. He was still the outsider.

He slapped his hands on the table and stood up. "Let's get to work."

All evening, no matter what he was doing, Patrick found

himself watching Darcy. Wondering why Nathan had confided in her.

Whatever the reason, she buried her reaction while she was working. She smiled, chatted with the customers, teased the cooks and busboys, like she did every night.

But when she was alone in the waitresses' station, getting bread or entering an order on the touch screen, her smile fell away. When she thought no one was watching, she let the weariness show. Along with relief and a bone-deep worry.

He wanted to know what was going on in his restaurant.

He wanted to know how Darcy was involved.

WHEN THE EVENING was finally over and everyone was leaving, Patrick put a hand on Darcy's arm. "Hold on a minute."

She tensed beneath his hand, then slowly drew away. "Why?"

"I need to talk to you. Alone." He saw Marco approaching and said under his breath, "Pretend you forgot something in the other room."

Her knuckles were white on the strap of her bag, but she turned and pushed through the swinging door into the now-dark dining room.

Marco paused on his way to the exit. "Darcy okay?"

"Forgot something," Patrick said easily. "Go ahead. I'll lock up."

Marco looked from Patrick to the dining room. "See you tomorrow, Paddy."

Luis and Jesse followed him out, and Patrick locked the door.

He strode to the swinging door and pushed it open. She stood in the dark, her bag in front of her like a shield.

"Everyone's gone," he said, stepping into the room. The darkness was intimate. Private. Maybe she would be more comfortable talking without the bright lights of the kitchen illuminating every expression on her face.

But before he could move toward her, Darcy straightened her shoulders and brushed past him into the kitchen.

He followed reluctantly. And when the door had swung shut behind them, she studied him. "What's this about, Patrick?"

The freezer hummed in the background, and the acrid scent of cleaning solution hung in the air. Bright light from the overhead fixtures bounced off the aluminum tables and counters.

Late at night, empty except for the two of them, the kitchen was a cold, stark place.

Darcy stood rigid in front of him, shoulders back, arms crossed in front of her, dark red hair tousled. Suddenly he wanted more than just to talk to her.

He didn't move.

Wasn't going to happen. He needed her help running Mama's, and he wasn't going to screw that up by hitting on her and having her walk. Without Darcy, he suspected the place would fall apart. It would also delay his return to Detroit, his return to his life. He wasn't going to risk that for a few weeks of fun and games.

That didn't stop him from wanting her.

"What do you need?" she asked.

She'd be surprised if he told her. "What's going on at Mama's Place? What are you and Nathan and Marco up to?"

She let the bag drop to her side and frowned. "What are you talking about?"

"You were shocked about Bridie Sullivan. You weren't expecting an old lady to be the one who hit Nathan. Which meant you thought it was someone else. Nathan and Marco had the same reaction. I want to know who. And why."

He watched her mentally scramble. Try get her thoughts in order. Finally she said, "Why wouldn't we be surprised? We all thought the driver was drunk."

"Nathan was relieved. Which means he figured he knew who was responsible." He moved closer to her. "He's stonewalling. Marco, too. So I'm asking you. You know about everything going on here."

"You think Nathan's in trouble." She frowned, as if surprised.

"Yeah. I want the details."

"I don't have any. I haven't seen any problems." Her gaze was clear and direct. Open.

She looked as if she was telling the truth about Nathan.

Which meant her shock about Bridie Sullivan was on her own account. She'd thought someone was after her. "So when that car hit Nathan, you didn't think it was after Nate. You assumed *you* were being targeted."

Her eyes widened. She swallowed. Her knuckles whitened.

There was the tell.

In the background, the freezer coughed and turned off. Silence pressed down on the room.

"That's ridiculous," she finally said. "Why would I think that?"

"I don't know. You tell me." He edged closer. "Did you think it was Theresa's husband? Some guy you're dating? Someone from your life before Mama's?" He moved closer. Intimidating her. Trying to fluster her. But she didn't budge.

"None of the above." She slid her half-clenched fist up and down the handle of her purse. "But even if you were right, why would it be any of your business?"

"Because it happened at my restaurant. On my time."

"Not your time," she retorted. "You weren't here."

"Nathan's, then." He loomed over her.

She stood her ground. "If I thought I knew who it was, I'd tell the police. I'd help them find the person who hit Nathan."

He shook his head slowly. "Lot of secrets in one small restaurant." He was close enough to see a flicker of fear in her hazel eyes. "Does Nathan know what you're hiding?"

"You're letting your imagination run away with you." Her voice was tinged with just the right amount of impatience. As if she'd practiced her response. "Do you think I'm stealing from Mama's? Doing something to hurt the restaurant?"

Another good technique—go on the offensive. "I never said that."

"Then why are you questioning me as if I were a criminal?" Her eyes flashed and her mouth firmed.

"Never implied you were a criminal." He studied her expression. "You've got secrets, though."

"Everyone does." She shoved her hands through her hair, ruffling it even more. Making it look as if she'd just gotten out of bed. "Including you. Do you want me to poke into your life?"

"Depends on why you're poking." He leaned in, close enough to smell her gingery shampoo, the lemon-lime soda she'd gulped as she cleaned. The closed-off, guarded Darcy had disappeared. The woman in front of him was vibrant. Alive. As vivid as her red hair. "Maybe I'd welcome your interest."

Her eyes darkened. She swallowed. Held his gaze.

Desire slammed into him. He'd been holding back with Darcy because Nathan needed her. Patrick hadn't wanted to screw that up.

But his brother was shutting him out.

So why should he defer to Nathan's wishes and stay away from Darcy?

Before he realized he'd moved, she was plastered against him, her back against the counter. He wove his fingers through her hair and cupped her head, lowered his mouth to hers.

PATRICK'S MOUTH WAS hard on hers. Almost rough. For a moment, Darcy was too stunned to move. Then she brought her hands up to shove him away.

Before she could, he softened the kiss. He touched his tongue to her lower lip and sucked gently. His hands shook, and he brushed his thumbs over her cheeks.

Her bag dropped to the floor with a heavy thud. She curled her palms into his shirt and held on. It had been so long since she'd felt desire. Since she'd kissed a man. Need raced through her like fire, making her burn.

Not with generic, impersonal lust. Need for *Patrick*. The

man who'd alarmed her from the beginning. Fascinated her just as much. She wanted to know what he tasted like. How he felt with his body pressed against hers.

Slowly, trembling, she wound her arms around him. His chest was solid with muscle, hard to her softness. She splayed her fingers on his back, and his muscles bunched and tensed. It was an effort for him to hold back. Go slow.

Suddenly, she didn't want slow. She wanted the flash and the heat and the mindless rush of desire. So she moved her hands to his head, speared her fingers into his soft hair and opened her mouth to him.

He froze for a moment, then he pressed closer. His tongue danced with hers, coaxing her to play. He slid his hands to her back, sweeping from her neck down her spine, cupping her rear. Lifting her against him.

His erection cradled against her belly, he groaned into her mouth and tugged her shirt from her waistband. He touched her belly, and her muscles tightened. For a moment, it wasn't Patrick kissing her. It was Tim, looming over her. Hurting her.

Darcy sucked in a breath, unwound her arms and pushed. It was like trying to move a boulder. She shoved harder, and he stumbled backward and let her go.

For a moment, they stared at each other. His face was flushed, his eyes darkened to navy. His face was all sharp planes and angles.

She was equally aroused, and she knew he could tell.

Her face burning, she bent and fumbled for her purse. Her hands shook as she picked it up. Without looking at Patrick, she slid past him and broke for the door.

"Darcy, wait."

She kept going. Outside into the darkness. She didn't even think about what could be hiding there.

Tonight, the danger waited inside the restaurant.

He grabbed the car door just as she was pulling it closed. "Don't go. Talk to me."

Yanking the door shut, she started the car with shaking

hands and drove away. As she turned onto Devon, her tires squealed.

She was fleeing.

Him? Or the secrets she kept?

CHAPTER EIGHT

DARCY GRIPPED THE steering wheel as she drove through the silent neighborhood. Her stomach churned and her chest ached. How could she have been so stupid?

She'd kissed Patrick. A *cop*. And not only had she kissed him, she'd liked it. Had wanted to do more than kiss.

The flashback to Tim had stunned her. She'd been so rattled that she'd run off like a panicked virgin who'd never been kissed. Mistake piled on mistake.

She should have stayed. Talked to him calmly, one adult to another. Told him she'd enjoyed kissing him, but nothing was going to happen between them. They worked together. He lived in Detroit, and she didn't do flings.

Instead, she'd fled. He'd noticed her panic. Her alarm.

Patrick noticed everything.

She slammed the flat of her hand into the steering wheel. Comfortable was making her careless. Careless was dangerous.

The flash of headlights behind her made her slow down and glance in her rear-view mirror. An SUV had followed her onto the side street from Devon. She turned two blocks early. The SUV did, too. Moments later, it pulled into a driveway and vanished into a garage.

Letting out a shaky breath, she made her way back to her apartment and turned into her own garage. Crickets chirped as she walked through the dark, silent backyard, and an owl hooted in the forest preserve a few blocks away. The scent of her landlord's mums was sharp in the cool fall air.

His light was off as she climbed the stairs, pepper spray clenched in her hand. When she reached her back door, she glanced at the tomato plant. It looked the same as it had when she'd left that afternoon.

Cat was waiting for her in the kitchen. Tossing her purse onto the chair, she went through her ritual of checking the rooms and windows and doors. Then she fed Cat and walked into the living room, throwing herself on the couch.

She'd screwed up tonight with Patrick. But at least the hit-and-run driver hadn't been Tim. That didn't make Nathan's injuries any less severe, but it alleviated some of her guilt. It should have relieved some of her anxiety, as well.

It hadn't. Everything that happened tonight only emphasized that she needed to leave. The itch at the back of her neck was worse; her whole body was shouting *go, go, go.*

If she'd been prepared this evening when Patrick told them about the old woman, she wouldn't have reacted. She wouldn't have given him anything.

But working together for the past weeks had lowered her barriers a little. Made her less cautious around him. And tonight she'd paid the price.

She'd kissed him. He'd seen how she really felt.

Reason enough to move on.

But she couldn't leave Theresa. No matter how much she needed to move on, she wasn't going anywhere until Theresa was safe.

Nathan got his casts off in three weeks. Then he'd be back at Mama's, and Patrick would be gone. Nathan wouldn't be able to do a lot of work right away, so she'd stick around another week or two, until he got back into the flow. She owed him that much.

Then she'd leave. She'd use some of her carefully hoarded cash to buy a new identity, find another city. Another restaurant.

It wouldn't be a hospital emergency room, but her nursing career was just another loss in a long string of them. She closed her eyes tightly, holding back the tears.

Waitressing wasn't the worst job in the world. It had a few

perks, like the constant stream of cash. Emergency money. Enough to get out of town on short notice.

Cat jumped into her lap, and Darcy ran her hand down the bumps of the animal's spine, smoothing the soft fur. He kneaded as he purred, nails gripping and releasing, digging into Darcy's thighs. Reminding her that every pleasure had an accompanying pain.

It was only late at night that Darcy regretted sacrificing her job to get away from Tim. In the cold light of day, she knew it had been necessary. She knew she'd do it again.

Patrick's face filled her mind, smiling down at her as they silently acknowledged their shared expertise the night Javier had been burned. The way they'd worked so seamlessly together.

That night had led to this one.

Worse, Javier's accident had stirred up memories. Memories that didn't want to go back in the box where they belonged.

Tomorrow she would force them there.

Tonight, she'd let herself grieve for what she'd lost.

And for what she'd never have.

THE REFRIGERATOR KICKED ON as Patrick stepped into Nathan's kitchen the next morning, and he tightened his grip on the banker's box he held. The low hum reminded him of the kitchen restaurant the night before. Darcy, in his arms. Kissing him. Wrapping her arms around him.

Kicking the pile of boxes out of his way, he dropped this one on the table and shoved the memory away. He'd spent enough time reliving it during the night. This morning, he needed to work.

Last night, he'd looked at the ledger in Nathan's computer. The amount of money in the deposit was five hundred bucks less than the amount Patrick had brought home.

What had Nate done with that five hundred?

This box was the last of six he'd carried down from the attic this morning. It was still dark outside and Nathan was asleep. Patrick was going to go through the restaurant's financial records, looking for any anomalies. He was starting from the year their parents had died. He knew that when you looked for patterns, you had to start at the beginning.

The top layer was income tax returns for the last two years of his parents' lives and beneath them the returns from the first five years Nathan was in charge of Mama's. The latter showed a drop-off in income the first year, then a gradual increase after that.

Made sense. Nathan would have been overwhelmed at first with new responsibilities. Patrick remembered how his brother had focused on his siblings, struggling to be a parent to seventeen-year-old Patrick, thirteen-year-old Frankie and ten-year-old Marco.

Nothing suspicious in those early years. He could always dig into the actual ledgers from the restaurant if he needed to, but first he was going to do a quick scan.

As he set the first envelope of tax returns back into the box, he felt the crinkle of paper beneath his fingers and frowned. He thought he'd taken everything out.

Standing up, he saw that the bottom was filled with loose papers. Photos. Folders. He pulled out the top one and stilled as he opened it.

It was a file of notices Nathan had gotten from their schools that first year. Detention slips for Frankie—talking back to the teacher. Fighting with other girls. Pushing a boy on the playground.

There were trips to the nurse for Marco—stomachaches. Headaches. Difficulty breathing. Each time, Nathan had gone to the school, talked to the nurse, talked to Marco. Usually brought him home.

There were papers from Patrick's high school, as well. Notices from his teachers about falling grades. Homework not turned in. Mouthing off in class.

God. The three of them had been screwed up. And Nathan had handled it all. Finally, after Frankie had run away, the school social worker had pushed Nathan to take his siblings to counseling. Patrick had hated it. He'd given the therapist the answers she clearly wanted and gotten out as soon as he could.

Frankie and Marco had done better. Gradually, their problems had eased.

Patrick slammed the folder shut and reached for the next one. As he cracked it open and saw the pictures, he almost shut it and tossed it back in the box. But he forced himself to look.

They were photos from the first couple of years after the accident. Family shots, mostly. In almost all of them, Nathan, Marco and Frankie were a tight cluster in the center. He was standing off to one side.

He knew why. He'd been eaten up with guilt. When he got to college, he'd finally matured enough to realize he needed therapy and it had helped some. But the distance between him and his siblings had widened, and it grew into a gulf when he joined the FBI and was assigned to Detroit, five hours away.

He slammed the folder shut and tossed it in the box. He didn't have time for a trip down memory lane. Shoving on the lid, he reached for the next box. He had a restaurant to run, and he needed to find out when things had gotten off the tracks. He was a forensic accountant. There would be evidence, and he would find it.

THAT AFTERNOON, Darcy arrived at the women's shelter for her regular shift, her head pounding. She'd hardly slept the night before, worries bouncing through her mind like a squirrel in a cage. She'd come to no conclusions, except that she couldn't leave yet.

That hadn't make it easier to fall asleep.

For the moment, though, she'd put her own predicament aside. The women at Safety Net had their own problems, and she was here to help them.

The aroma of beef stew lingered in the air as she walked into the house. In the living room, several women sat on the worn couches, watching television. The laugh track blended with the voices of the children playing with Lego blocks on the floor.

Kelly sat at her desk in her office, her head propped in her hand, doodling on a pad. Darcy stopped in the doorway. "Kelly? What's wrong?"

"Mary left today."

"Oh, no." Darcy walked in and slumped into a chair. "She took her kids back to her husband?" Darcy knew too well how an abusive relationship destroyed a woman's self-confidence and distorted her self-image. But it was still hard to understand how a mother could take her children back into a dangerous home.

"She said she was going to stay with her sister." Kelly tossed her pen down. "I hope she was telling the truth. And that she's safe there."

"Does the social worker know she left? The one who brought Mary here?"

"I called Emma right away. She's trying to connect with her."

"God! It never gets easier to watch women going back to their abusers. Or start up with the same kind of man. Why can't we learn our lesson?"

Kelly leaned back and studied her. "Who are you talking about, Darcy?" she asked softly.

"All of us." As she waved toward the women in the other room, Patrick's taste still lingered on her mouth. "Why are we so self-destructive? Why do we repeat our mistakes?"

"What happened, Darce?"

The understanding in Kelly's voice made her eyes sting. "Nothing. A moment of stupidity." She stared at the bookcases in the corner. "What is it about me and cops?"

"You want the long answer, or the short one?"

Darcy shifted her gaze to Kelly, who was smiling. "The short one."

"I'm guessing he was hot."

She stood up. "Who cares about hot when he's whaling on you?"

Kelly's smile disappeared and she half stood. "Did someone hit you?"

"No. And he wouldn't. I know that. But he's a *cop*. You know what that means."

She looked at her friend, sinking back into her chair. Kelly knew everything that had happened to her. She knew why a cop was so dangerous—a cop would be more likely to see through her cover story. More likely to be suspicious.

"So keep it light. Have a little fun." Kelly came around to sit on the edge of her desk and took Darcy's hand. "It's good that you're interested in someone. It's healthy. It's been three years."

"Yeah, yeah, I've had therapy. I know that. But a cop?"

"Is he a good man?"

"I think so."

"Then his job shouldn't matter. As long as you don't let things get too heavy."

"Easier not to get involved at all." She drew her feet onto her chair and wrapped her arms around her legs. Staring at the worn spot in the knee of her jeans, she whispered, "What if I did find someone? I'm not sure if I could give my whole self ever again. I'm not sure I could let go and allow myself to completely trust anyone."

"Before you can figure that out, you have to take a first step. Do more than work at the restaurant and volunteer here."

"I'm not sure I want to. Right now, I'm safe. Safe makes me happy."

"Maybe it's time to take a few chances, Darce. Let yourself live again."

"Not with a cop." Her voice was flat and final. "What's going on here tonight?"

Kelly held her gaze for a long moment, then nodded once. Conversation over. "Rosie wants you to take a look at Michael. She's worried about his rash. And Jessica found a lump. Can you see them?"

"I'm not a doctor, Kelly. We have one on staff. Why do they keep asking me about medical stuff?"

"Because they know you. They trust you. They don't know Doc Allison very well."

"Fine." She knew how important trust was. But every time she looked at a rash or a lump or a sprain, it was a little pinch at her heart. A reminder of her lost nursing career. "Go get Rosie and her baby."

Kelly walked across the hall, and Darcy plunged her hand into her bag to find the latex gloves she always brought to the shelter. Almost every time she volunteered, someone had a medical question. As she felt around for the gloves, her hand stilled as it brushed against her gun. Her very illegal gun. She never went anywhere without it. If it wasn't safe in her bag, it was on her nightstand as she slept.

If anyone found out she had it, she'd have a problem. A big one. But she'd rather be in legal trouble than dead.

Finally she found the gloves and pulled them out. A young brunette with a fading black eye walked into the office, cradling a six-month-old baby. Darcy forced a smile. "Hey, Rosie. Let's take a look at Michael's rash. We should be able to have him feeling better in no time."

She wished all problems could be solved as easily.

WHEN HE ARRIVED at Mama's that afternoon, Patrick automatically looked for Darcy's car. It wasn't there. Had she quit because he'd kissed her last night?

No. That would be stupid, and Darcy wasn't a stupid woman. Her style would be to freeze him out. Rebuild the wall that had been slowly crumbling.

He wasn't going to let her do it.

He'd kissed her because he was angry with Nathan. Not a good reason to kiss a woman, but once he'd tasted her, once he'd felt her response, he'd forgotten all about his brother.

Her sweetness, the tentative way she'd kissed him at first, her gradual participation had driven him wild. He closed his eyes as he remembered the tiny sound she'd made in the back of her throat when she'd finally wrapped her arms around him.

He'd been restless all night, his dreams vivid and arousing. Darcy would want to pretend the kiss had never happened. He'd remind her, every chance he got. Sooner or later, she'd kiss him again.

As he walked in the kitchen door, he asked Marco, "Darcy sick or something?"

His brother turned from the stove, frowning. "It's her day off, dude. Get your head in the game."

"Lot on my mind," he answered mildly.

The staff had Marco's tasting and the customers began arriving, but without Darcy, the evening was black and white. There wasn't as much laughing in the kitchen. No one teased the regulars at the bar about what they were watching on television. No one made Marco laugh.

The nights she worked, everything was in Technicolor.

He missed her. She felt like an ally, more than either Marco or Nathan. When she wasn't working, he felt stranded.

Hell of a thing.

As he was speaking to a couple at a table, a tall man walked into Mama's. He stood at the podium, looking around, cataloging the place. It was Danny Kopecki.

Thanking the couple for coming in, Patrick hurried to greet Kopecki. The cop was wearing a suit instead of a uniform, and he had a badge clipped to his belt. "Hey, Danny," Patrick said, holding out his hand. "Thanks for stopping by."

"How's it going, Devereux?" Kopecki answered. His mouth twitched as he studied Patrick's khaki pants and dress shirt. "Not often I get a Fibbie asking for favors."

"Yeah, yeah. I'll owe you." He nodded toward a table in the corner. "Have a seat. You want a beer?"

"Just went off-duty. Beer sounds great."

Five minutes later, Patrick set a pint of Guinness in front of his friend and slid into the seat across from him. Kopecki's eyebrows rose. "Remembering what I drink. Impressive."

"That's why I'm federal and you're local." Patrick rattled

the ice cubes in his glass of soda. "Heard you're a detective now. Congratulations."

"Thanks." Kopecki took another drink of the dark beer and set it aside. "What can I do for you, Paddy?"

Patrick glanced around to make sure no one was close. "It's complicated. I've got a guy who comes in here regularly. He's with a woman, and one of my waitresses thinks she's being beaten at home." Kopecki started to speak, and Patrick held up his hand. "He's not the husband. The woman calls him her 'bodyguard.' I think he's carrying."

Kopecki glanced around the restaurant, studying every couple. "They here?"

"Not now."

"You know their names?"

"Woman is Theresa Smith. Pretty obviously not her last name. Guy's name is Chuck. No last name."

"Description?"

"Theresa's between forty-five and fifty-five. Dark hair. Thin. Chuck looks like a thug. Lifter, maybe. Probably a juicer."

Danny drummed his fingers on the table. "I might know who they are. First names are right." He leaned forward and lowered his voice. "There's an alderman's wife named Theresa. He has a goon working for him named Chuck. I'll see if I can find pictures."

"God." What had Darcy gotten involved in? "I don't want some connected mope coming in here with a gun."

"Even if he's not the alderman's Chuck, we can take care of that."

"Soon would be good."

"Give me a call the next time they're here."

"Will do."

Kopecki finished his beer and stood. "How's Nate doing?"

"Better. Pissy as all hell about being laid up."

Kopecki shook his head. "Who can blame him? He coming back soon?"

"Few weeks."

"I'll be waiting for your call."

"Thanks, Danny."

Tension tightened Patrick's shoulders as he watched his friend walk out the door. If Theresa was the alderman's wife and her bodyguard was getting free drinks, did it mean the alderman was involved in whatever was happening at Mama's?

Chances were good that it did. Darcy needed to step back. She was putting herself squarely in the crossfire, and she could end up getting hurt.

He'd tell her to leave Theresa Smith alone.

CHAPTER NINE

As Darcy drove toward Mama's Place on Friday afternoon, she wasn't thinking about work.

The kiss she had shared with Patrick replayed itself on a loop, over and over.

Just like it had done last night. And the night before.

She told herself it was just a kiss. People kissed all the time, and most of them didn't spend two days brooding about it. Worrying what it meant. Trying to decide how to act when she next saw the guy she'd kissed.

She'd known why he'd kissed her. He was trying to intimidate her. Get her to spill her secrets.

It had morphed into something else almost immediately, but she didn't want to examine that. Didn't want to think about Patrick really wanting her.

Or that she wanted him, too.

She was pretty sure he'd pretend nothing had happened. That would be the smartest thing. The easiest thing, since they had to work together.

That would be her strategy, too.

As she pulled into the parking lot, his big, black SUV was parked directly in front of her. So he was here.

Her heart jumped and butterflies fluttered in her stomach. Of course he was.

The only spot close to the floodlight was next to Patrick's car. She pulled in there, ignoring the way the truck seemed to loom over her subcompact. Apparently, he liked to intimidate on the road, too.

The late afternoon air promised that winter was coming,

and she tugged her expensive fleece jacket closer. It had been a present from Tim, and she'd almost thrown it away. But pragmatism had trumped emotion. It was a warm jacket. She couldn't afford anything nearly as nice.

When she walked in the kitchen door, the familiar aroma of garlic cooking in butter surrounded her with its delicious scent. Settled her. She took a deep breath as she hung her jacket in the closet. "Smells great, Marco," she called.

From his position at the stove, he smiled. "I made it just for you, Darce."

"And I love you for it."

"Really?" a voice behind her said. Heat washed over her skin. "That's all it takes? I guess what they say about garlic is true."

Don't engage. Keep walking.

She glanced over her shoulder to see Patrick leaning against the wall next to the office. He wore a dark suit and a blue tie, which emphasized the width of his shoulders and the color of his eyes. "What do they say?"

His eyes darkened. "Garlic is an aphrodisiac."

Her heart raced and her palms got damp. "You're kidding me. Right?"

Patrick shook his head. "One whiff and you're telling Marco you love him."

"Marco?" She sucked in a deep breath, but managed to say, "You mean my annoying younger brother? Please."

"I heard that, Darce," Marco called. But she couldn't tear her gaze away from Patrick.

He was closer than she'd realized. "Someone else, then," he murmured, in a voice too low for Marco to hear.

"Don't know who that could be. Even garlic couldn't make me interested in any of the sad cases around here."

Patrick's lids were half-closed. "Could have fooled me."

He held her gaze, and she was the first to look away. Okay, then. Patrick wasn't taking the "pretend it never happened" approach.

Marco glanced over his shoulder as he threw more minced garlic into the simmering butter and waggled his eyebrows. "Something interesting going on over there that I don't know about?"

Horrified, she stared at Marco's back. How had her "ignore it" plan gone south so quickly?

Eyes twinkling, Patrick disappeared into the office.

"Of course not! Jeez, Marco!" She swallowed, but rolled her eyes for his sake. "Patrick and me?"

"Good to know you're saving yourself for me," Marco said with a wink.

"Don't hold your breath, dude."

He grinned and turned back to his garlic butter.

Patrick stepped out of the office again. "Marco?" he said, but focused on Darcy. "Could you help me out when you get a moment? I need to know about cheese."

Darcy finally turned away from Patrick. Her ears burned and her hands shook as she pushed through the door into the dining room.

This was bad. She'd hoped to be cool. Calm, with a hint of amusement.

She'd planned to avoid any mention of the kiss and figured Patrick would, too. After all, she'd shoved him away. Told him she wasn't interested. Patrick was a smart guy. He could take a hint.

Instead, he'd acted as if he was looking forward to the next kiss.

She remembered the taste of his mouth on hers, the pressure of his lips, the way he'd taken his time, as if he'd planned on kissing her all night. Heat washed over her and she closed her eyes.

It couldn't happen again. She'd be more careful. Starting immediately.

As she cut sheets of butcher's paper to cover the tablecloths, she realized that she was the only one in the room. Three other waitresses were supposed to be working tonight. Phyllis and

Carol were here every Friday, and Ashley was filling in for Rita. Carol and Ashley were occasionally late, but Phyllis was always prompt.

She had half the tables covered when Patrick stepped into the dining room. "Phyllis just called," he said. "She's watching her grandson and her daughter got held up. She'll get here as soon as she can, but you and Carol and Ashley are going to have to pick up the slack."

"We can do that."

He glanced around. "Where are those two?"

She laid another sheet of white paper over a tablecloth. "I have no idea." She wasn't about to tell Patrick about their tardiness. If he yelled at them, Carol would be more sullen than usual and Ashley would be more ditzy.

The dining room lights illuminated Patrick as he helped her tear off sheets. She watched him for a moment, his lean frame bending over a table, his hands smoothing the paper in place. When she caught herself watching his dark pants tighten over his ass, she looked away.

"Since you're doing all the setup, you can leave when we close. The others can do the breakdown."

"Thanks." She picked up the basket of cutlery and moved to a covered table. If she left early, there was no chance she'd end up alone with Patrick in the empty restaurant again. That was good. It was exactly what she wanted.

Jesse called Patrick into the bar, and he rolled a sheet of paper onto the last table and hurried out. Darcy took a deep breath. Clearly, Kelly had been right. Not dating for three years was a mistake. It made her too vulnerable to an attractive guy, even one she knew was trouble. Once she got out of Chicago and settled in another city, maybe she'd try to find a nice guy.

An accountant. A dentist. Anyone but a cop.

By the time she'd set the tables, her heart rate was back to normal, and she headed into the kitchen for the cheese.

As she was opening the walk-in refrigerator, a delivery truck's engine rumbled outside the propped-open back door.

Patrick appeared, carrying two cases of wine, and she pressed against the wall to let him through. He'd taken off his suit jacket and rolled up his shirt sleeves, and her gaze lingered on his defined forearm muscles and their dusting of dark hair.

Jesse followed him in, carrying a single case. As they walked through the kitchen, Ashley strolled in, pausing to watch Jesse and Patrick. "Dude, that man is fine," she said.

Darcy turned to the college student. "Really, *dude?* Patrick is old enough to be your father." Not quite. But close enough.

"Patrick?" The blonde with the ponytail grimaced. "Like, ewww. I was talking about Jesse."

"He's too old for you, too," Darcy muttered as heat crawled up her face.

The door to the bar swung shut, hiding both men. Ashley sighed. Darcy yanked open the refrigerator. "Hey, Ash, you'd better punch in and get busy. Patrick already noticed you weren't here."

"Darn it! I hoped he wouldn't."

Darcy watched the girl's ponytail bounce as she grabbed her apron and hurried toward the dining room. She'd been working with Patrick all this time and hadn't realized how observant he was?

It was the first thing Darcy noticed about him.

Maybe the second thing. As Ashley had said, the man was fine.

AFTER SHE'D DISTRIBUTED the cheese dishes on the tables, she went to the waitress station for a glass of water. Ashley was stacking clean glasses, and the restaurant was in that comfortable place when everything was ready to go but the first customers hadn't yet arrived.

Patrick walked over to her, as if he'd known, even from the bar, where she was. She set down her glass and waited for him.

"Before we get busy, Darcy, we need to talk."

She glanced toward the dining room, but Ashley was in the

far corner, not close enough to hear them. "We don't need to talk about it," she said.

"What's 'it'?"

She crossed her arms over her chest. "The other night."

"That wasn't what I meant, but we can talk about that, too." He smiled politely. "What did you want to discuss?"

"Nothing! It's done. We can't take it back. But we can forget about it. Which is what I'm going to do."

He leaned against the counter and studied her. "Would you take it back? If you could?"

"I… We…" *Tell him yes.* It had been stupid of her. Reckless. Dangerous. But the words wouldn't come out of her mouth. "It doesn't matter what I want. We can't."

He straightened with a faint smile. "That's what I thought."

"It's not happening again."

"If that's what you want." He paused for a beat. "Is it?"

"Yes! Of course. It would be…" *Amazing. Breathtaking.* "A mistake. We work together. And you're leaving in three weeks."

"I know that. But we could have fun in those three weeks." His eyes twinkled. "Does Nathan have a rule against coworkers kissing?"

"I have no idea. It never came up. But getting involved would be disruptive."

"If you kissed me in the middle of the restaurant when it was full of people, yeah. That would be distracting. Is that what you were planning?"

"No! I'm not planning anything."

"Good. Then we don't have a problem."

Oh, they had a problem. At least she did. Her palms were sweating and her heart battered against her ribs. "What's wrong with you?" she whispered. "Ashley's going to hear you. Or Jesse. Anyone could walk in from the kitchen."

"That's why I'm not going to kiss you now."

But he would kiss her again. Soon.

She stared at him for a long moment as her chest tightened. He was definitely dangerous.

She had to stay away from him.

Running her damp palms down her apron, she swallowed. "So. What did you actually want to talk about?"

His gaze lingered on her mouth for a moment, then he straightened. "Right. Business." He was silent a moment. "I'm concerned about your relationship with Theresa Smith," he finally said.

She struggled to switch gears from the mental image of her and Patrick entwined in the kitchen. "What do you mean?"

"I learned some things last night that have me worried. I want you to be careful around her."

"What kinds of things?" she demanded.

He glanced over his shoulder, and she saw that Carol had come in. "Not now. Just—don't do anything rash."

"In a restaurant full of people?" she said, throwing his words about a kiss back at him. "I'm not stupid."

"No, you're not, but I think there's stuff going on that you don't know about. I'm worried about you. I want you to be careful. I don't want you to get hurt."

"Talking to Theresa isn't going to hurt me."

"Look, Darcy, I get it. I think you were a victim of violence, probably domestic abuse, and you want to help her. But you need to step back."

She could focus only on the bomb he'd just dropped. "Why do you think that? That I was a victim."

"Because of your extreme care about going to your car alone. The pepper spray you carry when you jog in the daylight in a nice neighborhood." He paused. "Your secretiveness and your strong reaction to Theresa tells me it was probably domestic. You want me to go on?"

"No! My personal life is irrelevant. Anyone would want to help Theresa." How did he know? Had he really put it together from those clues? Or, in spite of what he'd said that night, had he gone looking for information about her?

"We'll talk about this later. I wanted you to know before Theresa came in tonight."

"Is all this protectiveness because I kissed you?" She stepped closer to him. "It was a nice kiss, but it wasn't *that* good, Patrick. Not good enough for you to get all caveman about me. I appreciate that you're concerned, but I'll do what's best for Theresa."

His jaw tightened.

"Are we done here?" she demanded.

"For now."

She turned and bumped into the counter. She steadied herself, then retreated. As she walked away, she buried her shaking hands in her pockets.

She headed to Theresa's usual table, knowing Patrick was watching. The paper slipped on the tablecloth as she smoothed it, and the napkin-rolled place settings skidded sideways. Patrick had shaken her. But she glanced at him, let their eyes meet.

I'm not backing down.

NICE? PATRICK FUMED as he shoved into the kitchen. That damn kiss had kept him awake most of the night. And she thought it was *nice.*

The next time he kissed her, no one would be using the *n* word.

"Everything okay, Paddy?" Marco asked.

"Why wouldn't it be?"

"You look upset."

"Too much on my mind."

Marco pulled a serving of ravioli out of the water and plated it, then reached for a pan of white sauce bubbling on the stove. "Darcy part of it? I saw the way you looked at her, bro. You interested?"

Yeah, he was interested. He wanted to chip away at her walls and discover the woman who hid behind them. "That would be stupid, since I'm only going to be here a few more weeks." As Darcy had pointed out. But maybe he could come to Chicago more often.

"Not what I asked." Marco poured a ladle of the sauce on

the pasta, then added sautéed ham, peas and mushrooms. The scent of garlic rolled over Patrick, reminding him of their earlier conversation about its aphrodisiac qualities.

He didn't need any help where Darcy was concerned. "What if I am?"

"You break her heart, Nathan will kill you."

"That's a federal offense," Patrick said, trying to lighten the conversation.

Marco pointed the ladle at him. "Watch it," he warned. "Nathan's very protective of her."

"Is he."

"Don't get your panties in a twist," Marco said. "Not that way. Like he is with Frankie."

"Thanks for the warning."

If Nathan had a problem with him and Darcy, he could tell Patrick himself. He'd welcome a good fight—it might clear the air.

"Anytime." Marco backed up to the door and bumped his way through. Before it closed, he added, "Come taste the specials."

"I'll catch them later." If he sat at the table with Darcy, he wouldn't taste a thing, anyway. *Nice.*

He couldn't wait to show her *nice* again.

CHAPTER TEN

As THE RESTAURANT began to fill with customers, it was easy for Patrick to keep his mind off Darcy. She was busy serving, he was busy making the rounds in the dining room. Ducking behind the bar to help when Jesse got behind. Going into the cold keg room and wrestling with the awkward barrels when the Guinness keg needed to be switched out.

Every time there was a lull, though, he found himself looking for her. And each time, she was in another part of the restaurant. Talking and smiling with the customers, delivering food. Not looking at him.

Just as well. She needed time to settle down.

So did he.

At seven o'clock, two hours after the restaurant had opened, she wasn't smiling as much. She glanced toward the host's podium several times, even when he was watching her. She didn't seem to notice him. He caught her checking her watch more and more frequently.

Finally he got it. Theresa Smith was late tonight. Darcy was concerned.

When she stepped into the partially concealed waitresses' station, he slipped in beside her. "What time does she normally show up?"

She didn't look at him, but her finger slipped while she was entering an order. She didn't answer as she painstakingly corrected her mistake. Finally, when she'd submitted it and returned to the home page, she said, "Six. Never later."

"Maybe she's not coming tonight."

"She's always here on Friday. She misses other days occasionally, but never Friday." She spun around to face him. "What happened the other night when Chuck stormed out with her? Maybe that's why she's not here."

Chuck had been angry. He hoped that wasn't the reason behind Theresa's non-appearance. "The restaurant is almost full. We're not going to discuss it now," he said beneath his breath.

She stared at him for a long moment, and he couldn't read a thing in her expression. She knew how to hide what she was thinking, to keep all emotion buried deep.

Who'd taught her to do that?

"I'm worried about her," she finally said, turning to concentrate on the soda she was dispensing.

"I know."

"I keep wondering…" She pulled the glass away from the machine.

"What, Darcy?"

"If there was some way I could have gotten her out before now. Something I didn't do or say."

"Women leave when they're ready to leave." *You should know that.* "You can't blame yourself. Or put yourself in danger."

"How could I do that? I don't even know where she lives."

"Look," he said, leaning closer. "I want to help Theresa, too. But I don't want you to become collateral damage."

"Don't worry about me. I can take care of myself."

"Yeah, well, I *do* worry. Deal with it."

She stared at him for a long moment, then set the drink on a tray and walked away.

He watched her go, then noticed that two groups were waiting at the podium. Closing his eyes, he took a deep breath, forced himself to smile and strode over.

"Welcome to Mama's Place." He pretended to study his seating chart to give himself a chance to regain his footing. The faintly exotic scent of Darcy's shampoo lingered in his head, and he clenched his fists until he could focus on the chart.

"Right this way," he said to the first group as he pulled menus off the stack on the podium.

Two hours later, after the dinner rush had passed and most of the customers left were lingering over coffee or after-dinner drinks, he saw Darcy pause while cleaning a table. She stared out the front window at a dark SUV making its way down the street next to the train tracks. As it passed, she stood on tiptoe and craned her neck.

Hell. Theresa and Chuck had left in a dark SUV the night Chuck had stormed out. Darcy was still thinking about them.

He'd bet a lot of money that she examined every dark SUV she saw in the neighborhood.

No one was seated close to her. He walked over. "Darcy. Things come up. Plans change. Don't assume the worst."

"She's never missed a Friday." She set the rolled silver carefully on the paper, adjusting it so it was completely straight.

"Doesn't mean something bad has happened. Heck, maybe she went to a shelter."

She looked up. "Really? You think she woke up this morning, figured out where the shelter was and got there by herself?" She slapped another roll of silver on the table. "If you do, you know nothing about domestic violence."

"Okay, she probably didn't go to a shelter. But there are other possibilities."

"Such as?"

"Maybe she went out with her husband. Maybe she's got a cold. Maybe Chuck had something else to do."

Her eyes narrowed. "Based on a couple of things Theresa said, I think she *is* Chuck's job."

"All I'm saying is, don't jump to conclusions."

"Did you ask Nathan why that jerk was drinking for free?" Darcy asked.

He held up his hands. "I didn't say anything about Theresa. There were…issues at the bar."

"That's why he left so fast and dragged Theresa with him."

She shoved a hand through her hair and closed her eyes. "What happened?"

He glanced around and saw several people watching them. "Not now."

She followed his gaze and nodded curtly. Her eyes promised she wasn't letting this go.

DARCY'S STOMACH churned the rest of the evening. What was going on with Theresa? Why hadn't she come to Mama's? What had Patrick said to Chuck?

By the time the restaurant closed, her head was pounding. She should take Patrick up on his offer and go home early. But she wanted to corner him and find out what had happened the other night. So she did her cleanup work, as usual.

"I told you to leave early," Patrick said from behind her as she slid the cheese containers into the refrigerator. "You don't have to clean."

"I know." She shut the refrigerator and turned to face him. "I want to hear why Nathan's letting Chuck drink for free."

There was no one in the back of the restaurant. Marco and the cooks were cleaning up in the kitchen. The dishwashers were finishing the last of the dishes. Spanglish filled the air, punctuated by bursts of laughter.

"I figured you wouldn't let this go." He closed his eyes, as if it had been a long night for him, too. "I haven't had a chance to talk to Nate about it, okay?" he said. Too carefully. Based on the way Patrick avoided her eyes, there was more to this story.

"I know there's something else. Is it about Theresa?"

He held up his hand. "I swear, I never mentioned her name. It was strictly about the scotch."

When he didn't look away, she knew he was telling the truth about that, at least. "Okay. Thank you."

"You ready to leave? I'll walk you out."

She shook her head. "I'll finish cleaning. We're almost done." There was nothing to rush home to, anyway. Only Cat waited for her.

"You going to stay for wine, too?"

If she left, Patrick would think she wanted to avoid him. Like she was afraid he'd kiss her again. Both might be true, but she didn't want to admit it to him. "Sure, why not? It's been a long week."

"Amen to that," he muttered.

Forty-five minutes later, she'd nursed one glass of wine as long as she could. She'd talked to Phyllis about her grandson, commiserated with Ashley about her lack of recent dates and joked with Luis and Francisco.

She'd teased Marco and Jesse.

She'd interacted with everyone except Patrick.

She'd chosen a seat on the opposite side of the table from him, but she'd made a strategic mistake.

She couldn't avoid his eyes.

He talked to other people, but his attention always returned to her. When she took a sip of wine, his gaze fell to her throat. When she shoved a hand through her hair, his pupils dilated.

Even when he leaned back in his chair and spoke to Jesse, sitting next to him, she knew Patrick's attention was still on her.

"See everyone tomorrow," she said as she pushed away from the table.

Patrick immediately stood up. "I'll walk you out."

Her heart began a slow thudding. "Thank you."

She stepped into the kitchen and removed her jacket and purse from the locker. He held the door open for her, and her heart rate increased as she brushed past him. He kicked the stopper in place, then followed her into the parking lot.

It was a crisp fall night. The cold air carried the tang of wood fires burning in fireplaces. The sky was dark indigo, and in spite of the light pollution from the city, stars glittered above her.

As she rounded Patrick's large SUV, she slowed. Her car looked as if it was listing to one side. Patrick stopped, too. He studied the vehicle for a moment, then moved to look at the other side.

Frowned. Poked at the tire.

He stood up, brushing off his hands. "You have two flat tires."

"Two?" She moved past him to check for herself. Both tires on the passenger side were almost completely deflated. "How do you get two flat tires at the same time?"

"Did you hit any big potholes?"

"Not that I remember."

"Damage like this, you'd notice the impact."

She looked at the rear tire, then the front one. Replacing both of them would take a good chunk of her emergency money. Damn it!

Patrick squatted by the rear tire, positioning himself so the floodlight illuminated it. He ran his finger over the sidewall, frowned, then stood up. "I'll be right back. I need a flashlight."

"What did you see?"

"Not sure. That's why I need more light."

"I've got one. Hold on."

She gave him the flashlight she kept in the glove box, and he trained it on in the rear tire. Then the front one. Finally he stood up.

"There are holes in the side of each tire. Possibly from a pothole, but I doubt it. You'd have to be really unlucky to get those from an impact." He glanced around the parking lot. "Have we had vandalism back here?"

Her teeth were suddenly chattering. "My car was broken into a few months ago. Some CDs and loose change was taken. I haven't heard about anything else." Of course she'd thought of Tim first. But nothing else had happened, and she'd finally relaxed.

"We should call the police and report this."

"No!" He raised his eyebrows. "I mean, why waste their time on something like this? They'll look at the car, say, 'Yeah, the tires are flat.' What else can they do? I'll just get it fixed."

"Maybe there have been other incidents around here. This could be part of a pattern."

"I read the police reports in the local paper. There's been nothing about flat tires."

"You read the police reports?"

Oh, God. That had been a mistake. "Doesn't everyone?" she managed to say. "I bet you glance at them every week in your own local paper."

"No, I don't."

"Yeah, well, you carry a gun," she retorted.

"If you're not going to call them, I will."

He pulled out his phone and she grabbed his arm. "I'll call them myself tomorrow." His muscles were taut beneath her hand, and his skin was hot. She let him go. "Thank you for being concerned," she said. "But waiting until tomorrow isn't going to make any difference."

He watched her as he slid the phone into his pocket, then nodded. "Let's take a look at the other cars. See if any of them have holes."

Should she hope that they did? At least it would mean no one had targeted her specifically.

She shivered in the cold as they stopped at each of the six cars left in the lot. All of them were fine.

Only her car had been damaged.

She wrapped her arms around herself, suddenly freezing. Had Tim found her?

Slashing tires wasn't his style. Lying in wait for her was.

Patrick gestured toward his SUV. "I'll call the neighborhood auto repair guy and have him change the tires in the morning. The restaurant will pay for it, since it happened in our lot. In the meantime, let's get in my car. I'll start the heater, and we can talk. I need to tell you some things."

Her feet wouldn't move. She hesitated too long, and he frowned. "What's the matter? Are you afraid to get into a car with me?"

"Of course not." That was mostly true. She didn't like being trapped with men, but that was a reflex. She wasn't afraid of Patrick. "Wouldn't you be more comfortable in the restaurant?"

"I don't want to talk about this in front of everyone else."

"Okay."

"I'll get my keys." He took a few steps and looked back at her. "You coming?"

"Yes." She followed as he hurried toward the restaurant, shivering when they passed the tall lilac bushes surrounding the parking area. The lilacs were beautiful every spring, but she hated them. The bushes were too big, too dense, too dark. A perfect hiding place.

Something rustled on the ground, and she moved closer to Patrick. It was probably a raccoon. Or an opossum. They tried to get into the Dumpsters all the time.

Heart racing, she reached for his arm. Hesitated, then let her hand drop when they reached the restaurant. When they stepped inside, the noise in the bushes stopped.

After Patrick called the service truck and arranged for them to change her tires in the morning, they headed back to the cars. "That's me," he said, pointing at the SUV.

She didn't tell him she knew. He'd think it meant she was interested—that she paid attention to him. Instead, she raised her eyebrows. "Big truck."

"I'm a big guy. I like to be comfortable." He clicked his key fob and the doors unlocked.

She walked toward the passenger side, but he reached it before her. His shoulder brushed against hers and both of them froze. Then he moved away and she climbed in.

The inside of the SUV smelled like Patrick—fresh air and a sharp, spicy scent she finally identified as muscle rub. He must leave his gym bag in the car. When he turned the car on, the radio blasted a rap song out of the speakers. He quickly turned it off, but she said, "Really? Rap?"

"I like it. Lots of energy."

Maybe he wasn't as white-shirt, gray-suit as she'd thought.

He turned the heat up high, and pushed a button on the console. The vents blew out cold air, but the seat got warmer. She'd had heated seats in a car once. But the price of that luxury, and all the other ones, had been way too high.

She leaned against the door to watch him. As he fiddled with the heater controls, the floodlight outside the car illuminated tiny lines around his eyes. The dark shadow of his beard. The hint of a bruise on his jaw. She curled her fingers into her palms to keep from touching it.

"You've been boxing again."

She hadn't intended to say it out loud. Patrick touched the bruise. "Not a good idea to spar when you're distracted."

"A lot to learn about running a restaurant."

"Not all that was distracting me."

He shifted so he was leaning against his door. Watching her. The message in his gaze was clear—*you're distracting me.*

"Won't be long before you can go back to Detroit and leave all this behind."

"Yeah. Thought I was looking forward to that." He shifted and suddenly seemed closer. "Now? Not so much."

"So spaghetti sauce runs in your blood, too?" She'd heard Nathan and Marco say that often.

"Not the sauce."

He didn't move. Awareness rippled over her skin, making her jacket feel too tight. Making her heart beat faster.

Never get in cars with dangerous men.

"Right. So. What did you want to tell me about Chuck and Theresa?"

CHAPTER ELEVEN

PATRICK SHIFTED, filling the truck with the whisper of fabric on leather. The rolled-up sleeves of his dress shirt bared his forearms, and he draped one over the top of the steering wheel.

"If I tell you, this goes no further. Okay?"

She forced herself to look at his face. Tried to focus. Nodded.

"As far as I know, only Marco, Nathan and I know about this. And Jesse, since he's the one who's been serving Chuck."

"Who do you think I'd tell?" she asked.

"A friend. One of the other waitresses."

"I know how to keep a secret," she said.

He nodded slowly. "Yeah. I figured you did. And you're involved, whether I want you to be or not."

"What are you talking about?"

Drumming his fingers on the steering wheel, he held her gaze for a long moment. Then he said, "I told you about Chuck drinking for free when he comes in with Theresa. That he's been getting our most expensive scotch."

"I remember."

"Nathan won't answer my questions. He told me to butt out. Marco claims he doesn't know a thing. Jesse says he's just following orders. Makes me think there's some connection between Nathan and Chuck."

The thought of Nathan connected to Chuck made a ball of ice form in her stomach. "I don't know anything about it, either." She'd worked with Nathan for three years. Clearly, she didn't know him as well as she thought she did.

"I assumed you didn't. If Nate won't tell me, I figure he's not telling anyone." Patrick slammed the fleshy part of his palm against the steering wheel. "Damn closemouthed bastard."

The steering wheel quivered, and Patrick wrapped his hand around it.

Darcy began to reach for him, then jerked her hand back. Patrick's gaze followed it, lingering even when she curled it into her lap.

"Sounds like Nathan is shutting you out. Marco, too."

He raised his head. "That's exactly what they're doing."

That wasn't fair—Patrick had disrupted his life to stay in Chicago and help run the restaurant. "If I know Nathan, he's frustrated and bored," she said slowly. "Antsy. He's at the restaurant every night it's open, but now he's forced to sit at home and let you do everything. Maybe keeping this secret is his way of feeling like he's still in charge."

"What are you, a psychologist?"

Thanks to living with Tim, she'd become an expert at reading facial expressions. Body language. Emotions. "Don't have to be. I've spent a lot of time with Nathan over the past three years."

His mouth thinned. "A lot more than me, right?"

"Of course I have." She frowned, wondering where this tension was coming from. "Four nights a week add up."

"Has Nathan been bitching about me not being around?"

"Why would he expect you to be? You have a job in another city."

He blew out a breath. "Sorry. Forget about Nathan. I shouldn't have said anything."

She didn't want to get in the middle of a fight between the Devereux siblings. She leaned against the door. "Don't worry. I'm not going to tell Nathan we talked about him. But maybe you need to have another conversation."

"Pretty hard when he won't answer my questions."

"You're an FBI agent, for God's sake." She frowned at him. "You know how to interrogate people. And it's not like he can run away from you."

He smiled. "Good point. But let's get back to Chuck."

The back door of the restaurant opened, and an arc of light appeared on the pavement. Marco, Jesse, the waitresses and the cooks hurried into the lot and headed for their cars.

Marco, who was parked farther down the line, slowed when he reached Patrick's SUV.

Patrick rolled down the window. "Darcy has a flat tire. We're waiting to see if the service truck can make it tonight."

"Yeah? Need help changing it?" Marco peered over the front of Patrick's vehicle, as if trying to confirm what Patrick said.

"Spare's bad, too."

"Want me to drive her home?"

"Nah, I've got it. Thanks."

Marco hesitated a moment, then waved at both of them.

Darcy waited until Patrick had rolled the window up. "Why didn't you tell him both tires were flat? That you suspect vandalism?"

Patrick shrugged as he watched his brother walk over to the small sports car Marco parked well away from everyone else. "No point worrying him. Nothing he could do tonight. And I didn't tell him the truck was coming in the morning because I didn't want to explain why we're sitting here and talking."

So Patrick wasn't going to be up front with either Marco or Nathan. God, were all sibling relationships this complicated? She wondered if Frankie knew how the three of them were posturing and bumping chests. "What else were you going to say about Chuck?"

Patrick didn't reply until Marco had roared out of the parking lot.

"Chuck was pretty angry the other night. You're always the one who waits on Theresa. I wondered if Chuck was angry enough to punch some holes in your tires."

"What?" She sucked in a breath. "Why would he flatten my tires instead of yours? You're the one who cut him off."

"Maybe he doesn't know which car is mine."

"How would he know *my* car?"

"Easy. Watch when everyone's coming to work. Or leaving."

"That's totally creepy." She remembered the rustling noise in the bushes earlier and wondered if that had been Chuck.

No. He was a thug. Slashing her tires would be about intimidation. He wouldn't bother to hide and watch her reaction.

"Chuck isn't a nice guy." He hesitated, studying her for a moment. "I'm pretty sure he was wearing a gun that night."

She slumped against the seat. "A gun? In Mama's?" Her conscience reminded her that she had a gun in Mama's every damn night. But hers was hidden in her bag, stashed in the locker.

"Yeah. Which is why I told you to be careful."

She narrowed her gaze, and he held up a hand. "I'm not telling you to stay away from her. But for God's sake, watch yourself. Chuck doesn't sit at that end of the bar for nothing. He's keeping a close eye on Theresa. You can bet he's noticed that you're the one who always waits on her."

"Which is why you think he might have slit my tires." She studied his face and noticed he didn't quite meet her eyes. "What are you not telling me?"

"That's all I know," he said.

"You're not telling me all you know."

"You don't need to know the rest."

"Don't make that decision for me. I'm an adult who can think for herself."

"Fine. I don't want to tell you." He straightened and leaned toward her. "I don't know anything else for certain. When I do, I'll tell you."

"Is that a promise?"

"Yes."

As she stared at him in the darkness, she believed him. When Patrick promised something, he delivered it. Maybe assuming that made her a fool, but she didn't think he was lying. "Okay."

"That's it? Okay? You're not going to badger me to reveal my deepest thoughts?"

"Would it work?"

He'd started the truck, and as it growled beneath them, he glanced at her. "You could probably talk me into anything."

Her heart kicked and began racing, and she couldn't look away. Neither did he. His eyes darkened, and she was pretty sure hers did, too.

Struggling to ease the sudden tension that stretched between them, she said, "I'll have to use my powers for good, then."

He grinned. "You do that."

Shifting into gear, he backed out and headed for the street. At the last moment, she twisted to look at her car, all alone beneath the light. Was there a darker shadow in front of it, in the lilacs?

"What?" Patrick asked. "What's wrong?"

"Nothing."

He slammed on the brakes. "Tell me."

She swallowed. "I thought I saw something in the bushes in front of my car."

He reached over her, his shoulder brushing her arm, and opened the glove compartment. He removed a black hand-gun. "Lock the door after me. And stay here. Do not get out of the truck."

He climbed out and loped toward the bushes, the gun held loosely by his side. He paused in front of her car, listening, then plunged into the bush and disappeared.

She hit the power lock and the reassuring click echoed loudly in the silence.

Patrick returned five minutes later. As he approached the door, he tucked the gun into his waistband at the small of his back. He swung into the truck, buckled his seat belt and put the SUV into gear.

"What? What did you see?"

"Not a thing. Thought I heard footsteps, but when I got through the foliage, I didn't see or hear anything."

Chuck wouldn't have hung around. Could it be Tim? Had he found her?

He reached over the console to open her hands. She hadn't realized she'd clenched them into fists.

"Relax, Darcy. It was probably nothing. After the flat tires, we're both jumpy."

"Yeah." Jumpy was good. It had kept her alive for a long time.

PATRICK GLANCED BEHIND him one more time as he waited for a car to go past on Devon Avenue. Nothing there. But Darcy was still staring over her shoulder.

Her knuckles were white where they gripped the arm rest. "If anyone was hiding back there, he's long gone," Patrick said. Why was she wound tighter than a spring? "You think it was someone besides Chuck?"

She faced forward and leaned her head against the seat, watching him out of the corner of her eye. "How many enemies do you think I have?"

"You tell me."

"Besides Chuck? The old man who yelled at me at Happy Foods last week because I had one too many items in the express checkout line. The librarian who got huffy because I lost a book. A couple of customers, maybe. That's it, as far as I know."

"Slashed tires don't scream 'huffy librarian.' Or old guy with a grocery cart."

"So we're back to Chuck."

Or whoever else was making her nervous. Her ex? "You want to tell me about the guy who beat you?"

She stared straight ahead, her face expressionless, her body rigid. She didn't breathe. Then she slowly turned her head, her eyes dark pools in her white face. "I never said anyone beat me."

"I'm not judging," he said.

"Good, because there's nothing to judge."

"Glad to hear that." He turned right onto Devon and felt her tense beside him.

"How did you know to turn right instead of left?" She gripped the door handle as if preparing to leap out of the truck.

"That day we ran together, you said you didn't go through the underpass. I assumed that meant you lived on the west side of the railroad tracks."

Some of the tension left her shoulders and her fingers loosened on the door. "Right. Of course. I'd forgotten that conversation." She glanced at him. "You're very observant."

"Comes with the job."

They bumped across the tracks and stopped at another light. "You want to tell me where you live?"

"Uh. Yeah." She cleared her throat. "Mayfair. 6330. Turn right three blocks after the light."

"Near the elementary school, right?"

"Yes."

She didn't say anything more, but she slid her hands beneath her thighs and leaned forward a little, as if she was checking out the exterior mirror on her side of the car. Was she always this alert? This watchful?

It would be an exhausting way to live.

A few minutes later he rolled to a stop in front of an older brick Tudor-style house. "This it?"

"Yes. I live on the top floor."

The blinds were drawn, but a light shone through the shade. There were no lights at all on the first floor.

She unbuckled her seat belt and opened the door. "Thanks for the ride, Patrick. I appreciate it. I'll see you tomorrow."

He opened his door and slid out as she stepped onto a sidewalk that ran along the side of the house. Apparently her entrance was in the back.

Out of view of the street.

"Hold on, Darcy," he said in a low voice. "I'll walk you to your door."

She glanced over her shoulder, already halfway to the house. "That's not necessary."

She fumbled in her bag, then pulled out something shiny.

A night insect chirped, and whatever she held fell to the sidewalk with a metallic clatter. Keys. She swiped two times before she retrieved them.

She was jittery as all hell.

It took only a few long strides to catch up with her. "Why don't you give me the keys to your car? I'll have the mechanic deliver it after he changes the tires."

When she'd removed the car keys and put them in his hand, he said, "Quiet neighborhood. Real safe." Up and down the block, dried leaves lay in piles between the street and the sidewalk. Their dusty smell filled the air.

"That's why I like it."

In a family neighborhood like this, it would be easy to spot someone who didn't belong. A stranger hanging around. He wondered if that's why she chose it. "You been living here long?"

"Since I started working at Mama's."

She stepped into the faint light spilling into the backyard and garden, and he saw that wooden decks had been added to the back of the house, similar to the ones on many Chicago two-flats. There were small porches on the first and second floors and stairs wound back and forth between them. Grabbing the railing, she nodded at him. Her jaw was tense and her shoulders hunched. "Thanks again for the ride."

"I'll walk you up," he said, swinging onto the stairs behind her.

She turned. "You don't have to do that. Seriously. I'm fine." She nodded at the second-story porch. "There's no one up there. Safe neighborhood, remember?"

He stood one step below her now. Eye to eye. The wind lifted her hair and its gingery scent drifted over him. Cool moonlight pearled her face. He wanted to cup it in his palm and feel her warmth beneath his hand.

"Are we going to have a staring contest, Darcy? Or something else?" He leaned forward and she made a tiny inhalation. Her pupils darkened and enlarged.

Abruptly she turned around and started walking again. "Suit yourself."

At the top of the stairs they emerged onto a tiny porch. One folded-up lawn chair was propped against the railing. A large pot beneath the window held a tomato plant in its death throes. One branch was broken and turning brown, pointing toward the window like an arthritic finger.

The kitchen light was on but blinds covered the window above the plant and the one in the door.

"All good," she said brightly, inserting the key in the lock. "Thanks again for driving me home." She smiled over her shoulder. "And for telling me about Chuck. You'll let me know when you find out more, won't you?"

"Yeah, I will."

"Good." She looked past him into the yard, then down at the floor as she turned the key in the lock.

"What?" he said as she froze, automatically reaching behind him for the gun he'd left in his waistband.

She pulled the keys out of the door. "There's mud on my porch. Footprints. They weren't there when I left for work."

CHAPTER TWELVE

WITHOUT THINKING, Patrick wrapped his hand around her upper arm and drew her away from the door. Even through the fleece, he felt the tension in her muscles.

"Do you want to call the police?" After her reaction to the same question earlier, he figured she'd refuse, but it was the smart choice. He'd give a lot to know why she wouldn't go that route.

"M-maybe it was my landlord," she said, her teeth chattering.

Patrick squatted on the wooden floor of the deck and studied the prints. They were faint, as if most of the mud had been worn off on two flights of stairs. But there was enough to get a general idea.

"These were most likely made by someone who's around six feet tall. How tall's your landlord?"

"Not that tall," she said.

"Anyone else come up here on a regular basis? Mailman? UPS guy?"

"No. My mailbox is downstairs. Any packages are left there, too." She was taking deep breaths and letting them out slowly, as if trying to calm herself. He wanted to wrap his arms around her, but he suspected that would freak her out even more.

"Okay." He studied the prints again. They went to the door, turned around and went back down the stairs. He didn't want to say it, but after the slashed tires, he had to. "Any chance Chuck could have followed you home one night?"

"No," she said immediately. "I pay attention to that."

He'd figured she did. But there were other ways of finding out where a person lived. "Where do you park your car?"

"In the garage."

She pointed to the structure behind the house, and moonlight reflected off a window. Easy enough to find her car.

"I'll check your house before you go in."

"You think someone's inside?" Her voice rose a little.

"No, I don't." He took her hand and tugged her down beside him. "See the prints? They lead up to the door, then away. But it would be smart to make sure."

She clung to his hand tightly as she studied the faint smears of mud. "So if he came up and went back down, it's probably okay, right? Thanks for offering, though."

She disentangled her hand from his slowly, letting go finger by finger. Finally, she pressed her palm to his for a long moment, then let her hand drop.

He itched to reach for her again. Instead, he stood up. "I think you're making a mistake, but it's your decision." He patted the gun in the small of his back, the metal warmed by his body. "As you pointed out, I do have a gun."

She stood as well, staring at him. "That's it? That's all you're going to say? That I'm making a mistake?"

"You told me you could think for yourself." He wanted like hell to take charge. To *tell* her he was checking, instead of asking. But she'd probably been in situations where she didn't have choices or control, so he chose his words carefully. "From my perspective, it makes sense to let me check your house. I'm armed. I know what I'm doing. This is my job. I want to protect you. But I'm not going to force you to do anything. You get to make your own decisions. Even if they're stupid ones."

"I know how to protect myself," she said.

"From someone hiding in there?" He jerked his head toward her apartment. "Waiting for you?"

Her hand tightened on the handle of her bag, and her face paled in the moonlight. "Yes."

"Like I said, your choice. I'll wait out here, though, until you're finished."

She inserted the key in the door, although it took two tries. She didn't turn it, though. She stared at him instead, and he wondered what she was thinking.

After a long few moments, she stepped to the side. "I'd like you to do it," she said. "Please."

"I'd be happy to." He slid his gun out of his waistband and turned the key. As he pushed open the door, a huge black cat meowed, then narrowed its eyes when it saw he wasn't Darcy.

Patrick relaxed a little. If the cat was waiting at the door, there probably wasn't anyone in the house.

It was easy to check the kitchen—small table, two chairs, old refrigerator and stove. No place for anyone to hide. He moved into the living room. No one under the couch. Closet empty.

No one behind the shower curtain in the bathroom.

Under the bed. Closet empty.

There was no one in the house. No sign that anyone had been here.

He slipped the gun behind his back again and turned slowly, assessing her living space. She had a double bed that she hadn't made that morning. The dark blue quilt was thrown back, revealing pale pink sheets. Two pillows, but only one slept on. Running shorts and a sports bra at the foot of the bed.

Her dresser was old and battered, with gouges in the wood and places where the varnish had worn off. The drawers looked as if they would stick. The scratched top held a few pairs of earrings and a couple of necklaces, as well as a handful of coins and a small, cheap lamp.

There were no pictures on the wall, no photos on the small night table beside the bed. It looked as impersonal as a motel room.

The bathroom was the same—nothing decorative. Nothing personal.

The living room, too. She had bookshelves that held some

paperbacks and a small television. The morning's *Herald Times* sat on a beaten-up coffee table, and the couch looked as if it had been rescued from Goodwill. Two tiny end tables held plain lamps.

She'd made no effort to personalize her living space.

He opened the back door and motioned her inside. "Everything is fine in here. Nothing's been disturbed, no sign of an intruder."

"Thank you," she murmured, dropping her purse on one of the two kitchen chairs with a thump. She glanced at him quickly, then fiddled with the teakettle. "You, uh, want some tea or instant coffee?"

He shoved his hand through his hair. "It's too late to dance around. If you want me to stay until you're comfortable, I'm happy to do that. If you want me to leave, tell me to get out."

The kettle clattered against the stove. "Would you rather have a beer?"

"Does that mean you want me to stay? I don't want to guess, in case I'm wrong."

Hope and fear battled in her eyes, and he didn't move as he waited to see which would win. Slowly her shoulders relaxed. She unclenched her fingers.

"Stay," she said in a rush.

"Happy to." He pushed away from the wall. "Beer sounds good."

DARCY PULLED A BOTTLE out of the refrigerator, opened it and handed it to Patrick. She'd only asked him to stay because she was rattled by the footsteps on the porch. If she was alone, she'd never fall asleep. She'd lie in bed, listening to every creak of the tree outside the living room, every whisper of wind through the badly sealed windows, every barking dog and suddenly silent night insect.

That wasn't the only reason she'd asked him to stay.

Ignoring the warning voice in her head, she took another beer out of the fridge. "I'm ready to sit down."

She headed into the living room and perched on one end of the couch. He sat at the opposite end, sinking into the cushions and stretching his legs out in front of him. She remembered how they'd felt against her the other night—solid. Strong. Muscled.

He lifted the beer and took a drink. When he set the bottle down on his thigh, a fleck of foam clung to his lip. He licked it off, and she swallowed.

Maybe this had been a mistake.

"Do you miss your job in Detroit?" she asked, desperate to banish the memory of his mouth against hers.

"Yeah. I left my partner holding the bag on our cases." He rolled his shoulders, tilted the bottle to his mouth, swallowed. "It's tough being here, when I'm needed there."

It felt as if the couch was listing toward Patrick. She planted her feet on the floor to keep from leaning toward him. A momentary weakness had made her ask him to stay. Her worst idea in a long time.

"I think everyone is glad you're here," she said.

"Not sure about that. But they're stuck with me."

Patrick turned to face her. Memories stirred of that night in the kitchen at Mama's. Her shirt against his. Her mouth against his.

"Why did you ask me to stay, Darcy?"

Their gazes connected, and her heart began pounding. *I didn't want to be alone. I feel safe with you.*

I wanted to kiss you again.

"I was a little shaken up."

"I could see that. How come?"

He was closer, but she hadn't seen him move. Her skin prickled and her chest tightened. "I thought someone had tried to break in to my apartment. Anyone would be upset."

"Yeah. But you never ask for help."

How had he figured that out in a few short weeks? She shrugged. "I wasn't asking for help. I wanted company for a few minutes, and you looked like you could use a beer." *She wanted more than company.*

"That was it? Really?"

"What else could it be?"

He slid closer. "You tell me, Darcy."

The light from the lamp illuminated the shadow of the bruise on his chin. He was a dangerous man. In so many ways. And she still wanted him.

Apparently, she was a slow learner.

"You know, I'm fine now. I don't want to keep you."

"You're not keeping me from anything." He lounged on the couch and lifted the beer to his mouth. Her gaze followed, and she watched the muscles in his throat ripple as he drank. She wanted to put her lips there and taste his skin. Feel his pulse race when she touched him.

She realized she was reaching for him, and she dropped her hand onto her lap. "Thank you for checking my apartment. I'll see you tomorrow, Patrick."

Before he could answer, Cat strolled in from the kitchen and jumped into her lap. He settled himself, then stared at Patrick.

Patrick's mouth twitched and he drained the last of the beer. Darcy stroked the cat's head, and loud purring filled the room.

"Nice cat," Patrick said. "What's his name?"

"Uh, it's Cat." Her hand must have tightened on Cat's ear, because he yowled and jumped down.

"Cat? That's his name?" Patrick sat up straight, frowning.

Brushing the hair off her thighs, she shrugged. "He was hanging around the back door, so I started feeding him. He sneaked in one day and wouldn't leave. I had to call him something."

He studied her closely. "You must have spent a lot of time coming up with that name. How does Cat like it?"

"He likes it just fine, since it comes with food and a place to sleep. I should have called him Dog. Then you wouldn't be looking at me as if I were some kind of freak."

"I don't think you're a freak," he said. "Just someone who's ready to pick up and leave at a moment's notice."

She swung around to look at him, her heart beating against her ribs. "That's an odd leap to make, just because you don't like my cat's name."

"Not just his name. The rest of the place tells me all I need to know."

"Really? After being in my house for fifteen minutes?" The beer bottle was slippery, and she set it carefully on the table. Wiped her hands on her pants.

"Took about five. Not hard to miss the signs. Bare-bones furnishings. No pictures or other personal stuff. Furniture that was really cheap and is easily abandoned."

His gaze touched on everything in the living room. Assessing. Cataloging. Understanding.

"The apartment came furnished," she said stiffly.

"You didn't add anything of your own. No personal touches."

"I didn't realize you moonlighted as an interior decorator," she said, trying to lighten things. To deflect his attention.

"Darcy, you didn't even name the damn cat." He leaned toward her, close enough that she could smell the beer on his breath, see the tiny lines around his eyes. "Does that mean you're leaving him behind when you run?"

Her gaze darted toward the kitchen, where Cat's food bowl clattered against the bottom of the cabinets. "It's always a mistake to get attached."

Patrick slid closer. His thigh was inches from hers, and his heat poured over her. "Tell me what's going on, Darcy. What are you afraid of? *Who* are you afraid of?"

"Nothing."

He leaned closer. "Who beat you? Who made you run? Who makes you carry pepper spray when you're out jogging?"

"You're making a lot of assumptions," she said, facing him. He would *not* make her retreat. She'd done enough of that in her life.

"I know what I'm seeing. I know what this means."

"Think what you want. You don't know anything about me, Patrick."

"You don't think so?" Frustration and desire swirled together in his eyes, turning them a stormy, midnight blue. "I know a few things."

"Like what?"

He leaned closer. "I know that one crooked tooth makes your smile unique. I know your eyes go unfocused when you're aroused." He drew one finger down the side of her face, and she shivered. "I know your heart races when I touch you."

His mouth was inches from hers. "I know your skin heats when I kiss you. And I know you want me. Almost as much as I want you."

"That's…that's…" She could barely draw air into her lungs. Her heart pistoned in her chest, her breasts swelled and her nipples rasped against her bra.

"You want to prove I'm wrong? Go ahead."

She stared at him, unable to move. Barely able to breathe. His eyes darkened even more. He grabbed her shoulders and yanked her against him. "Damn it, Darcy!"

Then his mouth was on hers, kissing her as if he would die if he didn't. Desire poured up from deep inside her, washing over her in a huge wave.

She slanted her lips over his and opened to him. He groaned into her mouth and his hands tightened on her. His grip was hard. Almost desperate, as if he was afraid she'd vanish if he didn't hold tightly enough.

She moved her hands through his hair, the silky strands sliding through her fingers as she learned the shape of his skull. He cupped the back of her head with his palm, urging her closer.

Their mouths moved over each other, hot and greedy, desperate to get closer. He swept one hand down her back, lingered at her hip, shaped the curves of her rear. When he slid a finger beneath her waistband, she sucked in a breath.

Then she was sprawled on the couch, his thigh between her legs, his body half-covering hers. He jerked her shirt out of her waistband and shoved it up, and his hands covered her breasts. The fabric of her plain blue bra rubbed against her nipples, making her squirm against him.

He tore his mouth away from hers, ripped the bra open and drew her into his mouth. She arched against him with a tiny cry as sensation overwhelmed her. Consumed her.

With his mouth still on her breast, he fumbled at her waist, then shoved her pants past her hips. Cool air stroked over the skin of her lower abdomen, then he slid on top of her.

She froze. For a moment it was Tim, holding her down. Overpowering her. Punishing her.

No. It's Patrick. Not Tim.

But the moment was gone. She turned her head and tried to push him away. His hands stilled. His head lifted. His eyes were dark. Wild with need. Glittering with desire.

Slowly, as if every inch of him hurt, he eased away. Rolled off the couch. Sat on the coffee table.

"Darcy." He reached over and lowered her shirt over her exposed breasts. "I'm sorry. I scared you."

She scrambled to sit up, fumbling to button her pants. "No." *Yes.* "I was just… We were moving too fast."

"Yeah." He held out his hand and she hesitated for a moment. Then she placed her fingers in his. He pulled her to her feet. As soon as she was standing, he let her go.

"Darcy, I'm attracted to you. I want you." He brushed his hand over her face, smoothed her hair. "I think you want me, too. But that's no excuse for being so aggressive." He leaned closer slowly, as if gauging her reaction. When she didn't flinch or move away, he cupped her cheeks.

His thumb slid over her lips, as if he were memorizing their texture. The shape of her mouth. "I was frustrated," he said, his voice low in the silent apartment. "Angry because you won't tell me what's going on. But I was wrong. Your story belongs to you. It's yours to share, or not."

His hands stilled on her face, then dropped to her shoulders. He held her softly, as if she was delicate. Fragile. Breakable.

She hated the feeling.

Hated that she'd let Tim make her feel that way.

"You okay alone?" he asked.

Deep inside, arousal still throbbed a heavy rhythm, but she nodded. Part of her wanted him to stay.

The part that didn't care Patrick was an FBI agent. Didn't care how dangerous he was.

But she'd learned her lesson a long time ago. You couldn't have everything you wanted.

CHAPTER THIRTEEN

"Darcy?" He brushed her hair behind her ears. "You okay? Say something."

"I'm fine."

"You don't look fine."

She managed to smile. "It was a kiss, Patrick. That's all. I'm not a shrinking virgin, scared by a kiss. It just got a little...out of hand."

"My fault. I should have known to be careful."

"Why?" Her temper stirred. "Because you think I'm damaged? That I've been traumatized by a man, so you have to walk on eggshells with me?"

Instead of saying something flip, he touched her chin. "I think you're one of the strongest women I know. When you decide you're ready, I won't hold anything back, and neither will you. But *you* get to decide when that happens."

"That was a hot kiss. I'll grant you that." It had set her on fire, and she was still uncomfortably aroused. "But it doesn't mean I'm going to sleep with you."

His eyes went all heavy-lidded again. "You want to."

"Doesn't matter. This can't go anywhere. Your life's in Detroit." Her heart thudded heavily as he held her gaze. If he kept looking at her like that, they'd be in her bedroom in minutes.

"It would be a fun few weeks," he said, his voice a low rasp.

Yeah, it would. But it was the kind of fun she couldn't afford. "I'm not interested in flings."

He shifted his stance, as if he was uncomfortable. "I didn't think you were, but it was worth a try." He smiled as he watched her. "And I'm not giving up."

Her breath caught. "I'm pretty good at saying no."

"I'll do my best to change your mind."

She found herself leaning toward him and straightened. She'd sworn she'd never rely on a man again. She would never allow herself to be exposed and vulnerable.

"You won't be successful."

"Can't wait to prove you wrong." He smiled and shrugged on his jacket, and she wrapped her arms around herself. His smile faded. "Are you sure you're all right by yourself tonight? I'll be happy to stay."

"I'm sure you would," she said dryly. "But I'll be fine."

"I didn't mean it that way. If you don't want to be alone, I'll sleep on your couch."

"It's about a foot too short for you."

"You think I care about that?"

He was serious. He would spend an uncomfortable night on her couch if she told him she was nervous being here alone, and the offer had nothing to do with trying to get her into bed.

He wanted her to feel safe.

He was even more dangerous than she'd thought.

"Thank you, Patrick." She reached up to kiss his cheek. "That's the nicest offer anyone's made in a long time. But I'll be fine. And Nathan needs you."

"I'd forgotten about Nate." He grasped her arms and pulled her closer. "You could stay at his house."

"I'm good. I'll see you tomorrow at work."

"Right." His hands tightened on her arms, then he let her go. "Check all the locks and windows after I leave."

"I always do."

She closed the door behind him, but he stood on the porch until she locked the door.

Without thinking, she headed for the living room and bent one slat of the window blind. Patrick emerged from the side of the house and paused before he got into his car.

He looked up, and even from a distance she saw him smile when he caught her watching.

After he drove away, a flicker of a shadow caught her eye. It came from a car parked in front of her neighbor's house. Almost as if someone was in the front seat.

She pressed the slat of the blind down farther and stared at the car. Dark sedan. Empty.

She turned off all the lights in her apartment and returned to the window.

The car was gone.

DARCY STUMBLED DOWN the stairs at eight the next morning, wearing her running shorts, leggings and a tight-fitting jacket. She'd barely slept the night before, and had been tempted to roll over and go back to sleep when the alarm went off. But a run would clear her head. And she always thought better while she pounded the pavement. There was something about the repetitive movements that kicked her brain into gear.

She didn't look at the traces of mud on the steps. She didn't want to think about that. Because thinking about an intruder on her porch would lead to remembering what had happened last night with Patrick.

As well as the car that had driven off after he'd left.

Her mind had leaped from one to the other. An unbroken loop.

The car would be a low-level worry, always there in the back of her mind. Patrick? She didn't want to think about him until she had to face him at work this afternoon.

It was Saturday. They'd be busy tonight. At least she wouldn't have time to moon over him.

When she reached the bottom of the stairs, she bent at the waist to stretch her legs one last time, then jogged out to the street. The gray sky pressed down and the wind rattled the last leaves on the trees that lined the street. As she reached into her pocket and pulled out a hat, she scanned the block for the dark car she'd seen last night.

It wasn't there.

No one had been hiding there, watching her. Someone had

gotten in the car, bent over to retrieve something from the floor, then driven away.

She'd just been nervous after her tires were slashed.

But she would keep her eyes open.

As she stepped onto the asphalt, she heard a car door slam behind her. Damn it! She'd been so tired she hadn't noticed someone sitting in a car. She closed her fingers around the pepper spray, then glanced over her shoulder, slowing to a stop at the sight of Patrick jogging toward her.

He wore running tights covered by a pair of baggy nylon shorts, a jacket similar to hers and sunglasses.

"What are you doing here?" she demanded.

"I figured you'd go for a run this morning." He stopped next to her. "Thought you might like some company."

"Why?"

"Last night? When you were freaked out about the car tires and the mud on your porch? I know you haven't forgotten."

"Of course I haven't. But I'm prepared." She tapped the pepper spray back into her pocket. "How long have you been waiting for me?"

He shrugged. "Not too long. Brought the paper and some coffee, so it was like sitting at home."

She scowled. It was either that or kiss him. "Don't you have better things to do than read your newspaper outside of my apartment?"

"Nope."

"You left Nathan alone?"

"Sound asleep."

"Well, I'm good. So you can go home."

"You kidding me? I'm running." He started to jog, then looked over his shoulder. "You coming?"

She should be running, too. In the opposite direction. But instead of telling him to get lost, she began moving. He'd gone to a lot of trouble to jog with her. She'd be snarky and ungrateful if she refused.

The view wasn't bad, either. His leg muscles bunched and

released in the running tights. The baggy shorts clung to his ass when the wind whipped around the corner. His stride was long and effortless, as if he could run for hours.

He glanced over his shoulder and slowed. "Am I going too fast for you?"

He was moving at the speed of light. She'd barely managed to crawl. "I'm getting warmed up. I'll catch you in a minute."

He smiled at her, and her heart fluttered. It must have shown on her face, because she recognized that bedroom-eyes expression. "You better watch where you're going," she managed to say. "Sewer grate ahead."

He jerked his head around. She took one more look at the view from the rear, then caught up with him. "Kind of gloomy for sunglasses."

"Had a few more beers when I got home." He glanced at her, and her cheeks burned. Yeah, he was going way too fast for her.

They ran another block in silence, and her muscles stretched out. She inhaled the cold air, fragrant with the scent of smoke and the last flowers of the season. It was kind of nice having company while she ran.

"You jog every day?" he asked.

"Pretty much." It was the best way to keep an eye on the neighborhood. "How about you?"

"Every day I don't box."

"Why boxing? That's a violent sport."

She felt him glance at her, but she didn't look at him. Finally he said, "I started in high school. Not long after my parents were killed. It helped me deal with…a lot of stuff. Now it's part of my routine. And it comes in handy once in a while."

A shiver rolled down her spine. "Like when?"

He didn't say anything for a long moment. They reached the tunnel and kept going. He must have remembered that she didn't like to run through it. Finally, when they were past it, he said, "I've never punched anyone outside the ring. But every once in a while, someone I'm arresting takes a swing at me. Knowing the defensive moves helps."

"I hadn't thought of that."

"I have a job that can be violent, but I'm not a violent man," he said quietly. "In case you were wondering."

She wondered a lot of things about Patrick—how he'd figured out so much about her.

How his body would feel against hers.

"I don't think you're violent, Patrick." But a part of her was wary. He was the first man who'd sparked her interest since she'd fled her marriage. Naturally she was a little nervous.

"You should be wondering," he said, surprising her. "You don't know that much about me."

"I know your brothers. Your sister, too, a little. I've worked with them for three years." She speeded up. "It's irrelevant, though. We're not in a relationship."

"Aren't we?"

"Two kisses, no matter how hot they were, doesn't make a relationship."

"Thank you."

"For what?"

"For not saying they were nice."

She remembered telling him after the first kiss that it had been nice, but nothing spectacular. She bit her lip to hide a smile. "Did that hurt your feelings?"

"Pissed me off, is what it did."

"Is that what last night was about? Trying to prove me wrong?"

"No. It was about wanting you. And don't get all smug, but you kept me awake all night."

"Guess you shouldn't have kissed me, then." *Flirting? Really?*

"Don't worry. I've learned my lesson."

"Good. That's good." Deflated, more disappointed than she should be, she glanced over at him. Big mistake. He was grinning.

"Next time, I'll go slow. So slow you'll be begging."

"In your dreams." Smiling, she began to sprint. They were

four blocks from her apartment. Her heart was going much faster than it should have been, and she needed time to settle herself.

He kept up with her easily. By the time they reached her house, her breath was sawing in and out. He was barely winded.

"You've got a nice kick," he said, leaning against the side of his SUV.

"And you look as if you've hardly broken a sweat."

He pushed away from the truck with a grin. "Need to give you a goal, don't I? You think you can beat me next time?"

"Probably not," she said, stretching. "Time after that, though? Watch out."

She stood abruptly. On what planet was flirting a good idea? There wouldn't be a next time. "Thank you for running with me," she said. "It wasn't necessary, but I appreciate it. I'll see you at work later."

He caught up with her. "I'll walk you to your door."

To make sure everything was okay. During their run, she'd forgotten about the mud on her porch. About Chuck. About Tim. About the car that had been parked next door last night. "Thank you."

He had thought about this. About reassuring her.

Keeping her safe.

She could trust Patrick.

He raised an eyebrow as he walked beside her. "No argument?"

"Would it do any good?"

"Of course not."

"There you go." She wouldn't tell him she wanted him to walk up the stairs with her. Couldn't tell him it made her feel safer. If you showed the chinks in your armor, people used them against you.

He wasn't Tim.

Patrick wouldn't hurt her. She trusted him.

They reached the top of the stairs with no signs of any intruders. The curtains hung over the windows as usual, and the mud footprints had dried to a crusty dark gray.

"You want me to check the inside?" he asked.

If he did, it would only be harder to walk into the place alone the next time. She had to get back on the horse right now, in the light of day. "Thanks, but I'm sure it's fine. It's daylight."

"Okay, then."

Instead of leaving, he waited. Did he want an invitation to come in for coffee? She was tempted. But she unlocked the door, turned and said, "Goodbye, Patrick. See you tonight."

Then closed the door firmly behind her.

THE NEXT MORNING, Patrick sprawled at the kitchen table as he turned the page of the Sunday *Herald Times* and took another sip of coffee. He glanced at Nathan, who was studying the sports section as he ate his omelet. "More coffee, Nate?"

Nathan looked into his cup, as if surprised it was empty. "Thanks."

As Patrick poured, he asked, "Cal coming over to watch the game today?"

"Said he was," Nathan said absently. "Did you see this story about the Cubs?"

"Someone's been hogging the sports page."

Nathan rolled his eyes, but smiled as he shoved the section across the table. "Give me Travel," he said. "I have to figure out where I'm going when I get some time off."

"I thought you were anxious to get back to work."

Nathan's smile faded. "I am. But sooner or later, things will…settle down at Mama's. Get back to normal. I'll take some time off then."

"You going to make Darcy a manager?"

Nathan rolled his shoulders. "Don't think she'd want the job. But I'll find someone."

"I think you're making a mistake," Patrick said as he glanced at a story about the Cougars, the football team his soon-to-be brother-in-law had played for. "She's bright, she's a fast learner and I think she'd do a good job."

"Yeah, well, it's my call. Not yours."

Patrick studied his brother. Maybe Nathan's weirdness about Darcy was related to the situation at the restaurant. "Is she involved with whatever's going on at Mama's?" he asked quietly. "I would have guessed no, but maybe I'm wrong."

"She's a waitress." Nathan pretended to be absorbed in a story about the new Cubs president. "That's it."

"Ah. So that's why you don't want her to manage. You're afraid she'll figure out there's a problem."

"Goddamn it, Paddy!" Nathan shoved the newspaper away and it fluttered to the floor. "You think you're so smart? So clever because you're an FBI agent? You got away. You got to pick your career. I was stuck here, running the restaurant, raising Frankie and Marco. So don't start with me. Don't act like you know better than me what's going on in my place. I might only be a restaurant manager, but I know what I'm doing. I've kept this family together. And made a few bucks for you along the way."

He jerked the wheelchair control and shot back into the wall. Then forward too far. As he tried to turn, Patrick leaped to his feet and blocked his exit.

"You resent my leaving? The fact that I didn't stick around?" He sucked in a lungful of air, trying to be rational. Thoughtful. But the words spewed out. "I couldn't stick around. Every time you or Frankie or Marco looked at me, I knew what you were thinking—he killed them. If it weren't for me, Mom and Dad would still be alive. So don't tell me about getting away. I can't get away from the guilt."

Frustration and anger roiled inside Patrick. The same emotions filled his brother's eyes. Along with fear.

Before either of them could speak, the front door opened.

The breeze ruffled the newspapers on the kitchen table and a page floated to the floor.

"Hey," Cal called. "What's the matter with you two losers? Why isn't the television on yet?"

CHAPTER FOURTEEN

NATHAN FUMBLED WITH the wheelchair control, and Patrick stepped aside. The hum of the electric motor revved as Nathan left the kitchen. Patrick heard him say, "Hey, Cal. Frankie. Glad you're here."

Patrick's heart battered against his chest and the sound of blood rushing through his head was all he heard. God, why had he let Nathan provoke him?

With a low growl, he moved to punch the wall, pulling back only at the last moment.

Damn it!

"Thanks for rescuing me," he heard Nathan say.

Rescuing him?

A ball of ice filled his stomach as he stormed into the living room. Then stopped abruptly. Not the time to continue that conversation.

Frankie stood at Cal's side, his arm draped casually over her shoulder, as if the two of them needed to be connected.

"It's my favorite sister," Patrick said, trying to smile. "And her shadow."

Cal kept his arm around Frankie as he grabbed the remote and turned on the television. He grinned at Patrick over his shoulder. "You got that right, Paddy. If I let her go, she might get away."

Frankie elbowed Cal lightly in the ribs. "Not ready to let you go just yet."

Patrick hadn't often seen this tender side of Frankie. He looked away, but not before longing washed through him. He wanted what his sister and Cal had.

Darcy's face filled his head.

"Hey, Cal," he said. "Want a beer? Frankie? How about you?"

"You don't have to wait on me," Frankie said. She let Cal go and reached up to wind her arms around Patrick's neck. "You probably do enough of that at Mama's."

Patrick squeezed her tightly and held on for a moment too long. Then he let her go. "Cal? Beer?"

"Little early," Cal said. "Got any coffee?" He elbowed Nathan. "I've got to keep my head with this one. We're going to be talking bets in a few minutes."

"Don't bother, Stewart," Nathan replied. "I've got it sewn up this week."

Patrick wondered if Frankie and Cal heard the strain in Nate's voice.

He retreated toward the kitchen, adrenaline still rushing through him. In a burst of anger he'd revealed that ugly hole inside him, and it was too late to take back what he'd said. "How about you, Nate? Want anything?"

Nathan glanced at him, and Patrick saw the regret in his expression. But there was still anger beneath it. And defiance. "I'll finish my coffee. Thanks."

Patrick walked into the kitchen and pulled a mug from the shelf. It was great of Cal to come over every Sunday and watch football games with Nathan. Cal's commentary on the games, especially when it was the Cougars, was insightful. Often hilarious.

Nathan looked forward to it. And it freed Patrick up to work on Mama's books. He'd only made it through the first few years after Nathan took over.

He listened to Nate and Cal laughing. Frankie said something, and Cal responded. Nathan chimed in, and Frankie laughed.

The three of them were comfortable together. Friends as well as family.

Him? He was the guy who got the coffee.

Frankie stepped into the kitchen behind him. "Let me help you with that."

"Thanks," he said without looking at her. "Nate takes cream and sugar."

"Got it," she said.

After she carried the two mugs to the other room, Patrick poured himself a cup and stared out the window at the backyard. The tire swing they'd played on as kids was still there, hanging from the huge oak tree, but the rope was dark and frayed. As the tire swayed in the breeze, water that had collected from the last rainfall splashed out.

What had happened to those kids who'd played together for hours?

Frankie stepped back into the kitchen and wrapped her arms around his waist. "What's wrong, Paddy? You missing someone in Detroit?"

No. He was missing his family in Chicago. He closed his eyes and forced himself to smile before he turned to face her. "You have romance on the brain, don't you?"

"Is there anyone back in Detroit?"

"Nah. I'm an all-work guy." He dated his share of women, but there'd been no one serious since the woman he'd lived with broke it off two years ago. Frankie didn't know about her, though. Frankie didn't know anything about his life.

Neither did Nathan or Marco.

But that was his choice.

"There was a woman a few years ago," he found himself saying. "Caroline. She was a high school teacher. We talked about getting married, but then she took a job a couple of hours away. Being apart killed it. Long-distance relationships don't work out."

"I'm sorry," Frankie said. "Even if it wasn't right, it still hurts."

"Yeah." He brushed his hand over her spiky hair. "You and Cal are good together."

"Better than good." Frankie glanced toward the living room,

as if she could hardly bear to have a room separating them. "We rock." She turned back to Patrick. "You and Nathan are having problems, though." She held his gaze, as if daring him to deny it.

He shrugged. "We've had our ups and downs. He doesn't want anyone else running Mama's. I've asked him some questions he doesn't like."

"We all appreciate you staying here and taking this on," she said quietly. "It should have been me."

That would have made things easier for him. He could have gone back to Detroit and picked up his life where he'd left off.

If he had, he wouldn't have gotten involved with Darcy.

He wouldn't have known about the problems at Mama's.

He wouldn't have realized how much he'd isolated himself from his family.

"You've got a few things on your plate right now," he said. "A wedding to plan, a teen center to run, Cal settling into his post-football life. And how's that pregnant girl you were helping?"

"Martha's doing okay," Frankie answered. "Had her baby, a little girl, and signed the adoption papers. She's back home with her parents, and they're all going to therapy." She tilted her head. "Yeah, we've got a lot going on. But there must be something Cal and I can do."

She didn't even need to ask before offering Cal's help—they were a unit. Patrick's parents had been the same way. How did you get that kind of bond?

He had no idea.

Patrick drew his sister to the kitchen table. "If you want to help, there's one thing you can do."

"Anything, Paddy."

"Tell me what's going on at Mama's."

Frankie frowned. "What do you mean by 'going on'?"

"That's just it. I don't know. But something is."

He stood up and looked into the living room. Cal was sprawled on the couch, next to Nathan in his chair. Both men were talking at once and pointing at the football game on the screen. "That's what I'm talking about," Cal said. "The guy is an idiot. Couldn't find his ass with both hands." He turned to Nate. "Total douche bag in the locker room, too. Thinks he's God's gift."

"Don't hold back, Cal," Nathan said with a grin. "Tell me what you really think."

"They're good for a while," Patrick said. He slid into a chair and waited for Frankie to sit. "Nathan's worried about something. Scared, almost, and he insisted on doing the books every night." He told his sister about their fights, about Chuck and the free drinks. "Since he was so determined to do the books, my gut told me it was about money. Then I found out some money was missing from a deposit. Now I'm going through all the old ledgers. You've spent a lot more time with him than I have. Do you have any idea what's bothering him?"

Frankie pulled a beer from the fridge. "No idea. He did say last spring that he needed to get away. That he was sick of the restaurant and wanted to do something else." She slid into a chair. "Seemed reasonable to me. He didn't get to choose his life. He was stuck with the restaurant, stuck with three kids to raise."

"Hey," Patrick said, trying to lighten things up. "That was two kids. I was practically an adult."

Frankie didn't smile. "You were more screwed up than me and Marco. You blamed yourself for Mom and Dad's death."

"I was driving the car."

"Jeez, Paddy. Haven't you figured out yet that there was nothing you could've done? The other driver ran a red light."

"So the therapists told me." His gulp of coffee scalded his throat. "Nathan told you he wanted to get away. Did he give you any reasons?"

She shrugged. "I thought it was pretty obvious. He needed a break. He did the big renovation last winter—replaced the stoves and freezer and refrigerator, put in new pizza ovens, updated the dishwashing system—and I know that was stressful. That he worried about it."

"Worried how?"

She rolled her eyes. "Obviously, you've never had any work done on your condo. It always takes longer than you think it's going to take. Costs more than you'd planned. And that's before you get the contractors involved."

"Was there something more specific about the renovation that was bothering him?"

She took another sip of beer and frowned. "I know he was worried about financing."

"Where did he get the money for the work?"

"Loans. I didn't ask for details. He said he'd taken care of it."

Patrick felt a familiar tingling at the back of his neck. This could be the link. He glanced at Nathan's computer, sitting on the dining room table. *Tomorrow.* "Thanks, Frankie."

THE SUN WAS JUST beginning to rise on Thursday morning when Patrick closed Nathan's computer and stared out the window at the eastern sky, washed with pink.

Bad weather coming.

Nathan had kept his computer close at hand on Tuesday and Wednesday, and Patrick hadn't had a chance to look at his spreadsheets. This morning, though, he'd gotten up way before dawn, snagged the computer from the table next to Nathan's bed and finally been able to examine Mama's books.

It had made everything more puzzling.

According to Nathan's spreadsheet, several lump sums had been paid into the restaurant account early in the year. Bank loans, he assumed, for the renovation.

Then, about a month after the last payment, there had been payouts every week. But the amount varied. There was no pattern. And there was no bank name attached to the payments.

He'd never seen a bank loan repaid like that.

He needed to see the paperwork from the renovation—it

should include the loan documents. After emailing the spreadsheet documents to himself, he dialed Frankie's cell number.

"Paddy? Is something wrong?" People yelled in the background, and a rhythmic thumping underlined Frankie's voice. One of the giant mixers they used at the bakery, probably.

"Nothing's wrong. Sorry. You're at work."

"No problem. What's going on?"

The thudding faded, as did the voices. A door opened and closed, and then there was only the whistle of the wind in the background.

"Look, Bunny, I'm sorry I'm calling so early. But I have a question and Nate is still asleep." And wasn't that a good excuse for not asking his brother?

"Shoot."

"Do you know where Nate would keep all the paperwork from the renovation? Receipts, building permits, that kind of thing."

"Yeah," Frankie said. "I know exactly where all that stuff is."

DARCY BRUSHED HER TEETH, wondering if Patrick would be waiting for her downstairs. He'd been there every morning since her car had been vandalized. On Sunday, she'd told him not to bother. That she was fine. On Tuesday, she'd rolled her eyes. Yesterday, she'd simply fallen into step as they jogged down the street.

Every night after work, he'd followed her home, walked her up the stairs and checked her apartment.

She would have thought he'd lost interest. But his gaze scorched her as he stood in her kitchen and said goodbye.

She knew what he was doing. If anything was going to happen between them, she'd have to initiate it. He wasn't going to push.

Getting involved with Patrick wasn't a good idea. But every morning when she saw him waiting at the curb, she wanted him a little more.

Patrick knew how to be patient.

She shivered, wondering if he was patient in bed, as well.

As she rinsed her mouth, someone began pounding on her door. Her heart jumped, then thudded with dread.

The sun was barely up. Patrick wouldn't be here for at least a half hour.

He always waited for her downstairs.

Spitting water into the sink, she threw on her bathrobe and grabbed her gun from the nightstand in her room.

In the kitchen she lifted the curtain and peeked out. Exhaled.

She dropped the gun into her pocket and unlocked the door. "Patrick. What are you doing here?"

His gaze swept over her, lingering at the deep V of her robe. She drew the lapels together and tightened the belt. But the weight of the gun pulled the right side down, baring her right breast beneath the paper-thin T-shirt. She clutched the top of the robe together. "Patrick. Eyes up here."

Instead of apologizing or making a joke, he just looked at her, his gaze heavy-lidded. "I should get here early every morning."

"Why *are* you here so early?" She was horribly conscious of the gun in her pocket. The illegal gun.

"I couldn't wait. We need to run. Right now."

"What's going on?"

He closed the door and leaned against it. "Get your running stuff on. We're going somewhere different today."

Ten minutes later, she followed him down the stairs and into the yard. They stretched for five minutes, then he led her into the alley. As they pounded down the broken cement, black trash cans stood as sentinels at each garage, silently watching their progress.

Normally, Patrick was relaxed when they ran, smiling, talking, teasing. Today, his mouth was a hard line and a muscle in his jaw jumped. He ran faster than usual, and she wanted to ask what was wrong. Instead, she sucked in a lungful of air and concentrated on keeping up. She didn't have any extra breath for questions.

A few minutes later they emerged onto Lehigh, the street running alongside the train tracks. They ran on the shoulder, which was gravel and dirt. She glanced at Patrick again. "Why are we running here, rather than through the neighborhood?"

"Tell you later."

Puzzled and faintly alarmed, Darcy kept pace with him. What had happened? He looked so grim. So focused. The way she imagined he'd look when he was on the job.

A bolt of fear shot through her. Had he found out about her past?

No. That wasn't Patrick's style. If he had something to say to her, he would have said it after bursting into her apartment.

This was something else.

When they reached the next intersection, Darcy hesitated. This cold, detached Patrick made her nervous. But as she slowed, he hooked his arm through hers and propelled her across the street.

On this side of Touhy Avenue, Lehigh ran through a maze of warehouses and small office buildings. Patrick turned onto a street that was still deserted—it was too early for any offices to be open. He finally stopped at a storage facility.

An iron fence surrounded it, and the gate across the drive was closed and padlocked. A small door in the fence was also locked.

"What's going on?" she whispered.

"Shhh. Don't want anyone to know I'm here."

Why the hell not?

But she stood beside him, breathing hard, and watched him unlock the door. He drew her through, then clicked the padlock back into place.

He led her away from the main building and down a row of storage units with corrugated metal doors. When they reached one in the middle of the row, he unlocked it, rolled the door up just high enough to get under, drew her inside and closed the door again.

Patrick reached into his backpack and pulled out a flashlight. The beam bounced off the metal walls and slid over boxes and ghostly shapes.

A long cord hung in the middle of the room, swaying gently. He yanked it, and the harsh light of a bare bulb illuminated stacks of banker's boxes along one wall. A few pieces of furniture were clustered together at the back of the unit, but the rest of the space was open.

"Okay, Mr. Secret Agent Man. What's going on?"

He switched off the flashlight and tossed it into the backpack, then laid it on the floor. "I have to find some records in here."

"And you couldn't drive over later this morning, walk in and pick them up?"

"No." He held her gaze. "Nate is in trouble. I'm not sure what kind of trouble, but I'm going to figure it out. I didn't want anyone seeing me drive in here to check his storage area."

"You think people are watching it?" She looked around the room, wondering what could be in here that was so dangerous.

"No. But the people who own the place might be keeping track of who comes and goes."

"There could be cameras. Did you disable them?"

At that he smiled a little. "You watch too much television. Or maybe you read too many books."

"Just saying."

"No cameras. I already checked."

She sank onto the top of a dusty box. "What kinds of records are you looking for?"

His smile disappeared. "Anything to do with the renovation of Mama's last winter."

"How do you know they're here?"

"I asked Frankie. She told me that right after Nathan was hurt, he asked her to bring them over here. He said they were taking up a lot of space in the spare room and he needed to get them out of the way so I could use it."

"That sounds reasonable."

Patrick glanced at the dates scrawled on the boxes. "He'd just been hit by a car. He was in traction, on pain medication. And this was the first thing he thought of?"

"Maybe. That sounds like Nathan—he thinks of everyone but himself. What did Frankie say?"

"She knows how Nate is. He's always taken care of us. She thought it was a typical Nate thing to do—think about where I would stay when he should have been thinking about himself. So she did it."

"And you knew this how?"

"Called her this morning."

Darcy scanned around the room, which was about twelve feet square. "Where do we begin looking?"

"Any box with the current year's date." He studied her for a long moment. "You're not going to ask me what's going on, what I'm specifically searching for?"

"Of course I want to know. I'm dying of curiosity." But if she wasn't willing to share her own secrets, she couldn't ask him to share his. "I can see this is hard for you, though. You're upset with Nathan. I'm not going to push." She wanted to reach out and smooth away the lines on his face. "You'll tell me when you're ready."

His expression was impossible to read as he stared down at her. "That's it? I drag you out of your apartment when it's barely light, make you run to this ugly-ass industrial park, and you'll wait for an explanation?"

"You didn't *make* me do anything. I *chose* to run with you. And yeah, I want to know. But I trust that you'll tell me what's going on when you can."

He looked vulnerable. Sad. Emotions she'd never seen in Patrick. Parts of himself he hadn't *let* her see. Without thinking, she wrapped her arms around him. Pulled him close.

She'd meant to comfort him. To make him feel less alone.

But she realized it was more than that. She needed to connect with him. To let him know he wasn't alone.

His arms tightened around her, and his lips found hers. He lifted her off the ground, supporting her against him. Then her back hit something cold and hard. The metal wall.

"My own brother doesn't trust me." He pressed kisses to her cheek, her neck, the sensitive spot beneath her ear. "But you do. God, Darcy." He returned to her mouth, his lips on hers. When she opened to him, he swept inside.

CHAPTER FIFTEEN

IT WAS COLD in the storage area, and her drying sweat chilled her. But she leaned into Patrick's heat and savored his kiss. She could taste his desolation, the anger and pain bursting out of him.

She should be afraid of his anger. The desire that consumed him. But instead, it fed her own craving. He'd needed someone, and he came to her.

He was angry and upset, but he was gentle with her. Careful.

So she shoved her fingers into his hair and held his mouth to hers. Learning his texture, his taste. Letting him learn hers.

With a rough sound, he shoved one hand between them and cupped her breast. It swelled in his hand, and even through her jacket, her T-shirt, her sports bra, his touch sent lightning crackling through her.

She hooked one leg around his waist and pressed closer, suddenly frantic to feel him there, to let him ease the ache. He yanked her jacket and shirt up, shoved the bra to the side and bent to take her in his mouth.

"Patrick," she gasped, arching her back. Rolling her hips against him, she tugged at his running shorts, but his jacket was in the way. Frustrated, she plucked at it, but her hand shook too much to pull it away.

Pressing her against the cold metal, he slid his hand into the back of her leggings, cupping her rear. His palm was shockingly hot on her cool skin. The rasp of his slightly callused fingers made her quiver. Every nerve in her body was alive. Throbbing. Needy.

When he dipped into her cleft, she arched into him with a

tiny cry. He stilled. His fingers trembled against her, then he slid his hand out of her leggings, excruciatingly slowly, as if he couldn't bear to let her go. He lowered her to the floor. Pressed his forehead to hers. Smoothed one hand up and down her back.

"I'm sorry, Darcy," he whispered, brushing his mouth over hers. "I was…worked up. And when you told me you trusted me, I lost it. I wanted you. Right now."

"And that's a problem because…?"

One side of his mouth curved up. "You are something else." He tugged her bra back into place, smoothed her T-shirt, straightened her jacket. "The first time we make love is not going to be up against a wall in a dirty, cold storage cell." He kissed her again. "And besides, I don't have a condom."

She raised her eyebrows. "You call yourself a cop? What happened to serve and protect?"

He smiled slowly and drew a line down the center of her chest, trailing fire. Making her shiver. "Trust me. Won't happen again." He leaned in and nipped at her ear. "And I can't wait."

She couldn't, either. And that was damn scary.

She disengaged from him slowly. "It's cold in here. Let's find what you need and get out."

THAT EVENING, as Darcy peered out the front window of Mama's once again, panic began to stir. Theresa often came in on Thursdays.

It had been a week since Darcy had seen her last.

Up until now, it had never been more than a few days.

"Darcy." Patrick laid a hand on her shoulder. Heat seeped through her blouse, and the weight of his fingers was comforting. "You have an order up in the kitchen."

She spun around in the almost-empty restaurant. "Something's wrong, Patrick."

He began to lift his hand, then let it drop. "Yeah. But you need to serve your order before it gets cold."

She nodded and stepped around him. He brushed her arm as she hurried to the kitchen, and she swallowed hard.

This was why workplace affairs were a bad idea. There was no thinking when Patrick touched her, even accidentally. There was only reacting.

She was careful to avoid him when she was carrying a tray full of food.

After backing out the door, balancing a pizza and two pasta dishes, she delivered them to a table in the corner of the room, brought all three customers another glass of wine, then checked her other tables. None of them needed anything, and she found herself scanning the room for Patrick.

He stood in the waitresses' station, rolling silver. She stepped in beside him. "That's our job."

"Slow night. Have to do something." He turned to face her. "I know you're worried, Darcy. Hell, I am, too. But there's nothing we can do about it."

"You could look her up. Try to find her address."

"Do you really think her name is Smith?" he asked gently.

"I don't." He glanced around the room, then moved closer. "I have someone checking on things."

His breath caressed the sensitive skin of her neck. Heat pooled in her abdomen, and she wanted to lean into him, to take comfort from his solid strength.

They were in the middle of a restaurant, in plain view of anyone who walked past. So she just whispered back, "What kinds of things?"

"Later." The front door opened. He dropped the silver in the basket and moved to the podium with a smile.

He'd gotten pretty good at managing a restaurant in the past four weeks, she thought as she watched him lead two people to a table. He chatted with the young couple as he motioned for Phyllis to take over.

The staff would miss him when he went back to Detroit.

She'd miss him, too.

The knowledge should have sounded alarm bells in her head. Should have had her scrambling to back away. Instead, she watched him walk to another table, let her gaze linger on his smile.

Let herself want.

After that kiss in the storage unit this morning, he'd expect her to ask him to stay tonight. But as her desire faded to a background hum, she'd been able to think logically again. She wanted to ask him.

It would be a very bad idea.

Still, she watched him stroll to the podium. Watched his long legs in the dark gray pants, the way the shirt made his shoulders look impossibly wide.

"You've got good taste," Phyllis said behind her.

Darcy spun around, color creeping up her neck. "What are you talking about?"

The other waitress jerked her head toward the podium. "Patrick. He's hot to the max."

"Phyll!" Darcy swallowed. "That's… You're…"

The other woman poked a friendly elbow in Darcy's ribs. "You telling me you haven't noticed?"

Darcy's face flamed.

"Yeah, that's what I thought. You two better get busy and do more than ogle each other. 'Cause if you don't, the eye sex is going to burn this place to the ground."

As Phyllis hurried off with a basket of bread, Darcy stared after her. Had everyone at Mama's noticed her and Patrick doing an intimate, private dance?

"Darcy? What's wrong?"

Patrick. Behind her.

"Nothing." She tossed a random number of silver rolls onto a tray. They landed with a clunk, and she snatched the tray up.

Before she could escape, he touched her arm. "Tell me."

"It was just Phyll. Saying typical Phyll stuff." *Eye sex.*

He turned her to face him, studied her for a moment, and grinned. "Can I guess what it was?"

"No! It wasn't important."

His smile widened. "I can get it out of Phyllis. She thinks

I'm hot." He nodded toward the front of the restaurant. "I seated a group in your section."

Phyllis was right, Darcy thought as she watched him walk away. Patrick *was* hot.

For the next fifteen minutes, Darcy's gaze flew to the door every time it opened. The hard ball of dread in her stomach grew larger each time someone walked in.

While she served drinks to the table of five, the door opened again. Chuck held it for Theresa, then walked through himself. Leaving her standing in front of Patrick, Chuck strode to the bar. A young woman was sitting in his usual seat, chatting with a guy. Scowling, Chuck took the next stool.

As Patrick helped Theresa into a chair at her usual table, Darcy forced herself to concentrate on her table's order. Then she slipped the pad into her pocket and hurried to Theresa.

Stopped. Put a hand to her mouth.

Theresa's left arm was in a cast that ran from her fingers to the middle of her upper arm. And not even makeup could hide the bruise covering the left side of her face.

She hurried toward Theresa, but Patrick stepped in front of her. Darcy had to rear back to avoid colliding with him.

"Easy," he murmured. "We have an audience." He jerked his head toward the bar.

Right. Chuck.

She stared at Patrick, took a deep breath, then nodded once. "Thanks."

Swallowing hard, she stepped to Theresa's table and smiled. The smile faded as she studied the woman's face. "What happened?" she murmured, touching Theresa's shoulder. Any acquaintance would ask the question.

"I fell," Theresa said, adjusting the neck of her high-collared sweater.

Darcy sensed Patrick behind her, then he placed a basket of bread on the table. Theresa began shredding a slice into tiny pieces.

"Would you like a drink?" Darcy asked.

"Yes, please." Her voice was low and raspy, as if she'd been yelling.

"The usual?"

Theresa nodded.

"I'll be right back."

Darcy's hand shook as she punched the order in, Chuck's gaze boring into her back. Forcing herself not to look at him, she waited for Jesse to mix the drink, then set it on a tray.

It was harder to avoid glancing at Chuck as she retraced her steps. He was staring at her, his eyes cold and flat. Unblinking. She shuddered, remembering the eyes of the Komodo dragon she'd seen at the zoo.

As she walked past him, she nodded, as she would to any customer. She felt his gaze on her as she delivered Theresa's drink. "Are you hungry?" Darcy asked.

"No. Thank you." She glanced at Darcy out of the corner of her eye. "Don't hang around. He'll be watching tonight."

"Right. Let me know when you need another drink."

Dropping her tray on the stack by the bar, she shoved through the swinging door into the kitchen. Leaning against the wall, she closed her eyes and took deep breaths. Theresa had come back. She was injured, but she wasn't dead. *Yet,* a tiny voice whispered.

There was still a chance to help her.

The door swung open, fanning air across her face. Patrick walked through. Focused on her. "Darcy, would you come to the office for a moment, please?"

She followed him to the cubicle at the rear of the kitchen, where he waited for her to enter before closing the door.

"Snap out of it," he said, grabbing her shoulders. "Right now. You want to help her? Then don't make Chuck suspicious."

"Did you see her face?" Darcy asked quietly. "I can't even imagine what the rest of her looks like." Tim had always been careful not to mark her face. He wanted the bruises hidden, where no one would notice and ask about them.

Theresa's husband apparently didn't care.

She shivered.

"I saw." He slid his hands up and down her arms. Comforting her. Warming her. "I know this is hard for you. But keep it together. We'll figure out what to do. Okay?"

She nodded. For Theresa's sake, she could pretend.

She'd become excellent at pretending when she was married to Tim.

As she walked out of the office, Patrick picked up the phone.

An hour later, Theresa pushed away from the table. Darcy hurried to the restroom. Better to be there already than have Chuck see her following Theresa.

In case he accompanied Theresa, Darcy stood at the sink next to the wall. Hidden there, no one could see her until they actually walked in. She used a paper towel to wipe up small splashes of water on the marble counter while she waited.

When the door opened, she turned. Theresa flinched and drew back. Exhaled when she saw Darcy.

"What happened?" Darcy whispered.

Theresa lifted one shoulder. "The usual. It got out of control."

Darcy took the woman's hand. It was cold and dry, and she warmed it between both of hers. "You can't stay there, Theresa. It's too dangerous."

Theresa stared at their joined hands. "I have nowhere to go."

"There's a women's shelter in this neighborhood." Darcy squeezed Theresa's fingers. "I know the place—I volunteer twice a week. They'll keep you safe and give you the help you need."

Theresa drew away from Darcy's clasp. "You don't understand. My husband is...powerful. He won't let me get away."

"Why not?"

"I know things about him. Things he wants hidden."

Dear God. Darcy had known things about Tim, too. That's why she'd changed her identity and fled to another state. If she hadn't, Tim would have come after her when he got out of jail. Killed her.

He'd told her exactly what he had planned.

"The first step is to get away," Darcy said. "Then we'll deal with the rest."

"I'm never alone. Someone is always in the house. Chuck goes everywhere with me."

"We'll figure something out."

"I don't know." Theresa's eyes darted around the room, as if looking for a hidden camera. "If he catches me..."

"I'm not going to force you to do anything, Theresa. But you need to get ready. To seize any chance you get. All right?"

"Maybe."

Darcy touched her shoulder. "Are there children at home?"

"They're in college."

"Okay. Do you have money stashed away?"

Theresa nodded. "I've been skimming from the household account. It's hidden where he won't find it."

"Good. Put it in the lining of your purse, so you're ready to leave anytime. Can you do that?"

Theresa nodded. The sliver of hope in her eyes was painful to see.

"Here's what we'll do." Darcy tried to be matter-of-fact and calm. "You have my phone number. If you want me to pick you up, call anytime. From anywhere. Okay?"

"Why are you doing this?"

Darcy took a deep breath. Let it out. "Because I've been where you are. I was in the same kind of marriage. I got away, and you can, too."

Theresa rubbed her shoulder absently. As if she barely noticed that it hurt. "Your husband—did he let you go?"

"Not by choice. But the shelter I went to helped me document the abuse, and I was able to get a divorce."

Before Theresa could answer, Phyllis poked her head in the door. "Everything okay in here?"

As soon as the door began to open, Theresa bent over the sink and pretended to wash her hands. "I'm fine."

Darcy shook her head at Phyllis, mimed zipping her lip and

nodded at Theresa. Phyllis's gaze shifted from one to the other, then she gave a tiny nod. "She's just washing her hands," she said to someone behind her. "Looks like it's awkward with the cast."

The door closed with a muffled thump, and Theresa's hands shook as she reached for a paper towel. Then, with a fearful glance at Darcy, she pulled the door open and walked out.

CHAPTER SIXTEEN

AFTER CHUCK SLID off his bar stool and headed for the restrooms, Patrick motioned Jesse over. "Chuck drinks well scotch tonight."

"Yeah, you told me that last time he was here. I got it."

"Any trouble, I'll handle it."

"He's all yours." Jesse glanced at Chuck. "Dirtbag doesn't tip."

"Now why doesn't that surprise me?" Patrick pushed away from the bar and spotted Chuck standing near the restrooms, behind Phyllis.

His stomach tightened. Darcy was in there. With Theresa. He curled his hands into fists as he stared at Chuck's back.

Was he the one who'd slashed Darcy's tires?

Touch one hair on her head, and I will destroy you.

As long as he was around, no one would hurt Darcy again.

Phyllis stuck her head inside the door, then said something over her shoulder to Chuck.

Patrick tidied the small glass jars of maraschino cherries, lemon and lime slices, olives and onions as he watched. Chuck hesitated, then nodded to Phyllis and made his way back to the bar. A few moments later, Theresa emerged from the restroom and walked carefully back to her table.

The bruise was a dark shadow on her face, and she moved stiffly. Patrick tightened his grip on the tray. Bastard of a husband.

Chuck followed Theresa's progress across the room, then his gaze returned to the ladies' room.

Stay in there, Darcy.

Patrick scanned her tables and caught the eye of an older man. He hurried over, took the man's drink order and brought it to the table. As he walked past Chuck, he noted the bulge beneath the guy's jacket.

Wearing a gun again.

As soon as Chuck's attention returned to the hockey game on the television, Patrick wandered through the back room, stopping at tables, talking to the customers. When he reached the alcove holding the restrooms, he tapped softly on the door to the ladies' room.

A few moments later, Darcy emerged. She glanced at him, and he held her gaze longer than necessary.

You okay?

I'm fine. Thanks for the all-clear.

Anytime.

Finally a smile lit her eyes, and her mouth curved slightly. Then she nodded, a movement so tiny only someone watching carefully would notice. When he nodded back, she hurried toward the kitchen.

Patrick watched until she disappeared. *God.* Now he was imagining he could read her mind.

And she could read his.

He found himself following her toward the kitchen. Then the front door of Mama's opened and Danny Kopecki walked in with his father.

"Danny," he said, changing course to shake the detective's hand. "Glad you stopped by. Mr. Kopecki." With one last look at the kitchen door, he focused on the two men. "It's been a long time. Good to see you."

"Call me Mitch, Patrick." The older man with the fringe of white hair smiled. "We go back too far to be so formal."

"Right, sir. I mean Mitch." It had been a while since he'd seen Danny's father. The elder Kopecki had been a cop, too, but around the time Patrick's parents died, he'd gone back to school, become a lawyer and joined the state's attorney's office. "How are things at the D.A.'s?"

"Busy as usual. There's never a shortage of criminals."

"Don't I know that." Patrick led them to a table in the corner, where Danny had a clear view of Theresa. Mitch sat opposite his son. "Hope you don't mind that Danny and I have a little business to take care of."

"Not at all. He filled me in on your situation. I'm just going to enjoy my dinner and keep him company. Be his cover," Mitch added with a wink.

"Let me get the two of you a drink," Patrick said.

"Thanks. Guinness'd be good," Danny answered. He appeared to be studying the menu, but his gaze was on Theresa.

"Same for me," his father said.

"Be right back."

As Patrick entered the order, Ashley emerged from the kitchen. He motioned her over.

"I ordered Guinnesses for the guys at your corner table," Patrick told her. "Their food and drinks are comped."

"Okay," the girl answered. She stood on tiptoes to look for Danny and Mitch. "Are they, like, famous?"

"Nah. The younger one is only a legend in his own mind." When Ashley frowned, bewildered, Patrick bit his lip to keep from laughing. "He's an old friend."

Darcy came out of the kitchen, slowed when she saw him talking to Ashley, then kept going.

"Cool." Ashley headed toward the bar for the beer, and Patrick watched Darcy for a moment. She was talking to a customer, smiling and gesturing. Then she scribbled on her order form and walked toward him.

He stepped aside so she could enter her order on the touch pad. As she typed, he leaned in. Inhaled her scent, even though he knew it was stupid. They were at work. "How's Theresa doing?"

"How do you think?" She didn't look at him. "Scared. Hurt. Ground down."

"Be careful around her. Chuck's suspicious."

"I know."

She finished her order and walked away.

A half hour later, when Chuck and Theresa left Mama's, Patrick slid onto a chair at Danny's table. Danny nodded, swallowed, then set his fork down. Mitch kept eating, watching both men. "Chuck Notarro. Used to be a bag man for Rizzulo. Freelances now. Total shithead. And you're right. Guy's carrying."

"How about Theresa? Did you recognize her?"

Danny took a long drink of beer, then leaned forward. "Yeah, I know her. Watch yourself, Paddy. She's Eddie O'Fallon's wife. Eddie's the alderman of this ward. Connected. Big-time."

"Your guess was right." Patrick glanced at Theresa's regular table.

"Yeah. There are wife beaters everywhere."

"You ever get any complaints from her?"

"Not that I know of. I'll check, though. On neighbor complaints, too."

"Can you get me his address?"

Kopecki frowned. "What are you planning, Paddy?"

"Nothing. Just want all the available info."

After a long moment, Danny nodded. "I'll call you."

"Thanks for coming by, Danny." He shook his friend's hand, then Mitch's. "And good to see you again, sir. Next time, let's make it social. Bring your wives."

"Don't have one of those anymore," Danny said. "How about you? That red-headed waitress going to join us?"

Patrick froze. "What are you talking about?"

Kopecki snorted. "You think I didn't notice the way you looked at her? And she looked back?"

"Your imagination, buddy."

"Don't think so. I'm a trained detective, and I detect something going on."

"Thanks for your help, Danny."

The detective grinned. "Anytime, pal."

After Danny and his father left, Patrick found Darcy in the kitchen. He drew her toward the office, where no one could hear them. "When did Theresa start coming into Mama's?" he asked.

"It's been a while." She stared at nothing and frowned, clearly trying to calculate. Finally she said, "We were in the middle of the renovations. It was crazy, and it took me a few weeks to figure out what was going on."

"Last winter, then?"

"That sounds right. Nathan started the project in January, since that's our slowest month. Theresa and Chuck started coming in a couple of months after that."

"Thanks, Darcy."

She waited a moment, as if expecting him to tell her what he was thinking. He shook his head. "Make sure there's no one waiting to be seated. I need to check on something."

She hesitated. Clearly, she wanted to press him. But finally she headed out the door. Patrick sank into the desk chair.

In the documents he and Darcy had retrieved that morning, there had been no loan papers from a bank. No evidence at all to tell him where Nathan got that money.

Theresa and Chuck had begun coming after Nathan started the renovations. During the spring, Nathan wanted a break from the restaurant.

During the spring, he'd begun making payments to someone.

He was willing to bet the two were connected. And the key to what was going on at Mama's.

SATURDAY WAS BUSIER than usual at Mama's.

A lot of groups came in, and almost all of them consisted of a few adults and several preadolescent boys. The noise level in the restaurant had risen to a high-pitched whine that made his ears hurt. Kids stood up at long tables, shouting to friends at the other end. Finally, Patrick asked one man if something was going on in the neighborhood.

"Hockey tournament," the guy said with a smile. "The rink

isn't far from here. Guy at the snack bar recommended this place for dinner."

"I always like to hear that," Patrick said, smiling. "Good luck in the tournament."

"Thanks." The guy counted heads as Patrick escorted his group to a table. By the time he'd made his way back to the front, two more groups were waiting to be seated.

As he called the busboy over and told him which tables to push together, he saw Chuck and Theresa at the back of the crowd. Chuck was gripping Theresa's arm. Hard. Trying to elbow his way through the pack of kids.

Patrick edged through the group and put his hand on Chuck's wrist. "Busy tonight. Let me help you."

He found the pressure point he wanted and squeezed. Chuck's hand opened and Theresa yanked her arm away.

"Sorry about the crowd," Patrick said with a bland smile. He wanted to twist Chuck's arm off and beat him with the stump. "Tournament in town. I'll help the lady through the crowd and get her settled at her usual table. You go ahead to the bar."

Chuck stared at him for a long moment. Finally he nodded once. Shouldering a parent aside, he marched to the bar and slid onto his usual stool.

"You okay?" Patrick murmured to Theresa.

"I'm fine." She rubbed her arm, cradling it next to her body.

Patrick fumed as he guided her to a table. She moved carefully, as if she was thirty years older than she looked.

"I'll get Darcy for you," he said once she was seated.

"Thank you. For what you did back there."

"Believe me, it was my pleasure."

He saw Darcy come out of the kitchen and let his gaze follow her across the room. As if she felt him watching, she turned toward him and began to smile. Saw Theresa and her smile fell away.

She nodded.

Theresa was still massaging her arm.

Patrick glanced at Chuck, who was sipping a scotch and

watching television. The guy didn't even care that he'd hurt the woman.

Probably enjoyed it.

Bastard.

He didn't want Chuck in his place. This ended tonight.

After seating the waiting group, he stepped to the side and pulled out his cell. Dialed Kopecki. "They're here again. I want this guy out of here permanently. Can you make it over here tonight?"

"I'll be right there."

Fifteen minutes later, Danny swung into a seat at the bar. He ordered a beer and struck up a conversation with the guy next to him. He didn't look at Patrick.

Chuck downed three scotches in forty-five minutes. As he signaled Jesse for another, Patrick stepped close. "Did you drive over?" he asked.

"Yeah. So?"

"You need to slow down," Patrick said in a quiet voice. "We have liability issues if a guest is overserved."

"I'll decide when I've had enough." Chuck tilted the empty glass back and forth, trying to get Jesse's attention. The bartender was carefully not noticing.

"Afraid that's not your call," Patrick said, still keeping his voice low.

Chuck let his glass drop. Swiveled on the stool. His chest seemed to swell as he confronted Patrick. "Yeah, it is. Where's your brother?"

"He's still recuperating," Patrick said coolly. "He's not part of the equation."

"Your brother and I have...an understanding."

"What would that be?"

"None of your business."

Out of the corner of his eye, Patrick saw Danny tense. Several other patrons were watching, as well.

Patrick focused his attention on Chuck. On frustrating him. Angering him enough to make him sloppy. "This place is my business now, and you're done. I don't want to see you here again."

He was taking a chance. If Chuck stormed out and didn't return, they had lost Theresa.

But he was betting that Chuck and Theresa had to be here for some reason.

"Tough shit. I ain't going nowhere."

"I think you are." He stuck his arm out, as if to escort Chuck from the bar, and Chuck reached inside his jacket.

Patrick didn't see Danny move, but suddenly he shoved Patrick aside. "You carrying?" he asked Chuck.

Chuck slapped his fist on the bar. "'Course not."

Danny pulled out his badge. "Police. Open your jacket."

Chuck stared at Danny. Danny stared back, but his hand slipped into his own jacket. Stayed there.

Chuck's gaze slid to one side. Then the other. The bar had fallen silent and everyone was watching.

"Hands on the bar," Danny barked. "Both of them."

Chuck stared at Danny and didn't move. Danny eased his gun out of his jacket and pointed it at Chuck's chest. "We going to do this easy? Or not. Your choice."

It felt as if the room had taken a deep breath. Finally Chuck put both his palms on the bar.

Still holding his own weapon, Danny flicked open Chuck's jacket to reveal the holstered gun. He stared at it for a long moment, then barked, "Hands on top of your head. Now."

Chuck scowled. "You're going to regret this."

"Don't think so. Carrying concealed is a crime in Illinois." He holstered his gun and pulled a pair of handcuffs from the back of his belt. Once Chuck's arms were secured behind his back, he pulled out his cell and called for backup.

"Get me a bag," he said to Patrick without looking at him.

"Jesse," Patrick said. "Give me one of the carryout containers."

A few moments later, the gun was nestled in a circular foil pan with a plastic cover over it. Takeout from Mama's.

Danny searched Chuck and found a knife strapped to his ankle. That went into another container.

The front door opened and two uniformed officers walked in. "Hey, Kopecki," one of them said when they saw Danny. "Whadda ya have?"

"Carrying concealed. The collar's all yours."

One of the uniformed officers took Chuck's arm. He shook it off and turned to Patrick, eyes blazing with fury. "What about the woman I came here with?"

"I'll make sure she gets home. I'll drive her myself."

"No. Call her a cab."

"When she's ready to leave, I will."

"Now."

"She can finish her drink first."

Chuck turned to Kopecki. "I want my phone call."

"And you'll get it, as soon as you're booked." He nodded to the uniforms. "Get him out of here."

Chuck struggled when they took his arms. By now, the whole restaurant had fallen silent.

When the police finally disappeared through the door with Chuck, people began talking again. The noise level rose, and Patrick saw Darcy, standing next to Theresa. As if protecting her.

He hurried over to her. "The lady's escort is indisposed. He requested that we call her a cab."

Darcy opened her mouth to say she'd drive Theresa home, but Patrick gave her a tiny shake of his head. "I'll call the cab. You wait outside with her. Make sure she gets safely into the taxi."

"Okay." Darcy swallowed. "I'll do that."

"Thanks."

He drew his car keys out of his pocket, and as he brushed past her, he dropped them into her apron. Disappearing toward the kitchen, he heard her say, "Are you ready to go, Theresa?"

CHAPTER SEVENTEEN

THERESA'S FACE WAS white. Her mouth trembled. As she looked up at Darcy, her expression showed both fear and hope. Finally she nodded. "Yes, I'm ready to go." She fumbled in her purse. "I need to pay my bill."

Darcy touched her hand. "You can get it next time, Theresa," she said, her voice loud enough for the neighboring tables to hear. "I know you'll be back."

For a moment, Theresa looked confused. Darcy held her gaze, and the older woman finally nodded. She understood.

As Theresa struggled to her feet, Darcy steadied her good arm. Her heart thundered in her chest, so loud she was sure everyone in the restaurant could hear it. She schooled her face into a polite, helpful mask.

Thank God she knew all about masks.

As they walked slowly toward the door, no one seemed to be paying attention. Finally, when they'd stepped outside into the chilly air, Darcy took a deep breath. "Do you want to get in that cab and go home? Or do you want to go to the shelter? It's your call, Theresa." She wouldn't take control away from the woman. As much as she wanted Theresa to go to the shelter, it had to be her decision.

Theresa swallowed. Stared at the cast on her arm. "I want to go to the shelter," she said, but her voice shook.

"Are you sure? I'm not going to pressure you."

"Yes, I'm sure." Her voice was stronger. "You figured out a way to get me free, and I'm going to take it."

"All right." She touched the woman's shoulder. "You okay?"

"I'm…scared." Her voice wavered.

"I know." She'd been terrified herself when she made the decision to escape. Afraid that Tim would catch her before she reached the sanctuary of the shelter. Afraid it was all a dream, that she'd wake up and Tim would be staring down at her, his fist raised.

She took Theresa's hand. Felt it trembling. "I'll keep you safe." She prayed that was true. Darcy looked around the quiet business district. Happy Foods grocery store was still open. So was the ice cream shop. Everything else was closed.

No one would be watching from a storefront, able to describe her and Theresa to a police officer searching for a missing woman.

They reached the edge of the parking lot, away from the restaurant windows. No one inside could see them, either. Theresa slowed. "What happened with Chuck? Why did the police arrest him?"

"I'm not sure," Darcy answered. "I didn't want to get too close and make Chuck suspicious."

Theresa's gaze drifted over the cars in the parking lot and paused at a large black SUV sitting in the corner. "My husband will come looking for me."

"And we'll tell him you got into a taxi. We assumed you were going home."

"Will it really be that easy?" she whispered.

"Getting into Patrick's SUV and going to the shelter? That's easy. The rest? Not so much." Darcy stepped in front of her and took both her hands. "It's scary, and lonely, and depressing. Completely disorienting. But sometimes, it's the only way to save yourself. The only way to be free."

"How long ago did you escape?"

"Three years ago. I'm still afraid. Still worry that he'll find me. But if I'd stayed, he would have killed me." *Just like your husband will eventually kill you.*

Theresa swallowed. "I've thought about this for a long time. So, yes. Please take me to the shelter." She seemed to stand straighter. "I need to do that before I can do anything else."

Thank God. "Are you sure?"

"Yes." Her voice firmed. Strengthened. "I am."

"Okay." They headed toward Patrick's vehicle, but Darcy faltered when she heard a rustling to her right. In the undergrowth at the corner of the parking lot.

She stared at the dense, bare-branched lilac bush, but couldn't see anything but shadows. Still, she reached into her pocket for Patrick's keys. Clutched them in her hand with the ends protruding between her fingers.

Chuck was in custody. There was no way Theresa's husband could know what was happening.

Maybe someone was watching Darcy.

Fear rushed through her. *Tim.*

No. Her ex-husband didn't skulk in the bushes. He confronted. Fists and feet ready to punch. Kick. Hurt.

Maybe someone was there. Or maybe it was an animal. Darcy shifted the keys so they were more comfortable, then closed her fist tighter. She wasn't taking any chances with Theresa's safety.

When they were finally inside the SUV, the doors locked, she took a deep breath. Let some of the tension ease from her shoulders. "The shelter is only a few minutes away."

"Okay." Theresa's hands shook as she buckled her seat belt. "I'm ready."

As they drove through the neighborhood, the streets were dark, with only the corner streetlights illuminating the way. Lights gleamed in the windows of most of the houses, but no cars drove past. No one was out walking.

The big black SUV passed through the neighborhood like a ghost, unseen and unheard.

Finally she rolled to the curb at the shelter. The fence surrounding it was high, but lights were on in the director's first-floor office, as well as several other windows.

"We're here."

Theresa gazed at the rambling colonial house that blended

in with the rest of the neighborhood homes. "It doesn't look like a women's shelter."

"They don't want to advertise." She jumped out of the driver's seat and hurried around to help Theresa. As they walked toward the gate, Theresa reached for her hand. Clutched it tightly.

Darcy remembered the day three years ago when she'd walked into a similar shelter. She knew her life had changed forever. She had no clue what the future held. She'd worried about what her friends would think.

And terror had been the slick, greasy glue binding it all together.

She also remembered the relief of knowing she was safe. Knowing that no one would hit her again. No one would threaten to kill her again.

"It'll be okay," Darcy murmured. "I'll introduce you to Kelly, the director, then I have to get back to Mama's. I don't want anyone to notice I've been gone."

Theresa gripped her hand more tightly. "You're going to leave me here?"

"I have to, Theresa," she said gently. "We don't want anyone missing me from the restaurant."

"Will you come back when it closes?"

She wanted to say yes. She knew how desperately Theresa needed to hold on to a familiar face. "I'm not sure that's a good idea, at least tonight." She wrapped her arm around the other woman's shoulders and felt her trembling. "Your husband will probably come looking for you. I don't want to lead him to this shelter."

"No." Theresa stared at the front door. "Me, either."

"I'll come back when I can. I promise."

Theresa turned her head slowly, as if her joints were stiff. Sore. She nodded. "Okay, Darcy. I believe you."

Darcy pushed the buzzer, and Kelly's voice came through the intercom. "Yes?"

"It's Darcy."

The gate buzzed, and they walked through. The sound of

the lock clicking into place behind them was reassuring. Comforting.

She was a big fan of locks.

Kelly opened the door as they approached. "Hi," she said to Theresa, holding out her hands. "I'm Kelly. Welcome."

Darcy sat in Patrick's car for a few minutes, staring at the closed door. Theresa had gathered the courage she needed to take the next step. To free herself of her past.

Did she have as much courage as Theresa? Could she take the next step, too? Free herself from the memories that wrapped around her like chains?

The past two nights, when Patrick had followed her home and checked her apartment, he'd wanted to stay. She'd wanted him to, as well. But she hadn't been able to force the words out of her mouth.

Maybe it was time to find that courage. To release herself from the past and become the strong woman she wanted to be.

Maybe it was time to ask Patrick to stay.

As Darcy pulled into Mama's parking lot, a cab was idling at the front door. She kept her head down as she walked past it, but out of the corner of her eye, she saw the driver talking on his cell. Suddenly, he tossed the phone onto the seat next to him, threw his arms in the air and pulled away, tires screeching.

Darcy hurried in. Patrick was standing at the podium, replacing his cell in his pocket. She nodded to him, saw his shoulders relax.

"Everything okay?" he asked in a low voice.

"Yeah. We're good." She edged toward the far side of the podium and scanned her tables. "You brought out my orders. Thanks."

"Not a problem."

She curled her hand around his keys and slid them gently into his pocket. The fabric of his pants made a warm rasp against the back of her hand. The material was softer than she'd expected. No wonder it hugged his butt like a glove.

As she slid her hand into his pocket and released the keys, his muscles tensed beneath her fingers. He stilled, and his gaze locked on her face. His eyes darkened.

She couldn't turn away. She'd started to lean toward him when the outside door opened, sending in a whoosh of cold air.

Her face flaming, she snatched her hand away. Stupid. Really stupid.

By the time she reached her cluster of tables, the heat was fading and she was able to smile. "How are you doing?" she asked a couple who'd finished their dessert. Their heads were close together, and they were holding hands. "Can I get you anything else?"

The man looked up at her. "Just the check, please," he said as he smiled at his date.

"I'll get it right away."

As she finished her shift, she thought about Theresa. Wondered how she was doing. Hoped she felt safe.

She glanced at her watch. Two more tables were getting ready to pay their bills. Once they left, she could start her prep for the next day.

The sooner she finished the sooner she could go home.

Would she be able to ask Patrick to stay tonight? Could she take what she wanted?

Her foot jiggling, she started her chores while she waited for her customers to study their checks and pull out their wallets.

"You're planning on going back to the shelter, aren't you?" Patrick murmured, touching the back of her hand as he appeared beside her.

Nerves jumped and her abdomen tightened at his quick caress. "Not tonight." She kept her head down and concentrated on picking up one spoon, two forks, one knife. Tried not to think about Theresa, alone at the shelter. "I don't want to take a chance on being followed."

His hand covered hers. "That's smart." He squeezed. "Hard, though."

"Yeah." Tears prickled her eyes, and she blinked them away. Theresa was safe. She had to remember that.

"You sticking around for wine?"

"God, no." It was the last thing she wanted to do.

"Maybe you should. After a night like tonight? The hockey crowd, the guy taken out in handcuffs, the woman who had to take a cab home? Everyone wants to talk about it. You disappear, it might look odd."

He was standing so close. All she had to do was move a few inches and they'd be touching. She wanted to lean into him. Wanted to soak up some of his strength. Instead, she straightened. "You're right. I'll stay."

"Good," he said quietly. "I'll be here, too. We'll get through this together."

PATRICK RETREATED to the podium, but he kept an eye on Darcy. She'd been shaky. Upset.

Taking Theresa to the shelter must have cut close to the bone for her. Brought back a lot of memories.

A few minutes later, he watched her head into the kitchen. She paused as she pushed open the door and caught his eye. Her expression softened. She smiled at him, then let the door close behind her.

One smile. A simple curving of a mouth, and he felt as if he'd taken a shot to his chest. He pressed a hand to his sternum, remembering how her mouth had felt against his two days ago.

She'd been off last night, and he'd missed her like hell.

After work on Wednesday, he'd followed her home and checked her apartment, but she hadn't asked him to stay. She'd acted like she wanted to, but hadn't been able to work up the nerve.

He wasn't going to push her. Instead, he'd gone back to Nathan's and pored over the documents they'd retrieved. He had to figure out what was going on.

Especially now. With Chuck arrested and Theresa disappearing, things were going to come to a head. He'd done what he had to do—he'd kept Theresa safe. But a shit storm was about to hit Nathan. And by definition, the rest of his siblings.

He'd set it off, and it was his responsibility to deal with it.

First step was getting everyone out of the restaurant tonight.

He walked through the room, saying good-night to the lingering customers. Thanking them for dining at Mama's.

When he was in the far corner, the slam of the front door told him they had another customer. Keeping his smile firmly in place, he headed toward the man standing at the podium.

The guy was tall, with thinning red hair. He'd probably been muscular and fit when he was younger, but now his bulk was running to fat. He scanned the room, his mouth a thin line.

"Can I help you?" Patrick asked.

"Where's Devereux?"

"I'm Patrick Devereux."

"Nathan's brother?" The guy finally focused on Patrick's face.

"One of them."

"I'm Eddie O'Fallon." He stuck out one beefy hand. When Patrick shook, O'Fallon squeezed hard. Patrick smiled, held on and squeezed back, equally hard. O'Fallon let go first. "My wife and one of my associates were in here earlier. They didn't come home."

"You're talking about Chuck?"

"And the woman with him."

"Your...associate had a run-in with an off-duty detective. Tried to pull his gun on him. The detective arrested him for carrying a concealed weapon."

O'Fallon's face darkened. "What kind of bullshit is that?"

Patrick shrugged. "Just telling you what happened."

"They arrest my wife, too?"

"Of course not. Chuck was concerned about her, and I offered to drive her home. He insisted I put her in a taxi, instead." He shrugged. "Thought it was odd, but I figured she didn't want to get in a car with a stranger. I called a taxi. She went out front to wait. Last I saw of her."

O'Fallon's hands curled into fists. "You see her get in the cab?"

"Sorry, but I didn't. We were busy this evening. Hockey tournament."

O'Fallon scowled.

"Maybe she went to visit a friend."

"She knows better than… She knows her friends are all out on a Friday night."

"Wish I could help you." Patrick smiled pleasantly and stared at the irate man. The guy took a step toward Patrick, tightening his fists. *Come on. Throw a punch. Please.*

Suddenly, as if realizing where he was, O'Fallon shoved his hands into his pockets. "Thanks for your help," he said stiffly. "I need to go look for my wife."

He turned and pushed out of the restaurant, letting the door bang shut behind him.

Patrick drew in a deep breath and spotted Jesse standing at the end of the bar. The bartender strolled over.

"That Chuck's boss?"

"Yeah."

"Guy's an asshole. Just like Chuck."

Patrick laughed. "Yeah. But I think we've seen the last of Chuck."

Jesse eyed him shrewdly. "Nice work, Patrick."

"What?"

Jesse shook his head as he walked away. "Wish Nathan had gotten rid of that guy a long time ago."

Patrick's smile faded. He needed to talk to Nathan in the morning, before O'Fallon got hold of him, and tell him what had happened.

Nathan wasn't going to be happy.

In the meantime, adrenaline buzzed through Patrick's veins. This was who he was—an FBI agent. Law enforcement. Putting the puzzle pieces together. Figuring out the big picture.

He needed to get back to this.

It had been great to help his family. Reestablish a connection with them. But the fire was back in his blood now.

In a couple of weeks, he'd return to Detroit. Get his life back. Leave Darcy behind.

The adrenaline faded, leaving him flat.

Yeah, he liked her a lot. Wanted her a lot. But his life wasn't about running a restaurant. It wasn't about staying in Chicago with his family.

She wasn't looking for long-term, either, he told himself. He was her bridge guy. The guy who would help her get her life back.

No matter how much he wanted her, there was no future for him and Darcy.

CHAPTER EIGHTEEN

AFTER DARCY CLIMBED into her car and locked the doors, Patrick clicked open his SUV and got behind the wheel. He started the engine and waited for the windows to defrost. Outside, he heard Darcy drive her muffler-impaired clunker out of the parking lot.

Once his windshield was clear, he threw the vehicle into gear and drove to her apartment. As he traveled down the quiet streets, he watched his rearview mirror, checked all the side streets. He was afraid O'Fallon might try to follow him.

Or Darcy.

He didn't worry that Darcy would head up to her apartment alone.

Following her home was their routine now. Expected. She waited for him to arrive before she got out of her car.

Baby steps.

As he pulled up to the curb, he scanned the dark street. The wind was blowing hard tonight, rustling the few leaves clinging stubbornly to the branches. The full moon scudded in and out of the clouds, illuminating the street momentarily like a strobe light, then hiding everything again.

He scrutinized the house on the other side of the street. The moonlight outlined every needle on its yew border clearly. Then the moon disappeared, leaving only a black shadow.

A movement behind the yews caught his eye, and he paused with his hand on the door. Watching.

Dark. Light. Dark again. A shadow crept out from behind the bush and disappeared into the foliage next door.

Patrick jumped out of his truck and ran after it. By the time he reached the house, it was gone.

Coyotes roamed the neighborhood at night, coming from the forest preserves on the other side of Devon. Maybe that's what he'd seen.

But it had looked too big for a coyote.

He touched the gun at the small of his back. Since they'd found the mud on Darcy's porch, he'd brought it with him when he checked her house.

Nothing moved. The only sound was the whistling of the wind.

Finally, he crossed the street and trotted between the houses to Darcy's garage. When she saw him, she climbed out and shut the door, but stayed in the shelter of the garage. "It took you a while to get here."

"After the night we had, I was more careful than usual." He waited until she was clear, then pushed the button to lower the garage door. He opened his mouth to tell her about the shape he'd seen, then closed it again. He didn't want to freak her out. "No surprises. That's my motto. Especially where you're concerned."

She glanced at him out of the corner of her eye. "I used to like surprises."

One tiny look. Innocent-sounding words. Probably no subtext.

Didn't matter. All the blood in his head rushed south.

He threw his arm across her shoulders and tucked her body against his. Her curves pressed into his side, and he curled his fingers into her coat to keep from exploring them. "Not all surprises are bad ones."

Another of those sidelong glances. "I know."

His heart thudded with a heavy beat that made his chest ache. She was different tonight. Not as nervous. Calmer. As if she'd finally figured something out.

He studied her face. The moonlight kissed her cheekbones and made her eyes huge and dark. Her hair, tousled from the long night, glinted in the pale light. She looked mysterious. Complicated. Beautiful.

As they started up the stairs, a stone scuffled across the alley.

He swung her behind him and turned around. Moments later, a cat trotted by.

"You're jumpy tonight," she said.

"And you're not. How come?"

She shrugged as she climbed the stairs. "I'm not sure. Theresa, maybe. I'm so relieved we got her away that I don't have room to worry about other things." She smiled. "At least for a little while. I'll think about all that stuff tomorrow."

All what stuff? He wanted to ask, but didn't want to break the mood. "So tonight we celebrate?" he asked lightly.

"Tonight I relax." She drew a deep breath. Faced him. "You make me feel safe, Patrick."

Safe. Normally, not what he was going for with a woman. Darcy was different. For her, it was exactly what she needed.

They'd reached her back door, and he held out his hand for the key. "Let me check the place before you start relaxing."

The cat was waiting in his usual place. By now he recognized Patrick, and whined for dinner.

Patrick stood in the doorway, scanning the living room, while Darcy opened the refrigerator and took out a can of cat food. As she bent her head to peer into the fridge, the pale skin on her nape was exposed. Vulnerable. He wanted to taste that spot, see if it was as sweet as it looked.

He'd told her the next move was hers, and he would keep his word. Even if it killed him.

He drew a deep breath as he checked the bathroom. The bedroom. She'd drawn the comforter over the sheets, and the moon dappled it with shifting patterns. Dark and light.

He closed his eyes and reached for control. That was his trademark. He was always contained. His body never ruled his mind.

Every minute he spent with Darcy tested that resolve.

Darcy listened to Patrick moving around her apartment as she scraped food into the dish on the floor, then petted Cat while he ate. Her hand was shaking, she realized.

Of course it was. She was nervous.

She stood and rinsed out the cat-food can, then tossed it into the recycling. She was going to try to seduce Patrick.

It had been a very long time since she'd done that. Almost as long since she'd wanted to.

She hadn't wanted to even think about sex. About baring herself to a man. Being vulnerable to him.

Wind gusted through her open back door, carrying the scent of the cold. Making her shiver.

She'd been thinking about sex a lot since Patrick first walked into Mama's. Specifically, sex with Patrick.

She wanted him.

Time to gather her courage and take what she wanted.

It was stupid. Foolish. Risky. They had no future together. It was time for her to move on. Find another city, another job.

But that was okay. She wasn't ready for a future with a man, even one as trustworthy as Patrick.

They had three weeks, more or less, until he'd leave. She didn't want to waste any more of those days. Or nights.

"Everything's fine," he said behind her.

She glanced over her shoulder. Smiled. "Thanks for checking."

His eyes looked darker than usual tonight. Tension rolled off him in waves. "You're welcome, Darcy." He straightened. "You need anything, you call. Anytime. You know that, right?"

She swallowed. "Yes. I do."

She gripped the doorknob tightly. Hesitated, then pulled the door closed.

Engaged both locks.

He'd been moving toward her. He stilled.

She turned and pressed her back to the door. "I have an open bottle of wine. You want a glass?"

He nodded slowly, never taking his gaze from her face. "I'd like that."

Her hands shook as she pulled out the cork and poured the wine. The burgundy looked darker, richer in the soft light of the kitchen. As she handed Patrick a glass, the wine slid around in the bowl, leaving a faint trace of color behind.

He took the glass, but kept her hand, as well. "You're cold," he murmured.

Nerves had her shivering as if she were standing in the walk-in refrigerator at Mama's. "Chilly with the back door open." She tried to pull away, but he tightened his grip.

"What's wrong?" he asked. He brought her hand to his mouth, kissed her palm. "Why are you so nervous? Is there something you haven't told me?"

Yeah. She wanted to get him naked, and it was scaring the hell out of her. What if she'd forgotten how to do it? What if her experiences with Tim had…changed something inside her? Made it impossible to enjoy being intimate with a man.

His hand tightened. "Is it Theresa? Are you worried about her? Nervous about what her husband is going to do?"

She shook her head. "No," she whispered.

"Then what?" He ran his finger along the back of her hand. "Talk to me, Darcy."

"I…I don't want to talk."

He closed his eyes, took a deep breath. Let it out slowly. "What do you want, then?"

"I…" She bit her lip but kept her gaze on him. She trusted him. He would never hurt her. "I want you, Patrick."

"You want me." He set his glass carefully on the counter, then took both her hands in his. She felt him trembling. "To fix your leaky sink? Play Monopoly? Go for a late-night run?"

He'd told her the next step was up to her. He wasn't going to assume anything.

She took a deep, shaky breath. "I want to make love with you."

Instead of wrapping his arms around her and kissing her,

he tucked her hair behind her ears and cupped her face. "Why is that?"

She frowned. "Because I want you."

"I know you do. And I want you, too. But why tonight? Why all of a sudden?"

"It's not so sudden," she said in a rush of breath. "The first time I saw you, I…noticed you."

"Yeah." A smile curved his mouth. "I noticed you, too. But you acted like I didn't exist."

"I wanted to pretend that you didn't." Her chest ached as she drew in air. "I haven't had sex in more than three years. And that was… It wasn't pleasant. I was horrified I wanted you that way. But when you took over after Nathan was injured, I got to know you."

"And now you're not so horrified?"

His thumbs caressed her cheeks, smoothing away her fears. Lighting tiny fires beneath her skin. Sending shivers down her belly. "Not horrified at all." She was needy. Reckless and edgy. Aroused.

He drew her closer. "If you want to stop, you tell me. At any point. I promise I will."

She closed her eyes and tried to swallow around the lump in her throat. "I know. I trust you." She reached up and cupped his face. "I didn't know it was possible to want like this. To feel as if I'll die if I can't have you."

"Right back at you." His hands slid to her shoulders, tugged her closer. "I've never wanted anything this much, Darcy." He brushed his mouth over hers, and she felt the touch deep inside. "Kiss me," he whispered.

She wrapped her arms around his neck and fitted her body to his. The muscles of his chest were familiar. Hot, even through his shirt. She pressed closer and felt her breasts flatten against him. Desire surged, and she lifted her face to kiss him.

His mouth was soft. Gentle. Instead of taking, he teased. He feathered kisses over her mouth. Nipped at her lower lip, then moved to another spot before she could react. He lingered at the corners, as if memorizing her texture. Her taste.

"Don't," she whispered, moving against him. "You're holding back. Trying to be careful. I don't want careful, Patrick."

"That's too damn bad," he said, licking her lips. "Because that's what you're going to get. I'm not taking you up against the wall." She felt him smile against her mouth. "Not this time, anyway. Later, we'll talk about next time."

Her heart expanded until her chest felt tight. Until it was hard to draw a breath. "I'll look forward to that talk."

"Me, too."

As he kissed her, his hands roamed over her back, down her spine, over her rear. Touching. Caressing. Loving.

She needed more. Opening her mouth, she welcomed him in. Tasted the wine he'd had at the restaurant, the coffee he'd gulped before he left. He shifted, and the ridge of his erection burned into her belly.

It wasn't enough. She leaned away, and his hands loosened. His mouth stilled. She tugged at his shirt, pulling it out of his waistband. Burrowed her hands beneath it, letting her fingers trace the hard lines of his muscles, the bumps of his ribs. When she reached his flat nipples, she shoved his shirt up and licked one, then the other.

"Darcy." His voice was a harsh rasp, and his hands tightened on her back. Slid lower and gripped her rear. "Don't do that again."

She reached up and sucked one nipple gently, swirling her tongue around it. "Okay," she whispered, letting her breath feather over him.

His belly twitched beneath her fingers, and she savored her power. Delighted in every little hitch of his breath, every tiny quiver beneath her hands.

"You're destroying me," he said, taking her mouth again. Without warning, he swung her into his arms. Carried her into the dark, shadowy bedroom. His kiss tasted of desperation. Of need that was out of control. She wrapped her arms around his neck and opened herself to him.

His mouth still locked to hers, he fell onto her bed, twisting so she landed on top of him. He rolled her over and fumbled with the buttons on her shirt. His fingers trembled, and it seemed to take forever for him to get it off. Finally, his hands covered her white cotton bra. He stared down at her, his face all angles and sharp planes.

"I need to see you, Darcy," he said, bending to suck at the thin material. She groaned and lifted to him, begging him to take more.

"Off," she said, licking his neck. Kissing a spot beneath his ear. "Take it off. I want to feel your skin. Your mouth."

He eased the blouse from her arms, tossed it away. Worked the front clasp of her bra until it separated.

Cool air moved over her, and she grabbed his hands to cover her breasts. He groaned, and she lifted into his palms. He was being so careful. So considerate. But she could sense his desperation, and loved that she was doing that to him.

When he raised his head, she dragged her eyes open to find him watching her. His hands shook on her breasts, his thumbs caressing her nipples. "Are you okay?" he asked.

Her heart cracked wide open. She cupped his face. "I'm good. More than good." She slid her hands down his chest, his abdomen, to his waist. Fumbled with his belt, heard the tiny clink of the buckle, the quiet rasp of his zipper. The hard ridge of his penis tented the fabric of his pants. "I could be better, though."

"Tell me."

"Take off your clothes. Please." She skimmed her hand along the bulge of his erection, and he hissed in a breath. Then let her go, his hands sliding away as if it was the hardest thing he'd ever done.

Standing in the pale moonlight, he shucked his pants first, then the rest followed. As the trees outside her window cast shifting shadows over him, he pulled a silver packet out of his wallet, tore it open and put on the condom, reaching for her.

Moments later, her clothes were in a pile on the floor. He traced her breasts, slid his hands down to her belly, down her legs, back up again. "You're so beautiful. More beautiful than I imagined."

She held out her hand. "Come to me," she said.

He kissed her again. Gently, as if he had all the time in the world. He touched her breasts, traced circles around her nipples. Roamed lower, tangled his hand in the curls between her legs. Brushed over her center.

By the time he reached her feet, she was panting. Aching for him. "Patrick. Please."

He took one nipple in his mouth, slid his hands between her thighs. Touched her once, and she climaxed against his hand.

Convulsing around him, she reached for him. As he slid inside her, tension built again.

They moved in unison, their arms wrapped around each other, their mouths fused together. As she tumbled over the edge again, he groaned into her mouth, joining her.

AFTER THEIR BREATHING slowed and their bodies cooled, he eased away then pulled her close again. She wrapped her arms around him and tangled her legs with his, nuzzling his neck. Inhaling his scent.

"Darcy." He brushed her hair away from her face. Kissed her again. "That was…"

"Amazing," she said, sinking into the kiss. Desire stirred again, and she wriggled against him.

She wanted nothing more than to lose herself in him again, to make love with him for the rest of the night. But as she breathed him in and listened to the steady beat of his heart, a tiny worm of shame squirmed inside her.

"Do you think I was using you?" she asked in a small voice.

His pause was a fraction of a second too long. "Of course not."

"Don't lie to me, Patrick."

He kissed the top of her head. "Okay. Maybe I thought I was your bridge guy. The one after a breakup. The one who gets you over the last guy so you can move on."

Of course he'd think that. She'd practically told him so. "No." She leaned back and looked him in the eye. He deserved the truth. "You're not. You think other guys haven't been interested in the last three years? Nice, normal guys? Good-looking guys that women drool over?"

He frowned, but his eyes twinkled. "Are you trying to make me jealous?"

"Of course not. I don't play those games. I'm just trying to tell you that I've had other…opportunities to get over my ex. I've never been interested.

"Until you walked in that day of Frankie's engagement party. I was working. I wasn't looking. But I saw you."

"You looked like you wanted to run the other way."

"I did." She couldn't tell him the whole reason—that he was an FBI agent. She was a felon. "I wasn't ready to get involved with anyone."

"But you succumbed to my devastating charm, right?"

"I succumbed to something." She let herself get lost in his arms, not quite ready to face him while she said the rest of what she needed to say. "You're honest, Patrick. To a fault. You're kind. You care about your family, enough to leave your job behind for months." *Everything I need right now.*

"You make me sound boring. Dull."

She slipped her leg between his. "You're not. You're sexy. Exciting. And you make me very hot."

His fingers tightened on her hip. "Tell me more."

"Isn't that enough?" she teased. "I'm at your mercy now."

He rose up onto one elbow, slid his hand down her leg. "Yeah? That opens up lots of possibilities." He leaned forward and kissed her. "But it's not enough, Darcy."

He wanted to know about her past. About Tim. And she

couldn't tell him everything. She could tell him some things, though. And she wanted to.

Just not face-to-face.

She slipped away from him, stood up and wrapped her robe tightly around her. Stared out the window at the night. A plastic grocery bag tumbled over itself down the street, catching momentarily on the bumper of a car parked across from her house. Breaking free and blowing away.

"You were right," she said, her voice quiet. "I'm just like Theresa. My husband knocked me around. Hurt me. So I finally left. I went to a shelter, got a divorce, came to Chicago and started a new life."

"Who was he?"

"I won't tell you that. I know you, Patrick. You'd go after him." That would be dangerous for both her and Patrick. Tim had gotten out of prison a few months ago. He was probably looking for her and the information she had. If Patrick got in his way, Tim wouldn't care that he was an FBI agent.

"I've been living in the shadows for the past three years. Watching Theresa walk into that shelter tonight showed me I needed to get some courage. To get past what happened to me. I need to be normal—the person I want to be. Because if I'm not, I'll always be T— His victim. Then he wins."

"I want to know more about you, Darcy." He paused. "Is that even your real name?"

She wrapped her arms around her waist. She wanted to give him more. But she couldn't. "That's all I can give you. I hope it's enough."

"Tell me who you really are."

"I'm trying to protect you."

"I don't need you to stand in front of me." The sheets rustled, then he was behind her. He stroked her hair, as if she was a wild animal he had to reassure. "You're not protecting me. You're protecting yourself."

"I'm doing what I need to do." She couldn't bear it if Patrick was hurt because of her.

He continued to caress her hair. "You running tomorrow morning?"

She struggled to drag her thoughts out of the deep hole of fear and dread. "Maybe. Later than usual, probably."

He kissed her head. "I kept you up past your bedtime."

"I'm glad you did."

"Me, too." His hands fell away, and she heard the clink of his belt as he pulled on his pants. The brush of fabric against skin as he buttoned his shirt.

When she turned, he was tucking his gun against the small of his back and stepping into his shoes. "Call me if you decide to run."

"Okay." God, she wanted him to stay.

But she couldn't ask. If he stayed, she'd end up saying things she'd regret.

"Promise?"

"I'll call, Patrick."

"Good."

She followed him out of the bedroom. Cat was curled on the sofa in the dark living room, sound asleep. Miffed, probably, that his spot in her bed had been usurped.

Patrick stood at the back door, his fingers hovering over the locks. Instead of turning them, he glanced over his shoulder. "Tonight was great, Darcy. Let me know if you want to do it again."

He opened the door, waited for her to lock it behind him, then ran down the stairs. Feeling desolate and more alone than she ever had, even in the darkest days of her marriage, Darcy hurried into the living room.

She was just in time to see Patrick trot to his SUV. As he slid behind the wheel, he glanced up and saw her. Nodded. Started the engine.

She pressed her palm to the window and watched as he drove away.

Their lovemaking had been beautiful. Earth-shattering.

So why did she feel so empty?

CHAPTER NINETEEN

PATRICK SLAMMED his fist into the steering wheel, jerked the gearshift into Drive, and pulled away from the curb. Sap that he was, he couldn't stop himself from looking up at her place.

She was standing in the window, watching him leave.

Wishing she'd asked him to stay?

Or glad that he was gone?

The wind pushed at his vehicle as he navigated the deserted streets to Nathan's house. The porch light was on, the house dark inside. Nathan wasn't waiting up for him.

Thank God. He didn't want to confront his brother right now. He'd rip him apart if he did.

Nathan was hiding too much from him.

Just like Darcy.

Both of them keeping secrets. Shutting him out.

Yanking the front door open, Patrick pushed inside. Stopped at the door to the den and watched Nathan, asleep in the hospital bed. As always when Nathan slept, the casts were all Patrick saw. They looked awkward. Uncomfortable.

A burden.

Patrick didn't care. Tomorrow, he and his brother would have it out. Nathan *would* tell him what was going on. Patrick had a pretty good idea, but he needed to hear it from Nathan. For his own protection.

Tonight, Patrick had stolen O'Fallon's wife and jailed his bully boy. The guy would put two and two together, and he would be out for blood.

Nathan's blood.

Patrick wouldn't let that happen. Nathan would accept his help, whether he wanted to or not.

He might be on the outside of the family circle, but it didn't matter. He was going to fix things. And he wasn't going back to Detroit until he did.

He made his way through the dark house, anger still boiling. He wanted to throw something. To hear something break. He yanked open the cabinet above the stove and reached for the Jameson's.

No. He didn't want a drink. He wanted to hit someone. Preferably Nathan.

His gym bag sat at the back door where he'd dropped it last time he'd gone to work out.

Perfect.

Slamming the cabinet closed, he grabbed the bag and headed to the all-night gym.

Two hours later, Patrick had put in ten miles on the treadmill, climbed about fifty stories on the stair-stepper and was beating on the small bag with a steady, punishing rhythm. Even through the bulky boxing gloves, his knuckles ached every time they connected.

This morning, Patrick would deal with Nathan. They'd have their come-to-Jesus talk. And Darcy?

The bag sang as Patrick pounded on it. Darcy was keeping him on the outside, too. He'd thought that asking him to make love with her meant she trusted him. Completely. But she'd only trusted him with her body.

Even the woman he…liked didn't let him inside her fences.

They'd had sex last night. Earth-shaking, twelve-on-a-scale-of-ten sex, but it didn't mean she had to share her deepest, darkest secrets with him.

She'd said she wanted to make love with him. Apparently, she'd meant sex. Not lovemaking.

He'd thought sex was all he wanted, too. Now? It felt empty. Unsatisfying. The guy who wasn't going to get serious about a woman, who wasn't interested in a long-distance relationship, suddenly wanted more.

How the hell had that happened?

Bang. Bang. Bang. He put all his weight behind the punches, and the bag flew into the spring holding it in place.

What was she doing now? Had she crawled back into bed and fallen asleep?

Or was she awake, too?

Feeling as hollow and lonely as he did?

His left hand flew past the bag, missing it completely. Before he could react, the bag slammed into him.

He staggered back hard as pain exploded on the left side of his face. The bag slowed and gradually stopped. Patrick ripped off the gloves and tossed them to the floor. Touched his face. No blood, thank goodness. But the eye was already swelling.

He walked unsteadily to the ice machine, grabbed a handful of cubes and wrapped them in a towel. Holding it to his throbbing eye, he dropped onto a weight bench. Perfect way to end this damn night.

THE SUN HADN'T RISEN yet when Patrick walked into the house an hour later. Nathan was up already, sitting at the kitchen table, staring into a cup of coffee. When he lifted his head, there were lines of weariness on his face, and his eyes were shadowed.

He tried to smile, though. "Looks like that hurts. You're losing your touch, bro," he said.

Patrick touched the swelling around his left eye. "Yeah. Don't box in the middle of the night." *Or when you're thinking about a woman.*

"Good rule to live by," Nathan said. He swiveled the wheelchair and followed Patrick into the kitchen. "Waited up for a while, but you didn't come home last night."

Patrick tried to block out the memories of Darcy. "There was some excitement at Mama's."

"Yeah? What was that?"

Patrick poured himself a cup of coffee and took a bag of

peas out of the freezer. Holding the bag over his throbbing eye, he sat at the kitchen table.

"Your buddy Chuck ran into trouble."

Nathan's knuckles tightened on his coffee cup. "What kind of trouble?"

"He was carrying. Tried to draw down on a cop. Got himself arrested."

"What the hell?" Nathan paled. "How could you let that happen?"

"How was I supposed to stop Kopecki from arresting him?"

"Danny Kopecki?" Nathan's gaze narrowed. "He's a buddy of yours."

"Yeah. We had some classes together at Saint Pats, and he still lives in the neighborhood. He was having a drink at the bar." Patrick tossed his coffee into the sink. What the hell did he feel guilty about? He was trying to help his brother.

"Oh, God." Nathan's hands tightened on the arms of his chair. "I need to make a phone call." He reached into the bag hanging from one of the handles of his chair and pulled out his cell.

Patrick leaned forward before Nathan could punch in a number. "The woman who came with Chuck? Theresa? We took her to a women's shelter."

Nathan dropped the phone on the table. "You did what?"

Both fear and relief flashed across Nathan's face, and Patrick eased back in his chair. "Yeah. She broke her arm last week."

Nathan clenched his teeth and stared out the window. "*She* didn't break it. Her bastard of a husband did that for her. Darcy has been worried sick about her."

"How could you cut a deal with the guy, knowing he was a wife-beating asshole?" Patrick shifted the cold bag over his eye and took a deep breath, struggling to keep his voice even. He needed to stay calm. It wouldn't help anyone, especially Nathan, if Patrick tore a chunk out of him.

His brother swallowed once, then again. He turned his head slowly to face Patrick. "How did you find out?"

"Did you really think you could keep it hidden? There was money missing from a deposit after I brought the books home for you. You're worried sick. I looked at the books and put two and two together."

Nathan's hand curled around the control of his wheelchair, as if he was thinking about making a break for it. Patrick tensed, ready to block his way. They were going to have this out. Right now.

But instead of putting his wheelchair in motion, Nathan slumped in the seat. "I didn't know about Theresa before I made my deal with O'Fallon. I swear. By the time I did know, it was too late. The money was spent."

The square yellow clock that had been on the kitchen wall since they were children hummed, and the black hand moved stiffly to the next minute. The coffeemaker gurgled once, and a drop of water fell from the faucet into the stainless steel sink.

"Tell me everything, Nate."

THE WEAK LIGHT OF early morning poured into the tiny bedroom at the shelter as Darcy sat with Theresa, holding her hand.

"Are you sure it was safe to come here?" the woman asked. Her voice sounded hoarse. Strained, as if she'd been crying.

"I was careful. No one followed me." She leaned closer. "Are you all right? You sound raspy."

Theresa touched her throat. "I…cried most of last night."

Darcy had cried, too, her first night in a shelter. She squeezed Theresa's hand. "I know it's terrifying. Your life is never going to be the same. But that's a good thing, Theresa. You made the right decision."

"I know I did." Theresa looked around the tiny room with its old, battered dresser and the small bookcase that held a mix of fiction and nonfiction. She ran a hand over the threadbare brown chair where she sat. "It was the first night in years that I didn't wake up twenty times, afraid he was coming into my room. The first night I slept in peace."

"The first of many. You don't have to make any decisions

today. Or tomorrow, or next week. You have time to figure out what you want to do. Kelly has therapists coming here every day. You can talk to one, if you like. They'll help you sort out your options."

"I've been thinking about escaping for a long time. I know what my options are. I know what I have to do."

"What's that?" Darcy asked softly.

"I have to disappear. I need to find someone who can get me a new identity and help me start a new life. Somewhere far away from Chicago." She watched Darcy steadily. "It's the only way I'll be safe. My husband's too powerful in this city."

Darcy's stomach roiled and her chest ached. "We can help you document your abuse. You can have him arrested. Tried. He'll go to jail."

Theresa snorted. "You're naive if you think that will happen. If he gets arrested, he'll be out of jail the same day. If he goes on trial, he'll be acquitted. My only chance is to vanish."

"You don't have to decide that right now."

"There's no decision to be made. It's my only chance." She stared at Darcy. "That's what you did, isn't it?"

"My circumstances were different than yours, Theresa." Actually, they were eerily similar. Her husband had been a powerful man, too.

"Do you know how I can get a new identity?"

"That's not the way to go, Theresa."

Please don't ask me to do it for you. To make that choice. She'd just begun to explore the possibilities with Patrick. If she helped Theresa get a new identity, she'd be committing a crime. She'd destroy any chance she had of making something work with Patrick.

Patrick or Theresa?

The future or her past?

Although she wasn't sure how she and Patrick could have a future.

She was going to have to run again. She'd known that she'd have to leave since she found out Tim had been released.

She didn't want to run. Wildwood, Mama's Place felt like home. The people she worked with felt like family.

But she didn't have a home anymore. She'd forfeited that when she bought a new identity and fled.

THE CLOCK IN THE kitchen counted down the seconds too loudly.

Neither he nor Nathan moved.

Nathan stared at his hands. Patrick watched his brother.

When Nathan raised his head, he looked ten years older than thirty-five. Beaten down. Defeated. "I screwed up, Paddy. Bigtime. I've been trying to protect you and Marco and Frankie, but I've made things worse. I'm glad you realized something was wrong. I don't want to keep secrets from the rest of you anymore."

Patrick reached across the table and squeezed his brother's shoulder. "Let us help, Nate."

Nathan nodded and sat up straight. "Call Marco and Frankie and have them come over. I'll tell you everything."

An hour later, Marco rubbed his red, bleary eyes, poured a cup of coffee and started another pot. "Is this so important that it couldn't wait a few hours?" he groused. "I didn't get much sleep last night."

"Your choice. Your problem." Nathan's voice was calm. Steady. He looked more like the older brother Patrick remembered, in control of himself and taking care of his family. "And yeah. It's important."

Marco sat down at the kitchen table, slumped in his chair.

A car door slammed, and moments later, the front door opened. Frankie appeared with Cal behind her.

"I thought this was *family* business," Marco said, glowering at Cal.

"Cal's family," Frankie said calmly. "You have a problem with that?"

"Fine."

"Knock it off, Marco," Nathan said. "Isn't it time you grew

up? The whole bad-boy attitude, drinking and catting around every night is getting old."

Marco scowled, but didn't say anything.

Patrick looked at Frankie and Cal, standing so close together. A unit.

Darcy's face filled his head, but he pushed her away. That wasn't what she wanted. She wanted to take care of herself. Protect herself.

Protect her heart.

He kicked a chair away from the table. "Sit down, Frankie. Cal. Nathan wants to tell us something."

Cal leaned back in his chair and looked at the Devereux siblings, then put his arm across the back of Frankie's chair. His hand was barely touching her shoulder, but she reached up and covered it with hers.

Whatever was going on, they'd face it together.

His hand was empty.

"Mama's is in trouble," Nathan said abruptly.

They all stilled.

"When I did the kitchen renovation last winter, I couldn't get a loan from a bank. Even though I had this house and the restaurant, they wanted more in collateral."

"Banks have been shitheads for the past few years," Cal said.

"You do have a way with words, Cal," Nathan said. "You're going to make a great teacher." His half smile disappeared. "So I couldn't get a loan. But if I didn't do the remodeling and renovating, I couldn't get Mama's up to code and the building inspectors were going to close us down. So in the time-honored Chicago tradition, I went to the alderman and asked if there was anything he could do."

Patrick leaned forward. "Why didn't you come to us? We could have pooled our money."

"Don't you think I thought of that? None of you had the kind of money I needed, even if you put it all together. You do okay as an FBI agent, but you're not swimming in it. Frankie was struggling to keep FreeZone together and was already in debt. And Master Chef over there?" He jerked his thumb at Marco. "He spends it as fast as he makes it."

Marco's face turned a dull red. "I knew something was wrong. Just hadn't figured out what. I could have contributed."

"So what did O'Fallon do?" Patrick had a pretty good idea where this was going.

"O'Fallon had a friend. The friend could lend me the money I needed. But the payments had to be in cash."

"So there'd be no proof if anyone investigated him," Patrick said. The Bureau's Chicago office was going to have a field day with this.

"Pretty much."

"And Chuck?"

"He was the bag man. I gave him cash every week, until I got hurt. Then he started coming over here to pick it up." He slid his gaze toward Patrick. "He waited until you went to Mama's."

"So why did he keep coming to the restaurant?" Patrick asked.

Nathan shrugged. "Intimidation, I guess."

"And Theresa was his cover," Patrick guessed.

"Yeah."

Patrick looked around at the rest of his family. Marco was sitting up straight, eyes focused. Frankie had taken Nathan's hand. Cal had taken Frankie's other hand. "Last night, Chuck was arrested for carrying a concealed weapon," Patrick said. "Theresa went to a women's shelter. So the shit's coming down the pike."

"How much do you still owe?" Marco asked.

"About a hundred thousand." Nathan's mouth twisted. "The interest rate was high, but I didn't have a choice."

"I can come up with forty thousand, give or take," Patrick said. He'd have to take the money out of his retirement account, but he'd do it in a second.

"I've, uh, got ten thousand," Marco said, staring down into his coffee.

"I'll get a mortgage on FreeZone." Frankie glanced at Cal. "We own it free and clear."

"I have a better idea," Cal said. He stared around the table. "Hear me out before you start yelling, okay?"

"Yell?" Frankie rolled her eyes. "Devereuxs never yell. All our discussions are rational, calm and reasonable."

"Right." Dropping a kiss on her head, Cal turned to the rest of them. "I made a lot of money playing football," he began. "I'd like to…"

Marco, Nathan and Patrick all began speaking at once. The volume in the room rose, but the overarching theme was "no." Followed by "way."

Cal leaned back, crossed his arms, and waited for the uproar to die down. When they were all finally quiet, he said, "Rational and calm. Right."

Frankie put her hand on his arm. "They'll be quiet." Her fierce gaze traveled from one brother to the next. "Won't you?"

Patrick nodded curtly, but the thought of letting Cal bail them out filled him with shame.

He guessed Nathan and Marco felt the same way.

"I'd like to invest in Mama's," Cal said. "I'll lend you the money you need to pay off the loan, and you can pay me back. I'd rather just give it to you, but I'm guessing that would be a big 'no.'"

"It's great of you to offer, Cal," Nathan said stiffly. "But we can't accept that."

"Why the hell not? Didn't I just hear all of you offer what you had?" He jerked his chin at Patrick. "You know how much of a penalty you'd pay if you took that money out of your retirement account?"

"I wasn't…"

"Shut up." Cal pointed to Marco. "And you? You're willing to give every penny you have?"

He turned to Nathan. "I'm guessing you already used all of your savings." He slid back into his chair and wrapped his arm around Frankie. "Was I mistaken, or did you all tell me I'm part of this family now, whether I liked it or not?"

No one in the room would meet his eyes.

"So if everyone else can offer their money, why can't I?"

"Because you have so much of it," Nathan muttered.

"Oh, there's a logical reason. Snatch the gruel from the starving kid, but leave the rich guy his roast beef dinner."

"When did we become the characters in *Oliver Twist?*" Marco whispered to Patrick.

Patrick's mouth twitched. "We don't want to take advantage, Cal," he said.

"That's bullshit. You're just too stubborn to accept help."

Patrick had said the same thing to Darcy last night.

Couldn't go there now. "The money's only part of it." He glanced around the table. "We have bigger problems than repaying the loan."

CHAPTER TWENTY

THERESA STRAIGHTENED in the chair. "I'm not going to the police. They won't be able to help me. They'll just make it worse." Her jaw was set and her eyes were determined.

"Then what are you going to do?" Darcy asked. "You can't stay here for the rest of your life."

"I have a plan."

Darcy waited, letting Theresa tell it in her own way. And her own time.

"I'll move to Minneapolis."

"Really? Do you have friends or family there?"

"I don't know a soul. That's why I chose it. That and the fact that it's cold. My husband knows I hate the cold. He'd never look for me there."

"You've been thinking about this for a while," Darcy said slowly.

"It was either make a plan or go crazy."

It felt as if Darcy was looking at a different woman than the one she'd gotten to know at Mama's. "You were never this determined at the restaurant."

"How could I be? Chuck reported everything to my husband. I had to keep my mouth shut and act intimidated."

"That was Oscar-worthy acting, Theresa." When the other woman smiled, Darcy continued, "So. Once you get to Minneapolis. What then?"

"I've got some money in a bank." She named one of the national chains. "I started saving years ago. Ever since..." She looked out the window.

"Ever since it started," Darcy murmured. She'd done the same thing.

"Yes." Theresa turned to her again. "And my husband keeps cash in the bottom desk drawer in his home office." A hint of a smile. "He thinks I'm too scared to look through his stuff. But I managed. And every time there was money in that drawer, I took some of it. Put it in the bank."

"So you have a nest egg. That's good. That will help."

The other woman nodded. "I'm going to get a new identity, find a job and be free."

"What about your children? You said they were in college."

Her eyes clouded. "Sooner or later, I'll tell them where I am. Right now, they're under my husband's thumb. They believe what he tells them. So I have to get away from them, too."

"Oh, Theresa," Darcy said, shifting to hug her tightly. "I'm so sorry."

She felt the other woman trembling, and rocked her gently. Finally Theresa straightened. "I'll send them emails."

"You can't…" Darcy thought of the friends she'd had in Milwaukee, how hard it had been to leave them behind. It would be so much harder to leave your children. "It's not a good idea to send emails. They can be traced."

"I know that. I'll send them from a different place every time." She reached for Darcy's hand. "All I need is a new identity. Is there someone here who can help me with that?"

"You said you know things that could be dangerous for your husband. Maybe you should think about the government's witness protection program."

"No! I can't do that. I have money. I can pay for a new identity."

"Why can't you go into witness protection?" Darcy asked carefully. "It was set up for people like you."

Theresa stared out the window, her eyes glittering with tears. "It's too final. Too drastic."

"Moving to Minneapolis with a new identity is pretty drastic, too."

"But it's on my terms. I don't want anyone to tell me what to do. Ever again."

"I understand that, Theresa. But you need help, and they can give it to you."

Theresa turned in her chair, slowly, as if she were an old woman. "You said you would help me. Get me what I needed."

"Yes, I did. But what you're asking is a felony."

"I don't care. I'm willing to take the chance."

It's a felony for me, too. And I don't want to do it. "I'm not the same person I was when I ran away from my husband," Darcy said slowly. "I'm not sure I'd go that route again."

"It's what I have to do. I don't have a choice."

Darcy had felt the same. Now? She would have found a different way to get free. She glanced at her watch. "I have to go, Theresa. I have to get ready for work."

"Will you come back tomorrow?"

"I'll try. But…I may have to run again. If I do, I won't be able to come back. If I can't, I'll call you when I'm safe."

Theresa paled. "Has your husband found you?"

"I don't know. Not for sure. But I'm…scared that he has."

Theresa took her hand. "Be careful, Darcy."

"I will. But if I don't see you again, make the right choice. Contact the witness protection program."

Theresa looked away. "I'll think about it."

Darcy drove home carefully, dread roiling in her stomach. Theresa wouldn't go to the government. She wanted to buy a new identity. She had the money to do it. And Darcy could help her. All she'd have to do was hand over a name.

One piece of paper. That was all.

She'd be an accessory to the crime.

And sabotage forever any hope of a relationship with Patrick.

Theresa or Patrick.

Patrick or Theresa.

She'd sent him away last night, and regretted it afterward. She'd been too guarded, too careful.

That was the way she'd lived for the past three years. The
way she had to live. But she wanted to open herself to him.

She wanted to tell him everything.

That was scary territory. Giving him her body had been
hard enough.

Giving him her heart would be terrifying.

As she idled at the stoplight at Devon and Caldwell, the forest preserve to her left was an imposing presence. Thick trees,
mostly bare. A tangle of creeping bushes beneath them, also
missing most of their leaves.

Even with the lack of foliage, she still couldn't see very far
into the woods. Only ten or twelve feet. The rest was a dark
blur.

Her future was a dark blur, as well.

The person in the car behind her honked, and Darcy jerked
her attention back to the road. The light was green, and she
accelerated through the intersection, then turned right toward
her apartment.

Maybe she should listen to what she'd said to Theresa. There
had to be another way to keep herself safe besides running.

She studied the neighborhood as she drove through it, but
nothing looked out of place. No one sat in a car, watching.
That's why she lived here, she reminded herself. Wildwood
was boring. Secure. Safe.

A few minutes later she rolled into her garage and turned
off the engine. It chugged twice, then quieted. The automatic
door rumbled behind her as she walked toward the house. She
looked up at her apartment, her usual habit.

The door was ajar.

Heart pounding, Darcy backed slowly toward the garage,
expecting someone to burst out of the apartment and run down
the stairs. She fumbled with the key pad on the garage door,
peering around the corner as it rose, excruciatingly slowly. In
her terrified mind, the noise was as loud as thunder crashing
over the house.

As soon as she could squeeze below the opening, she ran

to her car, threw herself into the driver's seat and locked all the doors.

Her breath heaving, she dug her phone out of her purse and pushed speed dial. The operator's impersonal voice said, "911."

"My house," Darcy managed to say. "The door's open. Someone broke in."

"What's your location?" the woman asked.

Darcy gave her address. "I'm in my car. In the garage at the back of the house."

There was a momentary silence, then the woman said, "Officers are on their way. What's your name?"

"Darcy," she said after a brief pause. "Darcy Gordon."

"Are you injured?" the operator asked. "Do you need an ambulance?"

"No." She struggled to catch her breath. "I'm fine."

"Okay. Stay on the line with me until they arrive."

Patrick. She needed him. He wouldn't panic. He'd know what to do.

"I can't. I have to call someone."

"Don't hang up," the woman said sharply. Darcy heard buttons being pushed in the background. "The police will arrive in less than a minute. You need to stay with me until they get there."

She heard the faint sound of sirens.

"I think I hear them."

"Good. It will just be a few more seconds. I'll tell the officers to look for you in the garage."

"I need to hang up." *Patrick.*

"Wait." Before the operator could say more, Darcy clicked off the phone.

As she pressed the speed dial for his number, she glanced out of the garage window and saw two police officers hurry down the walkway between the two houses. The tall man pulled his gun out of his holster and headed up the stairs. The shorter blonde woman ran toward the garage.

Her finger trembling, Darcy pressed Patrick's number.

The police officer ran into the garage as he said, "Darcy?"

"Patrick." She dragged in a breath. "I need you. Please."

"What's wrong?" he said sharply.

"Please. Come to my apartment."

The police officer pounded on the car window. "Ma'am! You all right?"

Patrick yelled something, but Darcy disconnected the call. Her hand shook as she slipped the phone back into her bag. Then she stepped out of the car.

"Are you injured? Do you need an ambulance?"

"No." Darcy clutched the handle of her bag. A tight band crushed her chest, pressing on her heart.

"Did you see an intruder?" the woman asked.

"N-no. My door was open when I got home."

The female officer scanned Darcy from head to toe, then let her hand hover over her gun as she studied the garage. She walked around the car, looked beneath it.

She pressed a button on her radio. "Clear in the garage, Tony."

"House is clear, too," came a crackly voice.

"Okay if I bring the owner up?"

"Yeah."

"Let's go up to your apartment. We'll need to ask you some questions."

Darcy nodded, her head trembling like a bobble-head doll. Where was Patrick? "Is your partner sure there's no one up there?"

"Yes," the officer said. "But you can sit in the patrol car if you'd rather do that."

"No." She didn't want to get anywhere near the patrol car. It would remind her too much of Tim. "I'll go upstairs."

The police officer waited while she locked the car, then lowered the garage door. As they walked toward the stairs, Darcy heard the screech of tires on the pavement in front of the house, followed by the slam of a car door. Moments later,

Patrick ran full-speed down the walkway. His right hand was at the small of his back.

"Darcy! What happened? Are you okay?"

She got a brief glimpse of bare legs and arms before he gathered her close. She wrapped her arms around his waist, and her fingers brushed cold metal. The gun. She slid her hands higher on his back and pressed her face to his chest. He smelled like sweat and coffee and the faint, unmistakable scent of Patrick.

"Tell me," he murmured into her ear.

"I came home and my door was open," she said. Her teeth were chattering. "I called the police, then I called you."

She felt him shift his head. "What have you found?" he asked the cop.

Darcy turned to look at the woman, who had straightened. Scowled. "Let's go upstairs. We need to ask Ms. Gordon some questions."

Patrick wrapped his arm around her shoulders and they started up the stairs, the police officer behind them.

"Hold it," the officer yelled. "Turn around. Slowly. Hands in the air."

Darcy raised her hands, felt them trembling in the cold air. When she turned to face the officer, the woman was holding her gun on them with a rock-steady grip.

Patrick turned as well. "I'm an FBI agent," he said calmly. "That's why I have the gun."

The cop narrowed her eyes. "Tony," she called. "Need some help down here."

Behind her, Darcy heard the heavy thump of feet on the stairs. Then the slide of metal out of a leather holster. "What the hell?" a male voice growled. "You think you're a tough guy? Bringing a gun to a crime scene?"

"Says he's an FBI agent." The woman hadn't lowered her own gun. "Find his ID."

"In my left pocket," Patrick said.

He looked completely at ease. Relaxed. But as Darcy shivered, she saw that goose bumps had raised the hair on his arms.

All he wore was a T-shirt with the sleeves ripped off and a pair of nylon shorts. A huge bruise circled his left eye.

"Your eye! What happened?"

"Later," he said, holding the police officer's gaze as he pulled Patrick's wallet from his pocket.

There was silence for a moment, then the officer said, "You can drop your hands, but keep them where I can see them. Turn around."

He glanced from Patrick to his wallet, then handed the wallet to his partner. "He's good."

She studied it for a moment, then handed it to Patrick. "We don't like nasty surprises. The next time you come charging to the rescue, mention that you're armed."

Patrick pulled Darcy close again. "Had other things on my mind."

"Let's go upstairs," Tony said, turning and leading the way.

When she walked through the door, Darcy gasped.

Everything in her cabinets had been tossed on the floor, the chairs and table overturned. Boxes of cereal and crackers had been crushed, crumbs spilling onto the cracked linoleum. Her refrigerator was emptied, as well. Shattered glass was smeared with broken eggs, a smashed stick of butter, a package of sliced turkey. Orange juice covered the mess like an oil slick.

Fear twisted her stomach. "This wasn't a robbery."

"No." The flat voice belonged to Tony. "Do you want to check and see if anything's missing?"

"Does the rest of the apartment look the same?" she managed to say.

"Pretty much," Tony said.

"My cat," she whispered. Oh, God, what had happened to him? Had the intruder hurt him? Killed him? "Cat! Here, baby."

She raced into the living room.

The destruction there was as bad as the kitchen. The bookcases were knocked over, the television screen was shattered.

"Cat," she screamed. "Where are you?"

Patrick came up beside her and put his hand on her arm. "Shhh," he said gently. "He's scared. Give him a minute."

She hadn't had a pet while she was married to Tim. She'd always been afraid of what her husband might do to it. "If that bastard hurt my cat, I'll…" Realizing what she'd almost given away, she stopped abruptly.

"What bastard would that be?" the woman cop asked.

Patrick watched her, as well.

"The…the one who broke in here," she finally said.

"That sounded personal. Do you have any idea who might have done this?"

She shook her head, glanced at Patrick. "Chuck?"

"Chuck who?" Tony asked sharply.

"Someone we had problems with last night." Patrick pulled out his phone. "Let me text Kopecki and see if he's still in jail."

"You know Danny?" the woman asked.

"Went to high school with him. He arrested the guy last night."

"You talking about Chuck Notarro?" she asked.

"Yeah."

"We still have him. He's waiting for a bond hearing. So it wasn't him."

Darcy hadn't thought it was. But it was the first thing she thought of to cover her slip. "Okay. Good. Thanks."

She felt Patrick's gaze but didn't meet his eyes.

"Anyone else you have a problem with?" Tony asked.

She shook her head, nudging one of the books with her toe.

"How about you, Devereux? You have any ideas?"

"Maybe."

Darcy barely suppressed a gasp as she jerked her head up to stare at Patrick. *No. Don't tell him. Please.*

"I followed Darcy home from work last night. I was worried about Chuck's…associates. When I parked in front of the house, I thought I saw something moving behind the bushes across the street."

"You get a look at him?"

"No."

"Sure it wasn't an animal?" Tony asked.

"Possible. It was dark. Hard to tell."

"Why didn't you tell me?" Darcy asked, anger overcoming the heart-pounding fear.

Patrick shrugged. "I didn't see anything clearly. Couldn't tell what it was. But in light of this…" He set her armchair upright. "Maybe it was a person."

Cat sat crouched on the floor where the chair had been.

"Cat!" She knelt in front of him and waited. His tail twitched once. Again. Then he walked over to Darcy and began licking his paw.

She swept him up in her arms and cradled him against her chest.

"So no one else you can think of who might have done this?" the woman persisted. "Someone who might have been watching you?"

Darcy shook her head, her face buried in Cat's fur.

"Are you gonna dust for prints?" Patrick asked.

Darcy held Cat more tightly. If Tim had done this, they might find his fingerprints. He was in the system. They'd get a match. She'd know if she'd been found.

But Patrick would learn who Tim was. He'd go after him.

Cat yowled, and Darcy realized she'd been gripping his fur. She loosened her fingers and he jumped to the floor.

"We'll check the doorknob. Don't get your hopes up, though. Everyone watches television these days. All the mopes know to wear gloves."

They talked awhile longer, gave her their cards, got her cell number and Patrick's, then the two officers left to talk to the neighbors. As their footsteps receded, Darcy was left alone with the ruins of her life.

And Patrick. Who hadn't been fooled by her claim of ignorance.

He set his hands on her shoulders. "You're afraid it was your ex, aren't you?"

CHAPTER TWENTY-ONE

Darcy tensed as she stared at the debris scattered around the living room. Was it Tim? Had he found her?

"If I knew, don't you think I would have told the police?"

"Maybe. Maybe not." His hands tightened. "You need to give me names. Yours and his."

She stepped away from him, then picked a path through the books and glass on the floor, stopping at the doorway to her bedroom.

Echoes of rage reverberated through the room. All the drawers of her dresser had been emptied, and everything on top swept to the floor and crushed. The bedding was shredded. Deep gouges had been carved into the mattress. One of her kitchen knives lay discarded on the floor.

"This was personal," Patrick said from behind her. He was close enough for her to feel his breath on her hair, but he didn't touch her. "Someone who knows you."

He was right. This wasn't a random act.

Tim.

How had he found her?

The shivering started deep inside her. Wrapping her arms around herself didn't help. Neither did the heavy jacket she wore.

She would never be warm again.

No one else hated her. She couldn't think of one other person who would break into her apartment and destroy everything.

Cat strolled into the room and jumped on the bed. He sniffed at the cottonlike tufts protruding from the mattress. Then he lay down and began cleaning himself again.

She had to leave. As soon as possible.

She'd been so confident when she debated between helping Theresa and being with Patrick.

As if she'd ever had a choice.

She should have paid better attention to that prickling at the back of her neck. Tim had been watching her. He'd seen her with Patrick.

That's why he'd destroyed her mattress and everything else she owned.

"Darcy." Patrick drew her back against him. "Could this be your ex?"

"Anything is possible." She tried to sound dismissive. Unworried. "But I don't know how he could have found me."

"What's his name? Where does he live?" He turned her around. There was only concern in his expression. He was trying to help her. And she couldn't let him.

"I can't tell you his name." She touched the bruise on his face. Patrick would have a lot worse than a bruise if he got in Tim's way.

"Why the hell not?"

"Because if you go looking for him, he'll know. Then you won't be safe, and neither will I."

"How would he know I was looking for him?"

She stared at the front of his T-shirt. It said Northwestern University in letters so faded they were almost invisible. Just the thought of telling Patrick anything more made her breathe harder. Made her heart race.

But she had to tell him. She had to make him understand. "He's a cop. *Was* a cop. He still has lots of friends on the police force. If you start looking for him, he'll find out. He'll figure out where I am and come after me."

He already knew. But if she told Patrick that, he'd never leave her side. He'd become a target, too.

He cupped her face and forced her to look at him. "Darcy, if he did this, he already knows where you are. I can protect you."

"Not 24/7," she retorted, wrapping her hands around his

wrists. She had to make him understand. "You can't stand in front of me all day and all night. If he finds me, he'll kill me. And if you got between us, he'd kill you, too."

He stroked his thumbs over her cheeks. "He doesn't have superpowers, sweetheart. Let me help you."

"You can't," she cried. "Don't you get it, Patrick? You can't do everything. You're not infallible. You couldn't protect Nathan from whatever he's done. You can't protect me, either."

His hands fell away. "I can try."

"I won't be responsible for getting you killed."

"Give me a little credit, Darcy." His voice rose and his mouth tightened. "I'm an FBI agent. I know how to protect myself and other people."

She grabbed his arms and shook him. "Do you have any idea how I'd feel if you were hurt? Killed? I couldn't live with myself."

"I know exactly how you feel." He shook her off and moved to the window. Stared down at the street, as if searching for something. "It was my fault my parents were killed. I have to live with that for the rest of my life. I'm not going to let something happen to another person I…care about."

Pain rolled off him in waves, and she moved toward him as if pulled by a string. She settled her palm on his back, kneading the tension in his muscles. "What are you talking about? Your parents were killed in an auto accident. Nathan told me about it."

"Did he tell you I was driving?"

She sucked in a breath. Wrapped her arms around his waist. "Oh, Patrick," she murmured. "Nathan said it was a drunk driver. How is that your fault?"

"I should have been more careful. I should have seen him coming, been able to brake in time. But I wasn't, and he broadsided us. Killed both of them."

"What happened to the driver?"

"He served twelve years in prison, got out recently."

"There's no way it was your fault," she said, laying her

cheek against his back. "If it was, the guy wouldn't have gone to prison. Nathan and Marco and Frankie don't think it was your fault, either. How could they?" She turned him around.

"If my father had been driving, it wouldn't have happened."

"You don't know that." *Oh, God.* Patrick had been carrying this burden for almost fifteen years. Was guilt the reason he didn't spend much time with his family? She had to make him understand. Grasping his upper arms, she said, "If he was driving, maybe all of you would have been killed. Is that what you wish? That you'd died with them?"

"Of course not. But the accident wrecked our family. Nathan had to drop out of school to run the restaurant and raise us. Frankie was so devastated that she ran away. Her life was changed forever. And Marco...he hardly got to know them."

"And you've let guilt rule your life." She shook him again. "Your parents wouldn't have wanted that. Your parents would be happy you survived. They would have wanted you to embrace that gift."

She held his face the way he'd held hers. The stubble of his day-old beard was rough beneath her fingers. She brushed her thumb along it, loving the sandpapery feel. "They would have wanted you to be happy, Patrick."

PATRICK STARED AT Darcy's face. She seemed so certain. As if it was a given. He shook his head. "If only it was that simple."

"It is," she said fiercely. "It's exactly that simple. He ran a red light, didn't he? How is that your fault?"

"You don't understand," he muttered. She had no idea how badly he wanted to believe her.

"I understand perfectly." She reared back and glared at him. "Is it my fault that my husband beat me?"

"Of course not. That's on him. Not you."

"Your parents' deaths are on the drunk driver. Not *you.*"

"How did we get on the subject of me, anyway?" he asked, desperate to avoid the discussion. If Darcy kept telling him it wasn't his fault, he might begin to believe her. Might begin to hope. "This is about you. It's your apartment that was trashed. Your ex that may be responsible."

"We were talking about you because you seem to think it's your job to protect everyone around you. To save everyone."

Her words made a knife twist inside him, so he tried to ignore them. "Right now, you're the only one I care about. I want to protect *you*. To save *you*. So tell me why your ex wants to kill you. Is it because you left him?"

"Partly. But mostly because I have some information that could get him killed."

His words came out on a rush of fear. "Goddamn it, Darcy! What kind of mess are you in?"

She rubbed her arms as if she were cold. "A bad one. I made a huge mistake, and there's no way of fixing it. That's why I changed my name and ran away."

"You changed your name." So he'd been right. "Got a fake identity?" She nodded.

"Tell me your real name."

She shook her head. "I can't."

"There's always some way to fix things."

"Not this time. Believe me, I've tried."

He'd never felt so helpless. So powerless. He had specialized training. Expertise. He could keep her safe. But she wouldn't let him.

Just like he wouldn't let his siblings in. Wouldn't let them close.

"You can't stay here," he said, grabbing some of her clothing off the floor. "You can stay at Nathan's." If she was living in the same house, he'd have a better chance of protecting her.

"I can't just leave this mess," she said. "I have to clean it up." But she glanced around as if she had no idea where to start.

"There are companies that can do that. You can hire one of them."

"I can't afford that. I'll clean it myself."

"And where will you sleep in the meantime?"

She looked at the bed, then quickly turned away. "The couch," she muttered.

"No. Come with me to Nathan's."

"What about Cat?"

"He can come, too." For an animal she claimed she didn't care about, she'd been awfully upset when she thought he might have been killed. "Nathan always wanted a cat when we were kids." He was making that up, but he needed to get her out of this apartment. Away from the memories and the fear that still had her face drawn and her eyes shuttered.

"Come on, Darcy." He smoothed his hand over her hair. "Throw some stuff in a bag, and let's get out of here. I'll make some calls, get somebody out here to deal with the mess. When you come back, it will look like nothing happened."

"I'll know something happened," she said quietly.

"Yeah, you will. But if it looks normal, you'll feel a lot better."

She turned and surveyed the room. "I don't know if I can ever live here again. It feels like I've been violated."

"You have been. But let's get the place cleaned up before you make a decision."

Staying a careful distance from the damaged mattress, she bent and petted the cat. "You're sure it's okay if Cat comes with me?"

"Of course it is."

"Okay." She straightened. Glanced around the room again. "Thanks. I'll feel safe staying with you and Nathan."

Thank God. "Great. How can I help you get ready?"

"Just stay here with me. I don't want to be alone."

"I'm not going anywhere."

As he watched her pick through the destroyed clothes and crushed jewelry, he curled his fingers into fists. He'd like to use her ex for boxing practice. *A cop.*

No wonder she hadn't wanted anything to do with Patrick when he showed up at Mama's.

But she'd told him her ex was a cop, and that she was using

a fake identity. That she'd made a huge mistake. That was the first step. Eventually, she'd tell him the rest.

And when she did, he'd track the guy down and beat the shit out of him.

Feeling much better than when she'd called him, he pushed away from the wall. "Do you have some kind of carrier for Cat?"

She looked up from the floor where she was untangling jewelry. "In the living room closet." She studied him for a moment. "For a guy helping his...helping someone with her trashed house, you look pretty cheerful."

"You're coming home with me. That's huge." He squatted down in front of her. "And you're not just 'someone.' You're important. You matter to me, Darcy."

Her lips trembled. "You matter to me, too, Patrick. Thank you for coming when I called."

"Always." He leaned forward and kissed her, and her mouth softened beneath his. Before it could go any further, he pulled away. They weren't going to do anything in this wreck of her house.

A half hour later, he held her hand as they walked into Nathan's. She'd stopped and told her landlord what had happened. He had just returned from his volunteer job at a local hospital, and he'd been horrified. Worried. But when she told him she was staying with a friend, he calmed down.

Nathan was parked at the dining room table, working on his laptop. When he heard the door, he turned. "Hey, Paddy."

His brother looked more relaxed than he'd been since Patrick arrived from Detroit. "Hey, Nate. Darcy's with me."

"Great." He actually smiled at Darcy when she stepped into view. Nathan's gaze lingered on their joined hands, and Darcy tried to let go. Patrick held on more tightly.

"How's it going, Darce?" Nathan asked.

Her eyes darkened and she untangled her hand from Patrick's. "Not so great."

"What's wrong?" Nathan swung the wheelchair around and headed toward her. "What happened?"

"Someone broke into her apartment and trashed it. She needs a place to stay for a few nights. I didn't think you'd mind if I brought her here."

"Of course not." Nathan didn't even look at Patrick. Instead, he pulled Darcy down into a fierce hug. "What can I do?" he murmured.

She sniffled on his shoulder, and Patrick was glad she'd ended up at Mama's. Glad she'd had someone like Nathan to lean on.

"Letting me stay here is huge," she said, finally straightening. "And putting up with Cat."

"You've got a cat?" Nathan bent his head to look into the carrier. "Cute. What's his name?"

Darcy reddened. "Cat."

"Makes it simple, I guess." Nathan switched his gaze to Patrick. "Why don't you find a room for Darcy?" he said. "You'll have to leave for Mama's soon."

God. He'd forgotten all about the restaurant. "Do you need the night off, Darcy?" he asked. "I can call another waitress to fill in for you."

"I'd rather work. I'd rather keep busy."

He wanted her at Mama's, as well. Close by. "Good." He picked up her duffel bag. "Let's get you settled in."

As Darcy walked out the back door of Mama's late that night, she stayed in front of Patrick as she scrutinized every car in the lot. After she identified all of them as employees' cars, she waited for him to catch up to her. He unlocked his SUV, helped her into the front seat and took his gun from the glove compartment.

"Stay in the car while I look around," he said. He didn't wait for her to answer before closing and locking the door.

She watched him poke through the bristling lilac bushes,

check the front of the restaurant. When he was satisfied, he swung into the driver's seat.

"I didn't see anything," he said. "I think we're good."

But he checked his rearview mirror every few seconds as they drove to Nathan's. Darcy kept her gaze on the side mirror, watching for the flash of headlights behind them. She saw nothing. No one followed them.

As Patrick parked at the curb, she relaxed her shoulders and felt some of the tightness drain from her muscles. She'd been ready to face Tim, she realized. She'd expected him to try something.

Patrick stood at her door, staring at the houses flanking Nathan's. Then he studied the houses on the opposite side of the street. After a very long minute, he opened her door.

Adrenaline drained away like air from a balloon. She slid out of the vehicle, stumbling as she stepped onto the ground. Patrick wrapped his arm around her shoulders, and the cold air slapped her face.

"Long night," he murmured as he led her toward the front door.

"Yeah." She'd been on edge the whole time she worked, and that had been foolish. Fear had muddled her brain. Tim wouldn't confront her in a restaurant full of people. Just like every other bully, he'd wait until the odds were in his favor. "You expected someone to be waiting here."

"It wouldn't have surprised me," he said as they entered the darkened house. "It's what I would have done. Stay away from the place they expected me to be. Surprise them after they've relaxed." He held her gaze. "If it was your ex, that's what he'd do. Cops usually think alike."

"I don't know how he could have found me." She should have used Google to search for her name as soon as she suspected he had, seen if there was anything that could betray her. But she'd stuck her head in the sand. Told herself she was safe.

She wasn't safe anymore. Now, she had to leave.

"If he was a cop, he'd have resources."

They'd both been speaking in whispers. The house was quiet, the only sound a hum from the kitchen. The single light was in the kitchen, and its warm glow spilled onto the table in the dining area.

Patrick paused at the door to a room off the living room. Nathan was asleep on the bed in an uncomfortable-looking position. Cat was tucked into the curl of his waist.

"Looks like Nate has a friend," Patrick said, a smile curving his mouth.

"Fickle animal," she murmured. But she smiled, too.

They ascended the stairs in the dark, quiet house. As they neared the top, Darcy's heart began to race. Earlier, when Patrick had taken her upstairs to choose a room, she'd picked what looked like Frankie's old room. Patrick had glanced at her but hadn't said a word.

Why had she been so foolish? She only had this one night left with Patrick. She wasn't going to spend it sleeping in a room across the hall.

As they reached Frankie's old room, she turned to face him. Patrick stood close enough for her to feel his heat, smell the faint scent of his aftershave.

The moment lengthened like a stretched rubber band. Finally, Patrick murmured, "Darcy?"

His breath stirred the hairs at her temple, making her shiver. Making her want.

"Patrick." She put her hands on his chest, felt his muscles tense beneath her fingers. "I don't want to stay in Frankie's room, after all."

"Thank God."

She touched his mouth, traced the seam of his lips. "I want to sleep in your room, Patrick."

Without saying anything else, he opened the door and drew her inside.

CHAPTER TWENTY-TWO

DARCY DIDN'T TURN on the light in Patrick's room, and neither did he. The faint glow from the streetlight illuminated a double bed, an old dresser, a bookcase packed tight with books, and an old Chicago Cougars poster on the wall. Team pictures lined the top of the bookcase.

Suddenly nervous, she picked one up. It was a high school football team. All the players looked ridiculously young. "Which one is you?"

"That one." He pointed to a grinning boy with windblown dark hair and a carefree expression on his face. It clearly had been taken before his parents died.

"Were you the star quarterback?" she teased. "Did all the girls chase after you?"

"I was a linebacker. I got to knock guys on their ass." He took the picture out of her hands and replaced it. "And I went to an all-boys high school."

"Bummer for you," she said.

"I made up for it in college." He turned her around. "Is that why you wanted to stay in my room? So you could look at my stuff and ask me about it?"

"No." She swallowed. Gathered her courage. "I wanted to be with you tonight." She wanted a lot more than tonight. But this was all they'd have.

He cupped the back of her neck and drew her closer. "I want to be with you, too," he murmured.

He brushed his mouth over hers, and she wanted to fall into the kiss. Wanted to lose herself in him, forget everything but this moment. But she forced herself to move away from him.

"I'm sorry about last night," she said. It was easier to say in the dark, silent room. "I wanted to tell you about my ex-husband. But I couldn't. I wanted you to stay, too. As soon as you left, I wanted to call you back. But I...I was scared." She still was.

"I know you were." He brushed his finger across her mouth. "I was hurt. I wanted you to trust me. I know that's hard for you."

"If I could tell anyone, it would be you," she said.

He cupped her face, stared down at her. "That's enough for tonight."

Shame rippled through her. He thought she'd open up eventually. Tell him everything. Instead, she was leaving. Sneaking away without even saying goodbye.

Her fingers were ghostly pale as she lifted her hands to unbutton his shirt. "I didn't come here to talk," she whispered. His shirt fell open, revealing the white T-shirt beneath. Leaving it, she let her hands drift down to his belt. Leather creaked and metal clicked softly as she unbuckled it.

Fabric rustled as she pulled down the zipper. The hard ridge of his erection beneath his black boxers brushed against the back of her hand, and she lingered for a moment. Curled her fingers around him.

His breath hitched, and she tugged his pants down his hips. Holding her gaze, he toed off his shoes and stepped out of them. Let his shirt flutter to the floor. Slowly, he pulled his T-shirt over his head and dropped it. Tugged his boxers off.

He stood in front of her, naked, letting her look. She put her hands on his chest, smoothed them over his ribs, his rock-hard muscles. Slid down until they hovered over his penis.

Slowly, she curled one hand around him. He sucked in a tiny breath, but he didn't move.

He was hot. Silky smooth. Hard as granite. As she touched the broad head, his muscles tensed. But still he didn't move.

"Is this okay?" she asked, suddenly worried. Before Patrick, sex had always been about the main event. Not this sensual exploration.

"Are you kidding me?" His face was taut, all hard angles and sharp lines. His eyes glittered in the faint light. "I've dreamed about your hands on me. Touching me." He caressed her cheek, and she felt his hand trembling. "Go ahead and play, sweetheart."

His voice was quiet. Tender, even though he clearly wanted to touch her, too. She'd never felt tenderness when she made love, and the softness in his eyes, the gentleness of his touch, made her shiver with need.

As she touched Patrick, it was as if all the ugliness in her past was wiped away. Desire sang through her veins, hummed in her nerves, made her hands tremble. She was finished playing. She took a step back and yanked her shirt over her head. As the slight illumination of the streetlight outlined her black bra, she tugged on the buttons at her waistband.

His hands closed over hers. "Let me." He shook as he undid the buttons, opened the zipper. Stroked the back of his hand over the triangle of her black panties.

"Two can play this game, you know," he murmured.

He knelt on the floor in front of her and removed her work pants, tossing them to the side. Then he cupped her rear, leaned in and kissed her belly. Went lower, until the heat of his mouth was at the juncture of her thighs.

Her legs couldn't support her, and she clutched his shoulders and gasped, "Patrick!"

"You like this game, too," he murmured against her. The vibrations from his mouth made her ache with need.

He backed her slowly toward the bed, yanked down the quilt, then eased her onto the crisp sheets. Took off her bra and panties, and stared down at her.

Fumbling in the nightstand drawer, he pulled out a condom, opened it and slid it on. Then he knelt on the floor in front of her, spread her legs and put his mouth on her.

"Patrick," she cried. She arched into him, impossibly

aroused. Desperate for him. But as she tugged on his hair, he ignored her pleas and kept kissing her. Loving her. As she coiled tighter, climbed higher, she panted, "Please, Patrick. Now. Please."

He drew her into his mouth, and she crashed over the edge. Wave after wave of release rippled through her, then his mouth was on hers, swallowing her helpless cries as he slipped inside her.

Tension built again and she wrapped her legs around him, moving perfectly together. When he shuddered and whispered, "Darcy," she joined him.

They lay tangled together as her heart rate slowed and her breathing calmed. She buried her face in his neck and held onto him, inhaling his scent. Memorizing the texture of his skin, the shape of his shoulders.

"My name was Beth," she whispered into his neck.

His hands stilled, then he kissed her.

"Thank you," he murmured. "Thank you, Darcy."

Finally, he cuddled her close and drew the covers over them. "I want to hold you all night," he murmured. "Wake up with you in the morning."

"Hmmm," she said, pressing a kiss above his ear. "Me, too."

"You're safe," he whispered. "You're safe with me."

She tucked her head against his shoulder and blinked away the tears that threatened. She knew she was safe with him. But he wasn't safe with her.

THE NEXT MORNING, Darcy woke up with sunlight on her face and Patrick spooned around her. His hand cupped her breast and her legs were tangled with his.

Contentment flowed through her in an endless, bubbling stream. She could stay like this forever.

Which meant she had to get out of bed. Sever this connection to Patrick before it was too late.

His steady, even breathing ruffled her hair and caressed her nape. She could allow herself another minute. A handful of seconds with him, to counter all the future mornings she'd wake up alone.

"Hey, Dar...Beth." Patrick's voice, drowsy with sleep, washed over her. He pressed his mouth to her neck. "Good morning."

"Hey, yourself. And it's Darcy. I'll never be Beth again." She spoke softly, trying not to break the spell. Wishing they were two different people, a couple who had many more mornings like this to savor.

His hand tightened on her breast, and she rolled over to face him. "I love how you smell in the morning," he murmured. "Warm and soft and sexy."

"I love how you feel," she whispered, her hand drifting through his soft hair, then down his back. "All relaxed and cozy."

"Not completely relaxed," he said, moving his hips against hers.

She smiled into his hair. "I stand corrected."

He slid one leg between hers and kissed her, and she pressed closer. As she opened to him, touched his tongue with hers, she heard a muffled thump from downstairs.

Patrick froze, then let her go. "Damn it. Nathan. I forgot all about him." He slid out of bed. "Sorry. I have to help him."

"Don't be sorry," she said, sitting up and clutching the sheet to her chest. "I understand."

He tugged on the sheet, a tiny smile on his face. "What's this about?"

It was one thing to be naked in the dark of the night. It was another to sit here, bared to him, in the bright sunlight. "I'm cold."

His grin widened. "Is that right?" He kissed her once more. "Too bad I can't stay and warm you up."

He pulled on a pair of sweatpants and a T-shirt. "I'll be back in a few minutes."

"No. I'll get dressed and come downstairs." No way could

she make love with him now, knowing Nathan would hear the bed creaking, hear the sounds she'd try to muffle.

His grin softened into a smile. "Okay. I'll put out some towels in the bathroom so you can take a shower."

He kissed her again and left the room. She closed her eyes and listened to him descend the stairs. Then, blinking back tears, she stood up and reached for clean clothes from her duffel.

DOWNSTAIRS, Patrick poured a cup of coffee for Nathan, then one for himself. As he sat down at the table, water rushed through the pipes. Darcy was taking a shower.

He wanted to be up there with her, their bodies touching each time one of them moved in the small bathtub. He wanted to slide a soapy washcloth down her back, wanted to watch as she did the same to him.

He wanted to press her against the wall and slide inside her as water sluiced over their joined bodies.

"Darcy sleep okay last night?" Nathan asked with a smile.

"What?" He jerked his attention to his brother, noticed the gleam in his eyes. "Yeah, I guess so. I didn't hear her up during the night."

Nathan's smile faded, and he set the mug on the table. "You break her heart, I'll kick your ass."

"I... Of course I'm not... What are you talking about?" God. He deserved to have Nathan kick his rear, just for that lame-ass answer.

"Give it up, Paddy. I saw the way you looked at her yesterday. The way she looked back. You two have something going on."

Patrick slumped in his chair, unwilling to look his brother in the eye and lie to him. "I'm not going to hurt her, Nate. I want to help her settle some...stuff. Clear the way so we can talk about the future."

Nathan leaned closer. "A future that includes moving back to Chicago?"

"Yeah. Maybe. I don't know." He shoved away from the table. "That's the last thing I've been thinking about." Although it wasn't. He'd been rolling the idea around in his brain for a while. "We have a lot of shit to straighten out first, between Darcy's issues and the alderman and the money. Okay?"

"Yeah, I know." Nathan drummed his fingers on the table. "We'd all love to have you closer. To see you more often."

"I'd like that, too. And even if I can't move here, I'll be coming back on a regular basis."

"Good for Darcy, if she got you thinking about that."

"It's not about Darcy." He wanted her with him, no matter where he was. "This is about you and Marco and Frankie. I've missed you. I want to spend more time with you."

"We want that, too." Nathan shifted in the wheelchair. "Who else but my hard-ass FBI brother would have forced me to deal with the money thing? Thanks for that. It was stupid to hide it from all of you. But once I had, I didn't know how to deal with it."

"You're welcome." He leaned across the table and knuckle-bumped Nathan. "It's a mess, but we'll get it straightened out. Together."

"Think we should take Cal's money?" Nathan asked.

Patrick scowled. "Sticks in my craw. You know?"

"Yeah, mine, too. But I think—as much as I don't want to do it—that it would be good for Frankie. Make her feel like we've accepted Cal. That he's one of us." He looked away. "I was tough on him in the beginning. Thought he was just using her."

"I hate it when you go all rational and reasonable."

"That's me. The rational guy who took money from a thug."

"There is that." As Patrick sat back in his chair and sipped his coffee, the water upstairs went off. He heard Darcy's footsteps heading into his bedroom. She'd be getting dressed. Coming downstairs for breakfast. But for now, it was just him and Nate. And he needed one more answer from his brother.

"Nate, do you think it's my fault that Mom and Dad died?"

"What?" Nathan stared at him, puzzled. "Why would I think that?"

"Because I was driving."

"Don't be an idiot. Did you run that red light? Were you drunk?"

"No," Patrick muttered.

"Then it wasn't your fault. I never once thought it was."

"I have. Ever since they died." As he said the words, it felt as if a boulder rolled off his chest.

Nathan shook his head. "I thought you were supposed to be the smart one, Mr. Scholarship-to-Northwestern. Now I find out you're a dumb-ass after all."

"If Dad had been driving, they might still be alive."

Nathan leaned toward him. "You can't think that way, Paddy. It was an accident. They happen." He narrowed his eyes. "You ran away to Detroit and never came home because you thought we blamed you for them dying. Didn't you?"

Patrick shrugged. "Maybe."

"Now that you know you're a dumb-ass, you need to come back home. Guy that slow needs his family around to point out when he's being an idiot."

"I'll think about it," he said, feeling lighter than he had in a long time.

DARCY PUSHED AWAY from the table and carried her plate, as well as Patrick's and Nathan's, to the sink. Patrick had made pancakes for breakfast, and as she rinsed the dishes and put them in the dishwasher, she said casually, "I promised Marco I'd be at Mama's this morning to accept the cheese delivery."

Nathan rolled his eyes at Patrick. "Did he have a hot date again last night?"

"Probably. He ran out like his ass was on fire."

"He shouldn't ask you to do his work," Nathan said to Darcy.

She shrugged. "I don't mind. He's done me some favors."

"Okay, but I'm coming with you," Patrick said.

She bent to scrub the griddle as tears threatened again.

"You don't have to do that. I'll park on the street in front of the restaurant and walk in the front door. Lock it behind me. I'll be fine."

"It would make me feel better," Patrick said.

"Listen to the dumb-ass," Nathan added. "He likes to protect people."

"I know he does." She turned around. "But in this case, it's not necessary."

"Maybe I'd like to come with you."

Her heart squeezed when she saw the concern in his eyes. The caring she'd miss when she left. "I know you have things you need to do, and I'll be home before noon," she lied.

Home? This wasn't her home. But it felt comfortable here with Patrick and Nathan. Easy. The conversation at breakfast had been fun. Nathan had taken turns teasing first Patrick, then her.

One more thing she'd miss when she left.

"Stay here with Nathan, Patrick. I'll be fine."

As she walked into the living room, Patrick followed her. "If anything freaks you out, anything feels wrong, call me. Please?"

"I will." She reached up and kissed him. "I called you yesterday, didn't I?"

His arms closed around her. "Yeah. You did. I never thanked you for that, did I?"

She kissed him again, lingered for a moment, then eased away. "Oh, I think you took care of that last night," she whispered.

"Hmmm," he said, kissing her again. "I can do better. We'll practice."

Her throat swelling, she backed away from him. "The, uh, cheese guy isn't coming for a couple of hours. In the meantime, I'm going to check some things on the internet. Do you have a laptop I could use?"

"Sure." He opened a briefcase and pulled out a laptop, turned it on and typed in his password. "You're all set."

"Thanks," she whispered. "I'll go upstairs so you and Nathan can spend some time together."

"You don't have to leave."

She forced herself to smile. "If I stay down here with you, I'll be distracted."

He took her hand and pressed his lips to her palm. "That's a problem for me, too. We'll discuss it later. In private."

"I can't wait," she murmured, then turned and ran upstairs before the tears could fall.

CHAPTER TWENTY-THREE

PATRICK WATCHED the sway of Darcy's hips as she dashed up the stairs. *Beth.*

She'd told him her name. Her ex-husband was a cop who'd probably been prosecuted for domestic abuse. It wasn't much, but he'd have an agent run it through the Bureau's system, see if anything popped.

He *would* find her husband. Make sure he could never terrorize her again.

She wanted to go to Mama's this morning, and his first reaction had been *No. You're not going anywhere without me.*

But maybe she was right. Maybe he was being overprotective. She wasn't going back to her apartment, for God's sake. The restaurant was on a main street. In broad daylight. She wouldn't be alone.

If anything, Patrick should be worried her ex had found Nathan's house. Worried that his brother, who couldn't defend himself, was in danger.

He pulled out his phone and called Danny Kopecki.

"Hey, Danny," he said when his friend answered. "You still have Chuck?"

"Yeah. Funny, but no one's showed up to pay his bail. Chuckie is getting a little worried."

"That right?" The alderman must be concentrating on finding his wife. "Maybe we can lean on him a little. Show him the advantages of cooperating with us. Can you keep him another day or two and let him think about why he's still there?"

"Not a problem," Kopecki said. "If O'Fallon wanted him, he'd be out by now."

"That's what I'm counting on. In the meantime, could you arrange for regular drive-bys at Nathan's place? Darcy, one of the waitresses there, is staying with us. Her place was trashed yesterday, and I don't want to take any chances."

"That the redhead you're interested in?"

Old friends had no respect for boundaries. "Ah, yeah. That's Darcy."

"Consider it done."

"Thanks, Danny. At this rate, you're going to be eating free at Mama's for a long time."

"Looking forward to it, pal."

Patrick turned off his phone and headed back to the kitchen. Nathan had moved to the dining room table and was studying the books from Mama's. Patrick sat across from him. "What day does Chuck pick up the money?"

Nathan didn't look up from the computer, but his face turned dull red. "Tuesdays. They wait for the weekend receipts, when they know we'll have some cash."

"So someone's coming over tomorrow?"

"Yeah. Chuck, probably."

Patrick smiled. "Not Chuck. He's still sitting in jail. Apparently, the alderman forgot to send over his lawyer."

Nathan raised his head. "That right?"

"Yeah. And I think it's our chance to finish this." Patrick hesitated. "You sure you want to take Cal's money?"

"No, I'm not. But maybe you're right. Maybe we have to do it for Frankie."

Patrick nodded. "Yeah, I think we do. Why don't you text Marco and get his okay. Then figure out how much you need, call Cal and tell him."

Nathan stared at the screen, then slammed the computer closed. "I know exactly how much I need. Every week, the total was carved into my brain. It went down way too slowly."

"See if Cal can get us a check by tomorrow. Then call the alderman. Tell him you're paying off the loan and he has to come himself. If he says no, bullshit him. Tell him your brother the accountant needs something from him in writing. Tell him there's a problem you need to discuss with him. Whatever you have to say to get him over here."

"What are you thinking, Paddy?"

He hadn't been here for Nathan while he was struggling with this problem. But he was here now, and he'd make sure this was solved, once and for all. "I'll talk to the FBI office in Chicago. We're going to nail that bastard and whoever he's taking orders from. The FBI will handle that part. All you have to do is get him over here tomorrow."

Nathan sat up straighter in the chair. "I can do that, Paddy." He clenched his fists. "Hell, I can't wait to do that."

"Your part consists of getting him here and introducing us. Period," Patrick said sharply. God! The last thing he needed was his brother playing hero from a wheelchair. "I'll take it from there. And don't say anything to Darcy when she comes downstairs."

"Why don't you want Darcy to know what's going on?" Nathan asked.

"I want to get everything set up before I decide where to stash her when the alderman comes by," Patrick answered absently, running scenarios in his head.

"Stash her? Darcy? Are we talking about the same woman?" Nathan shook his head. "She's not going to like that. Darcy isn't a doll you put away on the shelf when you don't want to play with her."

Patrick refocused his attention on his brother. "I know, and I don't care. I want her safe. I don't want her anywhere near the alderman. Especially since she helped his wife get away."

"Okay. You can stash her. But make sure you tell her it's your idea."

"I think she'll figure that out for herself."

WHEN DARCY REACHED Patrick's room, she closed the door. Then she sat on the floor next to her duffel, sorting through the clothes and toiletries she'd packed yesterday.

She couldn't walk out of here with her luggage if she was supposed to be going to Mama's. So she put the absolute necessities into the deep bag she used as a purse. She could buy whatever she needed when she reached her next destination.

Cat meowed outside the door to Patrick's room, and her hands stilled. Oh, God. She wouldn't be able to take Cat.

Rising to her knees, she opened the door a crack. The big black cat slipped inside and rubbed against her leg. Darcy dropped to the floor, scooped him into her lap and began to weep.

She had to leave him behind. Tears fell onto his back, the moisture making his black fur glisten. He licked her hand, and she closed her eyes as she swallowed the sobs.

"I'm going to miss you," she whispered, rubbing her face over the top of his head. "But you'll like it here with Nathan and Patrick. Heck, you were sleeping with Nathan last night."

While she slept with Patrick.

Tears pouring down her cheeks, she rocked the cat back and forth until he finally freed himself.

She let him go and watched as he roamed Patrick's room, sniffing, then jumped on the bed.

Patrick wouldn't toss Cat out the door. He'd take care of him. He knew how much Cat meant to her.

Swallowing the lump in her throat, she repacked her duffel bag, then pushed it into a corner. If it was out of the way, it would take Patrick longer to realize she was gone.

To St. Louis.

She'd researched a number of cities over the past three years and decided that would be her next destination.

It had a downtown area and suburbs that sprawled in every direction. Lots of small neighborhoods. She'd find another one like Wildwood and burrow in. And once she figured out how Tim had found her, she'd know what not to do the next time.

Taking a deep breath, she sat down on the bed and opened Patrick's computer. Entered "Darcy Gordon" into Google and watched as a number of entries popped up on the screen.

Most of them were clearly not her. There were a few Facebook profiles, a LinkedIn profile, a soccer player. A university student. But towards the bottom of the first page, she found a link to the Mama's Place website.

Her heart began thudding as she opened it. She clicked on each page and read it carefully. Nowhere was her name mentioned.

The last page was Private Parties. It explained the packages the restaurant offered for private events. There were photos, and one of them was from Frankie's engagement party.

Darcy's face took up one corner of the photo. Her hair was shorter than when she'd fled. It was auburn instead of blond. But anyone who'd known her well would recognize her.

How had Tim gotten her name, though?

Through the gang. She shivered as she realized what must have happened. The gang trafficked in stolen identities. Tim must have pressured them for a list of names they'd sold around the time she disappeared. Tracked down all of them until he found her.

She slumped against the headboard and stared at the photo for a long time. She'd been so careful. No Facebook, no smart phone, no email account, not even a computer in her apartment. She'd thought she was doing everything right.

One photo on the Mama's Place website. That's all it had taken for Tim to find her.

She wasn't sure how long she sat on the bed, staring at the computer screen. But when she heard a soft knock on the door, she flinched. Forced her shoulders to relax. "Come in."

Patrick walked in and sat down on the bed. "Find anything?"

She turned the computer and showed him the picture. "I'm assuming he got my name somehow. Once he did that, he had me."

"Damn it." Patrick stared at the screen. "Who does our website?"

"It doesn't matter. Whoever it was had no idea I was trying to hide. It's not their fault."

"I have to tell you some things," she said quietly. She owed it to Patrick to tell him everything. He needed to know enough to protect himself and Mama's employees.

"Okay. Hold on a minute." He stood at the top of the stairs. "Hey, Nate," he called down. "I'll be up here with Darcy for longer than I thought. Go ahead and make that phone call. Yell if you need anything. I'll leave the door open."

Darcy heard Nathan's laugh. "I need you to close the door if there's something you don't want me to hear," he called back.

"Get your mind out of the gutter, bro. Darcy needs to talk to me."

"Yeah, yeah. The oldest excuse in the book."

Darcy touched his face as he sat on the bed. "You and Nathan both seem happier today."

"Why wouldn't I be?" he said. "I've got you in my house every day, in my bed every night."

"That's good," she managed to say, although her throat was thick.

"And Nate and I worked out some of our problems."

She swallowed. "I'm glad, Patrick."

"Restaurant business. Family stuff." He picked up her hand and studied her fingers. "So what things do you need to tell me?"

She wanted to lean into him, to soak up his heat, but she didn't dare. So she straightened her spine. Took a deep breath, let it out slowly. Tried to calm her shaking hands. "My ex-husband's name is Timothy Reynolds."

Patrick whirled to face her, but he didn't say anything.

"He was a police officer in Milwaukee. We got married six years ago. I was right out of college, working as a nurse, and my mother had just died. I was...lost. Alone."

His hand tightened around hers. "Go on."

His voice was grim. Hard. Instead of looking at him, she focused on their joined hands. "The abuse was like every other story you've heard, I guess. Started slowly, built up. I called the police once, but Tim was one of theirs. Nothing happened, and the beatings got worse. I didn't call them again."

Patrick started to say something, and she put her hand over his mouth. "Let me finish before I chicken out, okay?"

She cleared her throat. "He started to buy things. Expensive stuff we couldn't afford. I asked him about it, and he told me to mind my own business. Then I found a program on his computer. He was running a business, so he kept records. Detailed ones." She closed her eyes, remembering the shock.

"He was working with a street gang. Collecting protection money from local businesses. Protecting drug dealers. He thought I was too stupid or too intimidated to break into his computer, but I was desperate. I dug deeper, and realized that he was skimming money from the gang and socking it away."

"What gang?" he asked, his voice flat.

"The King Cobras."

"What did you do, Darcy?" His voice was low. Expressionless.

"I put all the information from his books on a flash drive. Instead of going to work one day, I went to a shelter. Then I called the state police. Told them exactly where to find all the records, but I didn't tell them about the skimming. Which was really stupid, because if I had, Tim probably would have gone to jail for a lot longer. But I wasn't thinking straight."

"Then what?"

"He was arrested. Tried. Sentenced to eight years in jail. I had my lawyer contact him. I told him I had copies of the evidence of the skimming. I said that if he didn't agree to an uncontested divorce, I'd send that information to the gang. So he gave me the divorce. It was only after I got a new identity and left Milwaukee that I realized I'd made a mistake. By keeping the skimming records, I'd given Tim a reason to come after me. Although, truthfully, he probably would have, anyway. He doesn't like to lose."

"Why didn't you go to the police when you figured that out?"

"Because I knew I'd get into a lot of trouble."

"If he's in prison, how could he be the one that broke into your house?"

"He was released three months ago—crowded prison, time off for good behavior."

Patrick's hand tightened on hers. His eyes were blue ice. "And he wants the evidence."

PATRICK WANTED TO sweep Darcy into his arms and hold her close. Keep her safe. Protected.

He wanted to shake her until her teeth rattled.

"Yes," she said quietly. "He wants what's on the flash drive."

"If you had told me this right away, we could have caught the guy," he said, trying not to clench his teeth. "We would have gotten a picture. Had the cops looking for him."

"Maybe, maybe not," she retorted. "He was a cop, too. He knows all the tricks."

"Give me some credit, Darcy. I know a few, too."

She stared at the floor and rubbed her toe over a bare spot on the faded carpet. "I'm sorry. Maybe I should have told you. But I couldn't. I wanted you to be safe. And I didn't want you to see me as a victim. Someone weak."

Some of the anger faded. "You're not a victim, Darcy. You're one of the strongest people I know. To escape from your husband, protect yourself the way you did—no weak victim could have done that." He gripped her hand harder as the ball of ice in his chest grew and grew. "Did you think you couldn't trust me?"

"No! I was trying to protect you."

"*You* were trying to protect *me?* That's insane."

"And I wanted to keep you safe from my ex," she said quietly. Too quietly. "I couldn't tell you about Tim. If you didn't know about him, you wouldn't go after him." She rubbed her hands along her thighs. "Until we…got involved, Tim didn't care about you. He was focused on me."

He jumped up from the bed and paced the room. "Darcy,

that is the most asinine thing I've ever heard. Protecting other people, and myself, is my job. It's what I was trained to do. You should have told me as soon as you suspected it was him."

She stood up, too. "I didn't want you to get hurt. Do you have any idea how I'd feel if Tim shot you because you were trying to shield me? I love you, Patrick. Of course I want to protect you."

She stood toe-to-toe with him. By the time she'd finished, she was yelling. But her words stole all the breath in his lungs. "You love me?" he managed to say.

"Of course I do, you idiot. I wouldn't have slept with you if I didn't."

His pulse thundered in his ears. His chest tightened. "Darcy, I…"

"Patrick," Nathan bellowed from the first floor. "Get down here. We have a problem."

He grabbed Darcy's upper arms. "We're not done with this conversation." He kissed her, hard. "And I love you, too."

He ran down the stairs. By the time he reached the living room, Darcy was coming down, as well. He hurried over to Nathan. "What?" he said, more sharply than he should have. Nate didn't know what he'd interrupted.

"Just talked to O'Fallon. He says he's coming over here today. In a couple of hours."

"He can't do that. We don't have the money." Or the wire he was supposed to wear. Or the FBI agents in place.

"He was pissed off. He doesn't want the money. He wants to keep collecting the interest. I told him it was sign off the loan, or I'm going public."

"Did you call Cal?"

"Yeah. I told him what was going on, and he said he'd get here as fast as he could. Might take time to put the money to-gether, though."

"We can deal with that." He pulled out his phone, called the

Chicago FBI office and asked for the supervisor he'd spoken to earlier. "Change of plans. Has to happen today. In a couple of hours."

CHAPTER TWENTY-FOUR

DARCY SANK ONTO the couch in the living room, still shaking. Nathan and Patrick were talking, both of them agitated. Upset. But she couldn't concentrate on what they were saying. Her mind was trying to wrap itself around what she'd just done.

In the middle of a fight with Patrick, she'd blurted out "I love you."

And he'd blurted it back.

Tears prickled in her eyes. Why had she said that? Knowing Patrick loved her made it a thousand times harder to leave.

A tiny voice whispered that she didn't have to leave. She could stay here and let Patrick and the police find Tim. Have a happily ever after.

But Tim wouldn't let that happen. She knew him. She thought of her trashed apartment. He was enraged. Boiling over. He wouldn't listen to reason. He'd shoot first and ask questions later.

Patrick would step in front of a bullet for her.

It was even more important to leave now. She couldn't let him take those risks.

The couch dipped as Patrick sat down beside her and took her hand. "Nate and I have a bit of an emergency. Remember that problem at Mama's I mentioned? Turns out that Theresa's husband, the alderman, is involved in it. He loaned some money to Nate at an exorbitant interest rate. I'll tell you the whole story later, but O'Fallon's coming over here in a couple of hours to get his money, and we have to get everything set up."

"Okay," she said, trying to process what Patrick was telling her.

"I don't want you anywhere near O'Fallon. I don't want him to know you exist. So before he comes over, I'm going to have you leave. Could you go to FreeZone and stay with Frankie for the afternoon?"

"I'm going to Mama's this morning. Remember?" Her heart pounded in her ears, but apparently she'd managed to sound normal.

"Okay. That's okay." He shoved his hand through his hair. "When you're done there, go to FreeZone."

It was all falling into place. Patrick would be too busy with the alderman and whatever scheme he and Nate had concocted. By the time he realized she was gone, she'd be hours away from Chicago.

"All right. Give me her address and I'll use Google Maps to find it."

"I'll have Danny Kopecki follow you over there and make sure no one's on your tail. When we're done, I'll call you."

"Your friend doesn't need to follow me," she said, swallowing again. "It sounds as if you'll need him here. I'll park on the street in front of Mama's, park right at the door to Frankie's place. I'll be fine."

"All right." He cupped her face. "Sorry this is so rushed. But we have to deal with this right now." He kissed her. "After it's over, we'll get some dinner. Just the two of us." He kissed her again, lingered. "We have a lot to talk about."

"Sounds good."

His phone rang, and he grabbed it out of his pocket. He listened for a moment, then said, "Great, Kopecki. When you bring the wire over, could you stick around? We may need some backup."

After he disconnected, she glanced at her watch. "I need to get over to Mama's."

"Okay, I'll walk you out to your car."

"Let me get my purse."

She walked slowly up the stairs. Looked around Patrick's

room one more time. Inhaled his scent lingering in the air. Then straightened her shoulders and picked up her purse.

Patrick was distracted as he walked her out to the car. His phone rang again, and this time it was the FBI. While he talked, she opened her car door and set her purse on the passenger's seat.

Patrick touched the off button on the phone and slid his hands down her arms to her hands. "The police will find your ex. Lock him up. We'll get this thing with the alderman resolved. Then we'll have time to sort things out between us."

"Yes," she whispered. "I can't wait." Her lie made her feel dirty. Unbearably sad.

"Be careful," he said, pulling her close.

"You, too." She raised her head and kissed him, wrapped her arms around his neck and held him tightly. Poured her heart into it.

"Wow," he said, rubbing his finger over her lips. "If this is the way you kiss me when you go on an errand, I'll make sure there are plenty of them."

"Goodbye, Patrick," she said, letting him go and sliding into the car. He smiled and waved as she drove off.

When she turned the corner, she glanced back. Patrick still stood on the street, watching her disappear.

BEFORE SHE LEFT town, Darcy had to retrieve one last thing from her apartment. It wasn't smart to return, but she had no choice. Without her money, she wouldn't be able to survive.

She drove past Mama's, but didn't look at the building. She'd cried too much this morning. Now she had to toughen up.

As she got closer to her apartment, she gripped the steering wheel tighter. Tim wasn't going to be there, she told herself. The apartment and all her belongings were destroyed. He knew she couldn't live there.

But as she pulled to the curb and looked around, her heart battered against her chest. She drew in a deep breath. Everything seemed normal.

Darcy removed the clothes and toiletries from her purse and set them on the backseat. Then she got out of the car, slung the bag over her shoulder and plunged her hand inside. Curled it around her gun.

Tim wasn't around, but if she was wrong, she'd be ready.

As she edged up the back stairs, she stopped and glanced over her shoulder every few moments. Nothing moved in the alley. Birds chirped in the oak tree next door.

Normal.

A the top of the stairs, she saw something white fluttering on her door. When she was close enough to make out what it was, her stomach lurched and she began to back away.

It was a copy of her wedding picture. She and Tim, standing arm in arm, smiling. Happy.

The picture had been torn in half, right down the middle, then taped back together.

One of the knives from her kitchen pinned it to the door.

She needed Patrick.

No. She couldn't call him.

Tim had been watching her. He'd seen her come home with Patrick every evening, and jealousy would fuel his rage. When they were married, he'd constantly accused her of cheating on him.

Finally he had a focus for his fury.

Had he found Nathan's house? Was he also stalking Patrick?

The police knew about him now. They'd be watching for him. She didn't have to tell them about this.

The edges of the picture fluttered in the breeze, but she avoided looking at it as she inserted the key and opened the door. A sour, rancid smell wafted out.

Swallowing hard, she locked the door behind her and picked her way through the slimy mess in the kitchen. When she reached the bedroom, she scooted beneath the bed and ran her hands along the quarter-round until she found the loose piece.

Removing it carefully, she pulled out several packets of money, each in a sealed envelope. When all five were on her chest, she reached in one more time to double check. She should have taken it yesterday, but she hadn't wanted Patrick to think about her running away.

She replaced the quarter-round, edged out from under the bed and stood up. When she heard a noise outside the apartment, she froze then reached for her gun.

It was two mothers with strollers, walking past the front of the house.

She slid the envelopes into her bag and placed the gun on top. Within reach.

Once she had a new address, she'd get the rest of her money from the bank account she'd set up in another name.

She looked around at the wreckage of the apartment where she'd spent almost three years. This hadn't been a home. It had been a place to sleep. A place to hide.

That was all.

Seeing it for the last time didn't make her sad.

The people she was leaving behind, though…that was another story.

She'd miss her landlord, Henry. She'd miss everyone at Mama's—the waitresses, the busboys, the cooks. The bartenders. Nathan and Marco.

Patrick.

Her throat swelled and she choked back the tears. She wanted to stay with him. Love him. Build a life with him. But Tim was out there. Watching and waiting. And sooner or later, he'd come for Patrick.

PATRICK TUGGED ON the tape that held the small transmitter to his chest as he paced the living room. "Where the hell are they?" he muttered. "They were supposed to be here a half hour ago."

Nathan turned from his station at the front window. "A navy blue Taurus just pulled up. I'm betting that's them."

"Thank God."

He opened the door before the two agents could ring the bell. "Come in, for God's sake." As soon as they were inside, he grabbed his laptop and shoved it at them. "The software is loaded and ready to go. The mic works. Local cop set it up. Where do you want to wait?"

"Upstairs," the woman said. "You got the money?"

"Certified check." He patted his shirt pocket. He'd taken the check from Cal, thanked him and sent him back to FreeZone to keep an eye on Darcy.

"We want as much information as you can get out of him before we arrest the guy," she said. "He's part of an ongoing investigation. We need to know who he's working for."

"You told me that already. More than once. I got it, okay?"

The man held up his hands. "Fine. Good. We'll go upstairs."

Patrick gave them a few minutes before testing the wire.

"You hear me okay?"

"Loud and clear," came the answer through his earpiece. "We're set here."

"Then we're just waiting for O'Fallon."

The clock in the kitchen ticked, and the two agents upstairs said something in low voices. Nathan moved his wheelchair control from one position to another, each click loud in the silent house.

Nathan sat up straight. "He just pulled up."

A car door slammed, and Patrick adjusted the wire one more time. Then he waited for the doorbell to ring.

O'Fallon looked smaller somehow. As if he'd shrunk in the past few days. His fringe of red hair seemed duller. His skin grayer.

"Alderman," Patrick said. "Come in."

Before the door closed behind him, O'Fallon said, "Why are you screwing this up, Devereux? We both had a good thing going here. You got your kitchen rehab done, I was making a little money." He moved to Nathan, loomed over him. "Were we pressuring you? Making you pay more than you could afford?"

"Have a seat and we'll talk about it," Patrick said, shoving a chair at him. He sat beside Nathan, and O'Fallon sat across from him. "First of all, who's the 'we'?" he asked.

"Figure of speech," O'Fallon muttered. "My organization. People in my office."

Patrick leaned closer, and the alderman flinched. "Who gives you the money you loan?"

"I don't loan money. Devereux was a special case."

"Why is that?"

"How the hell should I know? Someone came to me, told me to make sure you had a loan. Gave me the money."

Patrick glanced at Nathan. *What the hell?*

His brother shrugged, looking equally baffled.

"Who was this mystery benefactor?"

O'Fallon stared at him with flat eyes.

"We'll find out eventually."

O'Fallon swallowed. His eyes flickered from Patrick to Nathan. "Not smart to look."

"Are you threatening us?" Patrick asked, incredulous.

"Just sayin'. Don't stick your nose where it don't belong."

Patrick stared at him for a long moment. O'Fallon shifted in the chair.

He'd leave it to the Bureau to make sense of this. They knew Chicago politics better than he did. Patrick took the check out of his pocket, pushed it across the table to O'Fallon. The alderman glanced at it, but didn't touch it.

"I'll need a receipt for that check," Patrick added.

"You're kidding me, right?" O'Fallon scowled at him. "That's not how it works in Chicago."

"I'm an accountant, and that's how it works in Detroit. You give someone money to pay a debt, you get a written statement."

"You're not in Detroit anymore, Devereux. We have a code of honor here. My…investor didn't need any receipts. Nathan's word was good."

"So what did you get out of it, O'Fallon?"

"A cut of the interest."

"That's it?"

"A little help when I need favors."

"What kinds of favors?"

"You know." He shrugged. "Someone's deadbeat brother-in-law needs a job, we find one for him. A kid needs to go to college, we find a scholarship. That kind of shit."

"What about the guy who provides the money? What does he get out of it?"

"How the hell should I know? Like I said, this was a special case."

Patrick pushed a piece of paper across the table. "Standard receipt. Sign it. Acknowledge that the amount is correct. That the debt is paid in full."

The alderman stared at the check, then the receipt. His hands tightened on the edge of the table. Patrick thought he was going to refuse and walk out.

He picked up the pen. Hesitated. Then scrawled his name and shoved the receipt back to Patrick.

"Wish I could say it was a pleasure doing business with you," he said as he shoved away from the table and headed for the door. He had it half-open when Patrick heard footsteps on the stairs.

"Edward O'Fallon, you're under arrest for bribery, money laundering and various RICO offenses." The woman pulled O'Fallon's hands behind his back. "You have the right…"

As the agent recited the Miranda notification, O'Fallon's eyes burned into Patrick's. Beneath the hatred, there was fear. Moments later, the FBI agents escorted him out of the house and into their car.

Neither Patrick nor Nathan spoke until the car drove away. Then Nathan slumped in the chair. "Thank God that's over."

"It's not over yet, Nate. This is part of a bigger corruption investigation, and they'll have lots of questions for you. But at least Mama's is safe. And you are, too."

"Thanks, Paddy."

"Let's call Darcy and tell her to come home. We have lots of celebrating to do."

CHAPTER TWENTY-FIVE

DARCY HAD DRIVEN more than a hundred miles and passed Bloomington, Illinois, when she started to get nervous. The same silver car had been behind her for the past hour.

At the next exit, she pulled off. As she slowed on the ramp, the silver sedan flashed past the exit without slowing down. It was an American car, going too fast for her to see the make, with only the driver inside.

Just to be sure, she turned right and pulled into a busy truck stop. Facing her car toward the road, she stayed close to the convenience store and watched for twenty minutes. Other silver cars got off the interstate, but none of them matched the one following her.

Even though her nerves were already twitchy, she opened one of the cans of Red Bull she'd brought and drank it down. Three more hours to St. Louis. She couldn't afford to let her attention drift.

Before she got back on the interstate, she glanced at the phone on the seat next to her. No missed calls. Patrick hadn't yet realized she was gone.

She accelerated onto the ramp and kept driving. Endless acres of farmland unrolled in front of her, most of them a plowed-under sea of black mud. Occasionally she passed a field with dried, broken-off cornstalks sticking out of the dirt like spears, lonely and abandoned.

She glanced at the phone again. Patrick would call as soon as she found out she hadn't gone to Frankie's place.

She sucked in a breath, fumbled for the phone and turned it off. She should have left it behind. Phones could be tracked via their GPS systems. An FBI agent would know exactly how to do that.

It was a link to Patrick. She couldn't toss it away.

Her hand hovered over the phone. If she turned it back on, Patrick could find her. Follow her to St. Louis.

When her finger settled on the power button, she threw the phone into the backseat. Yes, she missed him. Yes, it felt as if she'd left a piece of herself in Chicago. Yes, she'd do just about anything to turn the car around and go back to him.

But she couldn't do that.

At least he knew that she loved him.

Switching on the radio, she searched through staticky stations until she found one playing music, then pressed the accelerator harder. She needed to reach St. Louis before dark. Easier to find a motel in the daylight. Running down her mental checklist again, she assured herself that she hadn't overlooked anything.

She'd gone over that list every week for the past three years. She'd always known she'd have to leave Mama's and Chicago.

She just hadn't realized it would feel as if she'd torn her heart out and left it behind.

PATRICK PACED Nathan's living room as he dialed Darcy's cell. He needed to have her back here. He needed to hold her, inhale her scent, know she was safe.

Her phone went directly to voice mail, and he frowned. She knew he'd be calling. She knew she had to leave the phone on. Had she forgotten to charge it?

"I can't get hold of Darcy."

Nathan set down the beer he was drinking. "Frankie makes everyone turn off their cells at FreeZone. Adults, too. Darcy's probably just following orders."

"She should know better," he muttered. "She could have put it on vibrate."

"Call Frankie on the center's land line," Nathan suggested. "Tell her to put Darcy on the phone."

"You have the number?"

Nathan dug into the bag attached to his wheelchair, palmed his phone and looked it up. "Here it is."

Patrick tapped it in, then listened impatiently as it rang. Finally, Frankie said, "FreeZone. This is Frankie."

"Hey, Bunny, Patrick here. Can you put Darcy on the phone?"

"Darcy?" she said in a puzzled voice. "Why would she be here?"

He felt as if he'd been punched in the chest. For a long moment, he couldn't breathe. Finally he managed, "Has she left already?"

"What are you talking about? Darcy hasn't been here today."

"Not at all?" He clenched his phone so tightly that his hand ached.

"No. Paddy, what's wrong?"

He paced the living room, fear a cold lump in his gut. "The alderman left a few minutes ago in the custody of the FBI. I told Darcy to go to FreeZone and stay with you and Cal until he was arrested."

"Which she didn't do." He heard Frankie jump up and shut the door. "What do you think happened, Paddy?"

He blew out a breath. "Either her ex found her, or she ran. I hope to God she's heading away from Chicago."

"What ex? Why would she do that? Nathan told me you guys were, you know, together."

"She's trying to draw her ex away from me."

"Hold it together, Paddy. Cal and I will be there in an hour, as soon as the kids leave. We'll help you find her."

"Thanks, Frankie. I'll need you to stay with Nathan while I go after her."

"Do you know where she might have gone?"

"No, but I can find out. Get here as soon as you can."

He punched the off button and tightened his fingers around the phone. "I can't believe she did this."

"Tell me what's going on," Nathan said. "What did you mean, she's trying to draw her ex away from you?"

Unable to sit still, Patrick gave Nathan the *Cliff's Notes* version of Darcy's story, ending with, "She thinks her ex has found her. She thinks he's going to hurt me. So she took off. To protect me."

"That's whacked."

"Tell me about it. Damn it! I thought she trusted me. She said she lov…" He shoved his hands into his pockets to keep from punching the wall. "I trusted her when she promised to go to Frankie's."

"Calm down. We'll figure this out."

"Don't frigging tell me to calm down! You didn't see what that guy did to her apartment. He destroyed everything. Ground her belongings into dust. She has evidence that can get him sent to prison or killed. You think he's going to ask her nicely to hand it over?"

Nathan positioned his wheelchair in front of Patrick, then grabbed his wrist and yanked him down to eye level. "Listen to me. Go punch a bag if that's what you need to do. Stomp around the house. Then pull your head out of your ass and settle down. We'll figure out how to fix this."

His brother's words were like a splash of ice water to the face. Closing his eyes, Patrick took a deep breath. Then another one. Finally he stood up and stared at the gray, cloudy sky outside the window.

"God, Nate! I'm supposed to know how to deal with this stuff. I was trained to think logically. Even in a crisis."

"Hard to do when someone you love is in trouble."

He didn't even bother to deny Nathan's words. "Yeah. It is."

"Okay. How do we find her?"

"We hope." He loosened his hold on the phone and punched in Kopecki's number. "Hey, Danny," he said when the detective answered. "I need a favor. ASAP. Can you do a GPS search for this cell number? It's turned off now, but I need to know the last place it was." He read off Darcy's number. "Life and death, buddy. Her ex is after her, and she's disappeared."

He listened for a moment, then let out a breath. "Thanks. Talk to you when you get something."

Feeling steadier, Patrick tapped in the number for his boss in Detroit. When Neil answered, he said, "Devereux here. I need to talk to someone in the Milwaukee office. I have some information about one of the gangs there that the Bureau might be able to use. Can you have an agent call me?"

After his boss agreed, Patrick slipped the phone into his pocket.

"What did Kopecki say?" Nathan asked.

"They just got some new software. Can pinpoint her location within ten yards. He's going to run her number and let me know."

"Good thinking to call him."

"I have my moments." Unlike today. He shouldn't have told her to go to Frankie's. He should have asked Danny to take her there. He should have realized she'd be terrified. He should have paid more attention when she told him she needed to protect him.

When she told him her real name.

He should have connected the dots. Not let her out of his sight.

"I can't believe she was so devious," he muttered.

"Really? A woman who escaped from a vicious ex, who hid successfully for three years? Who was smart enough to find evidence of his crimes and use it to blackmail him into a quick divorce? Sounds like you seriously underestimated her."

"Yeah, rub it in."

"As soon as Danny gets a hit, take off. I'll be fine until Frankie and Cal get here."

"You sure?"

"Of course I'm sure. Do I look totally helpless?"

"Actually, yeah, you do."

Nathan grinned and held up his middle finger. "Screw you, buddy."

"Right back at ya." Patrick couldn't believe he was smiling, too. "How did you do that, Nate? Get my head out of my ass and functioning again?"

Nathan shrugged. "Little trick I learned when I was raising three kids. If you laugh at the drama, it's hard for them to take themselves seriously." He grinned again. "Remember that when you and Darcy have kids of your own."

Him and Darcy? Kids of their own? The puzzle pieces settled into place. Fit perfectly. Eased the ache in his chest. "Have to get her back first," Patrick said.

"You will."

Patrick's phone rang. His hand shook as he hit the call button.

"Got something," Kopecki said. "Last time the phone was on, she was thirty-five miles south of Bloomington, Illinois. Probably on I-55."

"Headed toward St. Louis," Patrick said immediately. That was her strategy. Go to another big city. "I'm on my way. Keep checking. Let me know the minute she turns that phone on again."

"You got it. Good luck."

He'd need it.

Darcy rolled to a stop in front of a bland chain motel in a St. Louis suburb. The neighborhood around it was full of cozy houses on tidy, well-cared-for lots.

The kind of neighborhood where kids played soccer on Saturday mornings and got ice cream cones at the Dairy Queen afterward.

For now, it was probably as safe as she could get.

But she sat in her car for a long time, watching. Checking every silver car that passed the motel. No one glanced at her. There was no one who even vaguely resembled Tim.

By the time she picked up the pulled pork sandwich she'd

purchased at the fast food restaurant before pulling into the motel, it was stone-cold. She ate it anyway. It was fuel. Nothing more. It meant she could lock herself into a room and not venture out until it was light again.

Finally, when shadows crept across the ground and the sky was beginning to darken, she checked in and asked for a room on the ground floor. If she needed to get away in a hurry, she didn't want to run down a set of stairs first.

She engaged all the locks, then tested them. She pulled the curtain tightly closed, so that not even a crack of light would show outside. She jammed the chair beneath the doorknob to slow any intruder.

Finally, when she was as secure as she could make herself, she sank onto the bed and stared at the door.

She was being paranoid. She'd watched her rearview mirror for five excruciating hours. The only suspicious thing she'd seen was that silver car, and after she'd gotten rid of it in Bloomington, she hadn't noticed anyone following her.

Tim was probably still in Chicago, waiting for his opportunity to grab her.

She slid one finger over the blank screen of her phone, guilt dripping like acid in her stomach. By now, Patrick would have realized she was gone. He'd be frantic. Wondering if she'd run away, or if Tim had found her.

How could she have been so cruel to leave without telling him anything? Fear had muddled her brain. Made her thoughtless and inconsiderate.

Made a mockery of her "I love you."

Pressing the on button, she waited impatiently for her phone to power up. When her home screen appeared, *twenty missed calls, ten new messages* flashed on her beach scene wallpaper.

She brought up Patrick's name and composed a text—I'm sorry. I'm fine. Will call soon. Then she pressed Send.

Would he believe her when she said she'd call?

Why would he? She'd already lied about going to Mama's. And she'd left him.

Saying it was for his own good sounded pretty lame right now.

Turning the phone off again, she reached into her bag, rooting through the clothes until she touched the cold metal of her gun. She set it on the small table between the two beds and dropped her purse between the bed and the wall.

Another car drove into the motel parking lot, went past her room and parked. Darcy tensed, then told herself to settle down.

It was a motel. People arrived by car. They parked in front of their rooms.

But she let her hand hover over her gun for a long time.

A HALF HOUR LATER, a tinny sound echoed through the quiet room as Darcy dropped an empty Red Bull can in the garbage container. Her hands shook a little and she felt as if she was climbing out of her skin. But she wouldn't fall asleep anytime soon.

Silent images flashed across the television screen, with the close-captioned words scrolling beneath the pictures. She'd know if someone was trying to get into her room. There would be no laugh track from a television show to hide the sounds of someone at her door.

Her fingers drummed on the coarse fabric of the bedspread as she clicked on the remote, looking for something other than sitcom reruns. She wasn't in the mood to laugh.

Something scratched at the door, and she froze. It sounded like the click of a key card missing the slot. She reached for her gun, but her trembling hand knocked it to the floor. It landed with a cannon-loud thud.

The noise stopped.

She retrieved the gun and pointed it at the door, but her hand shook so badly she knew she wouldn't hit anything she aimed for.

Damn Red Bull.

It wasn't only the energy drink.

It was one thing to shoot at a firing range. It was quite another to point the gun at a human being and pull the trigger. Even if it was her ex-husband.

Maybe it wasn't Tim. It could be someone who was trying to get into the wrong room. Someone who'd had a few beers too many.

She waited, heart pounding, mouth dry, body trembling. She didn't hear footsteps.

The noise came again, louder. As if the person trying to get in wasn't bothering to be quiet any longer. She fumbled with the phone, tried to dial 911, but her sweaty fingers slipped off the buttons.

With a loud bang, the door crashed open, knocking the chair over. Tim surged into the room. His head was shaved, his T-shirt tight over bulging muscles. Acne pitted his forehead and cheeks.

Teeth-clenching fury darkened his expression.

"Hello, Beth," he said. "I've missed you. Have you missed me, too?"

CHAPTER TWENTY-SIX

IN SPITE OF THE terror that made her heart race, Darcy pointed the gun at Tim's chest. "Get out. Or I'll shoot you."

He glanced at the gun, momentary surprise on his face. As if he hadn't expected her to fight back. Then he laughed.

"The way your hand is shaking? You won't be able to fire that thing." He took another step into the room and pushed the broken door closed behind him. It hung on two hinges, leaving a gap. A streetlight threw shadows over the dark parking lot. There was no noise—no yelling, no sirens. Apparently, no one had heard Tim kick in her door.

"You want to try me?" she said, bracing the gun with her other hand. The nose of the weapon wobbled back and forth, but she kept it level with his chest. "Take another step, and I'll shoot."

"Bethie! You've grown a spine." He smiled, showing yellowed teeth. The reek of cigarette smoke had followed him into the room. "You're going to be lots more fun than you used to be. But before we get started, give me that flash drive you have."

"You think I'm stupid enough to have it with me? It's in a safe-deposit box, somewhere far away from here." She swallowed, hoping she sounded calm. Confident. "But I'll make you a deal—as long as you leave me alone, it'll stay in the bank. I won't turn it over to the head of the King Cobras in Milwaukee—Aron Phillips, right?"

Anger flared in his eyes. "Give me the flash drive, Beth." He took a step closer, and she tracked him with the gun.

"Stop right now," she said. He was at the end of the bed.

Another step and he could grab her. "How did you find me, anyway?"

"Are you so stupid you didn't figure it out? I put a GPS unit on your car. Just had to stay back and follow you." He took another step. "But we're going to have to wrap this up. The police know where you are. They're probably on their way."

"How do you know that?" Damn the Red Bull. She had to raise one knee and rest the gun on it to keep it steady.

"I still have friends in high places." He smiled, and her skin crawled. "They've been a big help."

Without any warning he lunged toward her. She pulled the trigger.

The noise was deafening in the small room. The acrid smell of gunpowder floated in the air, and Tim stumbled backward.

"Damn." He glanced at the hole in the wall behind him. "Hope they didn't ask for a security deposit, Beth."

She'd practiced shooting until she could hit the target every time. "Get out, Tim. Someone heard that. They're calling the police."

"Then we'd better get this over with."

With no warning, he leaped for her. She got off another shot, but it went wide, as well. Before she could fire again, he had his knee on her forearm, pressing it into the bed. She couldn't turn her hand enough to point the gun at him.

He fastened his powerful fingers around her neck. "Tell me where it is."

"In the bank."

"You're lying." He tightened his grip, and she gulped in air. "Try again."

"In the bank."

"Beth, you know what happens when you lie." He let her go and backhanded her. Her head hit the headboard and bounced forward. Dazed, her ears ringing, her face throbbing, she struggled to free her arm. He pressed down harder and squeezed her neck again.

"I know you have it with you. So if you don't tell me, I'll

just kill you. Then I won't have to worry about you contacting Phillips."

He was going to kill her anyway. Fury danced in his eyes, reddened his face. He began to choke her, and she gasped for breath. Her vision grayed as she punched at his face.

She jammed the heel of her hand into his nose. When he flinched, the elbow holding her down shifted, freeing her. As blood poured down Tim's face, she turned the gun and fired.

PATRICK HEARD TWO gunshots as he pulled into the motel parking lot, tires squealing. Darcy's car was parked several spots down from a room whose door was hanging off the hinges. When he heard a third shot, he threw his SUV into Park and leaped out.

Pulling his gun from its holster as he ran, he kicked the door open.

Darcy was sprawled on the bed, a man on top of her. They were both scrabbling for a gun lying next to her.

"Hands in the air," Patrick yelled.

The guy's hand closed around the gun, and Patrick grabbed his collar and pulled him off Darcy. Kicked the gun out of his hand. Punched him. Once to the cheek. Hard. Another to the jaw. Even harder.

The guy's head snapped back, but he continued to struggle. Patrick kept punching until the man's head lolled on his neck and he became dead weight, dropping to the floor. Blood streamed from the dirtbag's nose and a gash in his side, but neither wound looked life-threatening.

Rolling him onto his stomach, Patrick pulled a pair of flexcuffs tight around his wrists, then leaped over him to Darcy.

Blood spattered her chest. Her face and neck were red and bruised, and she was pulling herself to a sitting position.

"Darcy!" He slid an arm around her and lifted. After he'd settled her against the headboard, he ran his hands over her sides, her legs, her abdomen. "You're bleeding. Where are you hurt?"

"Patrick." Her dazed expression faded, and she stared at him as if he was a mirage. "What… How did you get here?"

"In a minute. First I need to know if you're okay. Where are you bleeding?"

"His blood. Broke his nose, I think." She touched her cheek. Winced.

"You sure?"

"Yeah." She brushed her fingers over his face. "You're here. I thought I'd never see you again."

"So did I! Why did you run away, you idiot? If I hadn't broken the speed limit all the way down here, that asshole would have killed you."

"I'm sorry." She reached for him, let her hand fall to her lap. "But I did what I thought I had to do."

"You said you loved me. But you didn't trust me."

"Of course I trusted you."

"Just not enough."

The sound of sirens grew closer. Heavy vehicles rumbled on the street in front of the motel. "We'll talk about this later." He put his hand on her cheek, caressed her skin. He should be angry. Furious. And he was. But he was so damn glad to see her.

"How did you find me?" she asked in a small voice.

"Pinged your phone."

She frowned. "But it was off."

"Not until you were already on I-55. When I realized you were heading toward St. Louis, I followed you. You turned it on again when you got to this motel. Just for a moment, but it was enough to pinpoint your location." Thank God he'd told the FBI what was going on. They were sending the local cops.

She swung her feet over the edge of the bed and swayed a little. Her face was pale around the ugly bruise, and red fingerprints circled her neck. Patrick wrapped his arm around her shoulder to steady her and glared at Reynolds, still unconscious. He wanted to pull him off the floor and punch him a few more times.

She tried to stand, and he tightened his hold. "Paramedics are almost here. Sit still." He glanced at the gun on the bedspread. "How did you get the gun away from him?"

"It's mine."

"Yours? Where did you get it?"

"I've always had it. In my purse."

"You have a permit?"

"Of course I don't."

"You've been carrying an illegal gun around with you?" he asked, incredulous.

"Yes. Good thing, too. If I hadn't had it, he would have killed me."

"Keep your mouth shut about the gun. They'll assume it was his."

"Patrick, I…"

"Not now." Not until he'd calmed down. He didn't want to discuss her illegal gun, her boneheaded flight from Chicago, the fact that she could have died.

"He knew police were on their way," Darcy said quietly. "How did he know that?"

"I have no idea." Patrick studied her. "You sure about that?"

"Positive. Hard to forget stuff when someone's trying to kill you."

He tugged her closer until their thighs were touching. Until he could smell her skin and her hair. Reassure himself she was alive.

Doors slammed outside the room, and two local cops ran in, guns drawn. Patrick fumbled in his pocket for his badge. "I'm an FBI agent. The guy you want is on the floor between the beds. Cuffed."

The cops lowered their weapons, but didn't holster them until they saw that Reynolds was still out. Then they pulled him to his feet and studied the bruises on his face. "He get these falling to the floor?" one of them asked.

"Resisting arrest," Patrick answered.

"With this wound?" The cop studied the man sagging from

his grip, then shrugged. "Looks like he's juiced. Probably never felt the injury."

"Probably not. Better search him, though. I didn't get to it."

One cop held Reynolds up and the other patted him down. Found two knives. "Knives and a gun? Your boy was looking for a fight."

"Yeah. Get him out of here."

One paramedic put Reynolds on a gurney and began assessing him. His partner squatted in front of Darcy. When Patrick didn't move, the woman raised an eyebrow. "You want to get out of my way?"

He let Darcy go and slid a foot to the side. Took her hand.

The paramedic rolled her eyes. "I like a sappy love story as much as anyone. I get it. Now get the hell off the bed and let me examine her."

As the paramedic shined a light into Darcy's eyes and studied her reaction, Patrick's phone rang. He glanced at the screen and stepped out of the room to take the call.

"What day is it today?" the paramedic asked her.

"Monday. And it feels as if it's lasted forever."

The woman smiled. "Yeah, I bet it does." She took Darcy's blood pressure once more, then folded the cuff and wrapped the tube around it. "Your blood pressure's a little high."

"Too much Red Bull," Darcy told her.

"Take it easy with that stuff. You'll have a headache for a while, but it'll pass. Tylenol or Advil should take care of it." She reached into her tackle box and pulled out an ice pack. Cracked it to activate it, then handed it to Darcy.

"Keep this on your face. Ten minutes on, ten off. It'll help with the swelling."

"Thank you—" she glanced at the woman's name badge "—Sasha."

"My pleasure."

As she repacked her box, Patrick's voice drifted in from

outside the door. "Damn it, Jackson! I'm not going to do that."
A few moments later, he said, "You are going to regret this."

As he stepped back into the room, he shoved his phone into
his pocket. "You done here?" he asked brusquely.

"Yeah. Sasha says I'm fine."

"Just a headache and some nasty bruises." The paramedic
pointed the blood pressure cuff at him. "You make sure she
takes it easy. Nothing strenuous."

"Don't worry," he said. He looked far too forbidding, and
Darcy wondered why. "She won't be doing much of anything
for a while."

Sasha nodded, picked up her box and walked out of the
room. Patrick stared down at her, and Darcy shifted uncomfortably.

Was he going to turn around and drive back to Chicago,
leaving her behind? He seemed angry enough to do that.

He'd held her against him, even when the paramedic showed
up, but now he was distant.

How could she blame him? She'd lied to him. Run away.
He'd had to drive five hours to save her from Tim. Save her
from her own stupidity.

He stared at her shirt, touched one of the drying blood spat-
ters with his index finger. His hand was warm, even through
the fabric. She wanted to lean into his touch, but he stepped
away.

"You have another shirt somewhere?"

"In my bag. On the other side of the bed."

He dragged the leather satchel up and handed it to her. "Put
on a clean one."

Darcy pulled a long-sleeved, green T-shirt out of her bag,
took off the bloody shirt and dragged the clean one over her
head. Patrick watched her face, his expression grim.

She grabbed her bag and stood up. When her head spun,
she swayed a little and sat back down abruptly.

Patrick glanced at her, then turned away and focused on a
spot on the wall. "Beth Reynolds, you're under arrest for iden-

tity theft and withholding evidence in a federal case. Anything you say can and will be used against you." As he finished the Miranda warning, he slipped handcuffs over her wrists.

The metal was cold against her skin. He closed them carefully, leaving them loose on her wrists. She stared down at her lap dumbly.

She'd committed the crimes. But handcuffs? "You really think I'm going to run away?" She felt so wobbly, she was going to have trouble walking.

"Cuffs are standard in an arrest," he said, his voice terse.

At least he hadn't made them tight. She should be grateful, but all she could do was stare at the cold metal around her wrists.

He helped her stand up then supported her with one hand on her back, the other on her upper arm, and slipped her bag over his shoulder. "Can you walk to the car?"

"Are you going to drag me if I say no?"

His hand tightened on her arm, then he steered her out the door and toward his SUV, parked on an angle in the middle of the pavement. An ambulance idled behind it, the back doors open.

Sasha stepped out and frowned when she saw them. "We're arresting victims now?"

"You do your job, I'll do mine," Patrick answered curtly.

Darcy stared at her cuffed hands as heat rose in her face. She stumbled over a chunk of loose asphalt, and Patrick tightened his hold on her.

She tried to wrench her arm away from him. "You can let me go. I'm not going to take off."

"Damn it, Darcy!" They'd reached his SUV, and he yanked the door open. She started to climb in, but couldn't balance with her hands cuffed in front of her and slipped. Swearing beneath his breath, Patrick lifted her, slid her onto the seat and buckled her seat belt. He slammed the door harder than necessary.

Sasha stood next to the ambulance and watched their progress as he maneuvered around the boxy truck. Darcy stared at her hands, watching the lights from the parking lot reflect off the silver metal around her wrists.

Tension coiled tight in the car as Patrick sped through the quiet streets. Finally, still jittery and becoming more anxious by the moment, Darcy asked, "Where are you taking me?"

He glanced at her out of the corner of her eye. "St. Louis FBI office."

"Are you putting me in jail?"

"Goddamn it!" He slammed his fist on the steering wheel, and the car swerved to the right. "You think I wanted to do this? I was ordered to arrest you. Would you rather I do it, or some stranger?"

"My ex-husband almost killed me tonight," she retorted. "If I hadn't had that false identity, he would have done the job much sooner. Is that why you're arresting me? Because I didn't die a few years ago?"

"You should have turned that evidence over to the authorities. Maybe Reynolds would still be locked up."

"I was scared. Not thinking straight. But I can't go back and change things now." Knowing Patrick was right didn't make it any easier.

Darcy stared at the cuffs on her hands. When she moved her fingers, the chains between the two bracelets jangled quietly. "Are these really necessary? Do you think I'm going to jump out of a moving car?"

"I'll take them off when we get to the office. It's about a half hour away. Relax."

"'Relax'? On my way to the FBI office in handcuffs? Right."

A muscle jumped in his cheek and his hands tightened on the steering wheel. Neither of them spoke until they drove into a garage beneath a skyscraper in the downtown area.

"Can you walk to the elevator?" Patrick asked gruffly. "It's about twenty-five feet away."

"What's the alternative? Crawling?"

"I can carry you."

"I'll walk."

With every step a pain shot through her face. Her head pounded, and her throat was raw. Patrick tried to wrap an arm around her shoulders, but she shook him off. Once in the elevator, he stood too close, but he didn't try to touch her again. Waves of tension poured off him. She wanted to lean against him, wanted to soak up his strength, but she wouldn't let herself do it.

This was her fault. She'd hidden the evidence, she'd bought the stolen identity. And now she'd put Patrick in the terrible position of having to arrest his former lover.

She thought she'd lied to protect him, but her lies had hurt him. Badly.

Finally the door pinged and they stepped into a brightly lit corridor. The door in front of them said Federal Bureau of Investigation.

Patrick steered her inside. Several people glanced at her handcuffs and then at Patrick. He ignored all of them and led her into a small office. Closed the door.

"Don't say a thing," he warned.

In moments, a man dressed in a dark gray suit, wearing a white shirt and a dark blue tie, walked into the room. "Hello, Ms. Reynolds. I'm Special Agent in Charge Leo Jackson." He dropped a folder onto the table and sat down across from her, nodding to Patrick. "Uncuff her."

Darcy massaged her wrists rather than look at either of them. After a few moments, Jackson leaned across the table. "You've withheld valuable information from federal authorities. Information about Timothy Reynolds's gang activities. You also purchased a stolen identity from the King Cobras street gang. You're looking at five to ten years in federal prison."

She lifted her head and stared at the other agent, but didn't speak. Beside her, some of the stiffness left Patrick's shoulders.

"Do you understand what I'm saying, Ms. Reynolds?"

She pressed her lips together. Patrick had warned her not to say anything.

After an uncomfortably long silence, he leaned back in his

chair. "Looks like you have an uncooperative witness, Jackson."

Jackson glared at Patrick. "What did you tell her, Devereux?"

"I Mirandized her. That's it."

"You sure you didn't coach her?"

"You ordered me to arrest her. I did."

"We want some answers, Ms. Reynolds," Jackson demanded.

She wanted to tell him that wasn't her name. That it hadn't been her name for a long time. She felt Patrick's gaze, but she continued to stare at Jackson.

Finally Patrick leaned forward. "I'll tell you how this is going to work, Jackson. Ms. Gordon is willing to give you the information she has on Timothy Reynolds. In exchange for that, you're going to give her immunity from prosecution. If you're unwilling to do that, Ms. Gordon will keep her information. In addition, she'll get hold of an investigative reporter for the *St. Louis Post-Dispatch*. She'll tell him all about the leak in your department. How at least one of your agents is involved with the King Cobras in St. Louis. How that agent was in contact with Timothy Reynolds, supplying information to him. Information used in the execution of a crime."

"You're out of your mind, Devereux. How could she possibly know anything about that?"

"Reynolds told her he was going to have to kill her fast because the police were on their way. He said he had friends in law enforcement here. Only the FBI knew I was following her and what was going on."

"You're bluffing."

Patrick shrugged. "Suit yourself. Ms. Gordon will sit in federal lockup tonight. Maybe tomorrow, too. But the story will be all over the paper." Patrick smiled. "'Abused wife protects herself, FBI arrests her.' Sounds like the kind of story Washington would love to see in the local paper, doesn't it?"

Jackson held his gaze for a long moment. Then he scowled

and straightened the papers he held. "I'll have to check with the U.S. Attorney's office."

"You do that, Jackson."

"Your SAC in Detroit is going to hear about this."

"I'm sure he'll be appalled at what's happened tonight."

Jackson held Patrick's gaze for another long moment, then stormed out of the room.

As soon as he was gone, Darcy said, "Patrick, I…"

He put his index finger on her lips. "Anything you say can and will be used against you."

She frowned. "Is this room…"

"Darcy. Shut up."

They sat silently in the room for more than an hour. Finally, Jackson returned. He didn't look happy.

"Immunity from prosecution. In return, we want the information she has and assistance interpreting it, if necessary. And we want the name of the person who sold her the stolen identity."

"No," she said. "I won't give up the person's name."

"Why not?" Jackson asked.

"That person helps domestic violence victims escape from their abusers. I'm not going to be responsible for putting him or her out of business."

"Ms. Reynolds, the government will provide new identities to abuse victims. The person who sold you that identity is using those women's misery to make money. That's all."

"The answer is still no." She glanced at Patrick. He'd know if she should give up the name. But she wouldn't do it for Jackson.

She turned to stare at the agent. He stared back. Finally he shoved some papers across the table at her.

"Read and sign these. Then tell us where to find the information."

She read the legalese, then glanced at Patrick. When he nodded slightly, she signed. Then she extracted the flash drive from her bag and set it on top of the papers.

"She'll need a receipt for that," Patrick said.

Jackson pushed another paper across the table. Patrick read it. Nodded. Folded it and slid it into his jacket pocket. "Interesting working with you, Jackson."

Then he slid his arm around Darcy, helped her up and led her out the door.

She should be happy. Patrick had stayed with her instead of abandoning her to Jackson. He'd made sure she was off the hook with the FBI for the crimes she'd committed. They were leaving together.

But all her emotions, her feelings, were covered with a layer of ice.

CHAPTER TWENTY-SEVEN

NEITHER OF THEM spoke until they were in the elevator. Then Patrick said carefully, "Do you think you can drive back to Chicago tonight?"

He assumed she was going back there. With him? Some of the ice inside her melted. "If we have to. I'm a little tired, though. I'll need another Red Bull."

"You've had enough of that stuff. We'll stay here tonight."

"I don't want to go back to that motel." The thought of that room, those memories, made her shiver.

His arm tightened around her. "You don't have to. There's a hotel right across the street."

Now that the drama was over, now that she was safe, the buzz from the energy drink dissipated like air out of a balloon. By the time they exited the building to walk across the street, Darcy had to concentrate on putting one foot in front of the other. Patrick's arm was steady around her shoulders. Unwavering.

A chilly wind blew up the street and swirled around her. She'd left her jacket at the motel, and goose bumps rose on her exposed skin. Patrick slid his hand up and down her arm, warming her. She wanted to lean into him, but forced herself to stay upright. She wasn't a victim and wasn't going to act like one.

After crossing the street, he opened another door and they walked into a building that smelled like fresh flowers. A hotel lobby. It took only a minute to register, and she clung to the counter as Patrick passed the clerk his credit card and signed the form.

The elevator ride took moments, and when they stepped into the corridor on the tenth floor, Patrick lifted her into his arms.

"Put me down," she said, struggling. "I'm perfectly capable of walking."

"Maybe I want to carry you," he murmured.

Before she could argue, he stopped in front of a room, inserted the key card and pushed the door open. Out the window, she saw the Arch, St. Louis's signature landmark, spotlights reflecting off its silver surface. Patrick set her down on the bed.

"You want help getting undressed?" he asked.

"I can do it myself."

His expression tightened, but he nodded. "I got a couple of toothbrushes and toothpaste from the clerk. I'll leave them in the bathroom."

She stumbled through preparations for bed, then, still shivering, she crawled beneath the blankets. As she drifted into sleep, she heard Patrick speaking in a low voice. "Yeah, I have her. She's bruised but otherwise okay." There was a pause. "I don't know. I'm not sure what she wants."

SHE WAS FINALLY WARM.

Darcy opened her eyes slowly and looked around. The room was bright with sunlight. She was in a bed, and there was a second bed next to it. A table between them.

A hotel room.

She lifted her head, and pain stabbed her cheek. Groaning, she lay back down. Memories crowded in—her drive from Chicago. The motel in St. Louis.

Tim. Choking her. Slapping her.

Patrick.

Arresting her.

She clutched the blanket and turned over slowly. Patrick was lying next to her, his eyes open. Watching her.

"How do you feel?" he asked.

"Sore." She touched her throbbing face.

He swung out of bed. "You were shivering for too long last

night. I slept with you to warm you up." Wearing his T-shirt and boxers, he padded across the floor and picked up a small vial. He shook two tablets into his hand, and gave her the pills and a glass of water. "Ibuprofen. You should have taken it last night, but I didn't want to wake you."

She sat up and swallowed the pain medication, then gulped the glass of water. Her throat ached, but she hadn't realized how thirsty she was.

"Are you hungry?" he asked.

She thought about it for a moment. "Yeah. I think I am."

"I'll order breakfast."

By the time she'd eaten some pancakes and had drunk two cups of coffee, her head wasn't throbbing as much. And she didn't feel so muddled anymore.

Patrick had watched her eat, but hadn't said much. And why would he?

She'd lied, run away and almost gotten killed. She'd broken trust with him, and he had every right to be angry.

Where did that leave them?

She didn't know. When she'd first met him, she'd had no idea what he was thinking. As she got to know him, she'd grown much better at reading him. At knowing what he was thinking.

Now? It was as if they were strangers again.

Was it just twenty-four hours ago that she'd told him she was going to Mama's and then taken off? She wished she could roll back the clock. Wished she could change everything that had happened between yesterday and today.

But she couldn't. She had to move forward. Figure out what she wanted to do with the rest of her life. She could go back to nursing. Live a normal life, in the open, wherever she chose.

The only life she wanted was with Patrick. And this morning, it sure didn't look like he was interested in that.

She would deal with it, just like she'd dealt with everything in her life. She'd put her head down and go forward.

"Reynolds is in federal custody," Patrick said. "We got him

from the local cops, who arrested him for attempted murder. You didn't do any serious damage when you shot him, so he was patched up and is sitting in the federal lockup."

"He had a GPS unit attached to my car. So he always knew where I was."

"Yeah, the local cops found it."

All her efforts to protect Patrick and Nathan and Marco had been futile. Tim had always known where to find her. He'd known who'd sheltered her after he destroyed her apartment.

Her flight from Chicago had been the most dangerous thing she could do. "What will happen to him?"

"He'll be convicted, and he's going to federal prison for a very long time. If he gets out of the federal lockup, he'll go to prison in Missouri for attempted murder. You won't have to worry about him again."

Darcy swirled her fork in the maple syrup pooled on her plate. Fear had been her constant companion for the past three years. She should feel lighter. Free. Happy.

Instead, she just felt tired.

Sad.

"You arrested me. Walked me out of that motel room in chains. In front of the paramedics and everyone else."

"In chains?" A tiny smile played across his mouth. "For God's sake, Darcy. They were handcuffs."

"I was scared." She chopped the remaining half pancake into tiny bits until there was nothing but syrup-soaked crumbs on the plate. Then she tried to make them smaller. "You could have told me it would be okay. That they would make a deal with me."

"I didn't know that." He leaned across the table. "I was scared, too, Darcy. For more than five hours. All the way to St. Louis, tearing down I-55 at ninety miles an hour—I had no idea if Reynolds had found you. No idea if you were alive or dead. How do you think that made me feel?"

In his shoes, she would have been frantic. Terrified. Out of her mind.

Feeling ashamed, she said, "I guess I deserved to be treated like a criminal. That's what I am."

"Yes. You are. And making you wait to find out what was going on? Maybe I shouldn't have, but I was really angry."

He had a right to be.

"I'm sorry, Patrick. Sorry for everything. For lying to you, for running away. For not trusting you." Tears pricked her eyes, but she refused to let them fall.

He pushed away from the little table, stood up and began pacing. "So what do you want to do? You can become Beth Reynolds again. Go back to Milwaukee and get your nursing job back. Look up your old friends. Resume your old life."

Was that what he wanted? For her to walk away? Her hands began to shake, and the fork she was still holding rattled against the plate.

She dropped it and folded her hands together tightly in her lap. "I don't want to go back to Milwaukee. And I'll never be Beth Reynolds again."

"All right." He shrugged. "Then you can stay here in St. Louis. This is where you were heading, isn't it?"

"Only because it was a big city. And in the opposite direction from Milwaukee."

Patrick didn't look at her as he paced. He was the closed-off man she'd met right after Nathan's accident. She had no clue what he was feeling.

Finally he stopped in front of her. "What *do* you want, Darcy?"

She wanted to be with him. Wanted to go back to Detroit with him. Make a life with him.

But she was afraid to say so. Afraid she'd ruined everything. Afraid to hear him say he was done with her.

He stood in front of her, waiting.

She'd faced Tim and survived. Defeated her tormentor. Surely looking at the man she loved and saying she wanted *him* wasn't that hard.

But it was harder than anything she'd ever done. Because it meant more than anything.

She wanted Patrick to be her future. Wanted to hear him say he wanted the same thing.

If he said he was through with her, that she'd killed his love for her, it would be far worse than anything Tim had done to her.

But she had to take the risk.

Closing her eyes, she took a deep breath, then she let her gaze meet his. "The only thing I want is you, Patrick. I love you. I want to be part of your life. Is that possible? Can you ever forgive me?"

He stopped pacing and stood in front of her, but he didn't touch her. "I thought about this all the way to St. Louis. I was angry."

"I know," she said, drawing a shaky breath. Her heart thundered and her chest was too tight.

"It hurt," he said quietly. "That you didn't think I could protect you."

"That's not what I thought! I was trying to protect *you*."

"Yeah, I got that. But this is what I do, Darcy."

She jumped up and stared out the window at the Arch and its reflection in the brown water of the Mississippi. "Tim made me less than myself," she said quietly. "He diminished me. And I let him. When I got away from him, I swore I'd never be that woman again. That I'd be strong. Capable. Stand up for myself. I guess I never looked at it from your point of view. That taking care of myself, and trying to take care of you, would make *you* feel diminished."

"Maybe we both have some things to learn." He stood close behind her, close enough that she felt the heat from his body, close enough for his scent to wrap around her.

"Yes. I guess we do." Did that mean it wasn't too late? Her palms were sweaty, and she rubbed them against her thighs. "Can we… Are we going to have a chance to work on them?"

"I'd like to," he said. His hands settled on her shoulders and he pulled her against him. "How about you?"

"Yes," she breathed. "I love you, Patrick."

He turned her around. "I love you, too, Darcy." He cupped her face and his thumbs caressed her cheeks. "I think it's going to take a long time to figure things out, though."

She swallowed. "How long?"

"A lifetime. I won't settle for less." He brushed his mouth over hers. "Marry me, Darcy. Please."

"Is it really that easy?" she whispered. "To forgive me like that?"

"I was pretty pissed off. I planned on doing a lot of yelling when I found you. Let you sweat for a while."

"What changed your mind?"

"I heard gunshots as I drove into the motel parking lot. When I ran into the room, Reynolds was trying to shoot you. There was so much blood. I thought I was too late. I thought you were dead. I forgot about being pissed. Forgot about yelling, about making you suffer. I just wanted you to be alive."

He lifted her hand and kissed her palm. "I just wanted you, Darcy. That's all. Nothing else mattered."

"I'm so sorry," she whispered. "I almost turned around a hundred times. You were all I thought about as I drove away."

He leaned forward and kissed her, but his mouth was gentle against hers. Tender. Desire stirred inside her and she wrapped her arms around his neck. Tried to draw him closer.

He eased away. "I know your head still hurts." He touched her bruised cheek, her reddened neck, and his eyes darkened. "Your throat must be sore. No strenuous exercise for a while." He twined his fingers with hers again and kissed the back of her hand. "We have a whole lifetime ahead of us."

"I love the sound of that," she whispered.

He brushed the back of his knuckles against her bruised cheek. "I've been thinking about Chicago. How would you feel about living there?"

"That would be wonderful. But your job is in Detroit."

"I think I can get a transfer. We have a good case against O'Fallon, and I want to work it. I want to find out who he was working for. Most of all, I want to be closer to my family."

"That sounds perfect. And I'm so happy that you've found your family again."

He drew her against him and kissed her once more. "Then let's go home."

THEY ARRIVED IN Chicago five hours later. She'd driven behind him, and when they parked the cars in front of Nathan's house, she ran to Patrick as if it had been days instead of just a few hours. He kissed her, then wrapped an arm around her shoulders and held her against his side.

When they walked into the house, Nathan, Marco, Frankie and Cal were waiting. They all leaped to their feet and crowded around.

Nathan looked at the two of them, still pressed together from chest to thigh. "You couldn't have told us everything was okay?" he demanded.

"I told you we were coming back."

"Not that you were coming back *together,*" Frankie said. She reached out and embraced both of them, then leaned back. She touched Darcy's face. "We need to get some ice on that."

"How come I'm the last one to know anything?" Marco groused.

Darcy heard a plaintive meow, looked up and saw Cat running down the stairs. She swept him into her arms, hugging him tight. "Were you afraid I'd left you forever?" she murmured to him.

When he began to purr, she smoothed his black fur with one hand, holding him close with the other. After he'd licked her hand, he jumped from her arms and strolled into the kitchen.

Patrick wrapped his arm around her shoulder and wiped tears from her face. "All of us missed you," he said.

The room had fallen silent. Darcy struggled to smile as she

looked around at everyone. "I'm sorry," she said quietly. "I hope you can forgive me."

"You think you're the first one in this family to screw up?" Frankie asked. "Join the crowd."

Still holding her, Patrick steered her to the couch. "We'll tell you everything that happened in St. Louis. But first, what's the news on O'Fallon?"

"He's not talking," Nathan said. "He won't rat out the guy he's working for. Kopecki told me he watched your boys interrogate him. Said O'Fallon looked terrified."

"Good. The Bureau will need more agents to work on this case, and that means my transfer to Chicago should go through with no problems."

Frankie leaped at Patrick, enfolding him in a huge hug. Nathan and Marco and Cal began talking at the same time. Frankie let go of Patrick and threw her arms around Darcy.

"Thank you for convincing him to come home. I've been waiting *years* for this."

"It was all Patrick's idea," Darcy said.

"I'll get a bottle of wine to celebrate," Marco offered.

"Make it champagne," Patrick said. "We have more than a move to celebrate. Darcy and I are getting married."

Frankie hugged her again. "Finally I'm getting a sister."

Nathan, Marco and Cal hugged her, too. Her face hurt and her head throbbed, but happiness made her heart swell until she thought it might explode.

Frankie wanted to know when they were getting married. Nathan told Patrick about houses for sale in the neighborhood. Marco recommended caterers for their wedding reception. Which would be at Mama's, he declared. Just like Frankie and Cal's reception would be.

Darcy leaned against Patrick's side, smiling until her face hurt.

So this was what a big family felt like.

Her own home had been quiet. Reserved. Orderly.

She liked the Devereux model much better.

"You okay?" Patrick asked quietly. "We can be a little overwhelming."

"I'm wonderful. Thank you."

"For what?"

"For bringing me home."

* * * * *

REQUEST YOUR FREE BOOKS!
2 FREE NOVELS PLUS 2 FREE GIFTS!

◆ Harlequin®

Super Romance®

Exciting, emotional, unexpected!

HSR11

*What happens when a Texas nanny learns she is
the biological daughter of a prince? Her rancher boss
steps in to help protect her from the paparazzi, but who
can protect her from her attraction to him?*

Read on for an excerpt of
A HOME FOR NOBODY'S PRINCESS
by USA TODAY *bestselling author Leanne Banks.*

Available October 2012

"This is out of control." Benjamin sighed. "Well, damn.
I guess I'm gonna have to be your fiancé."

Coco's jaw dropped. "What?"

"It won't be real," he said quickly, as much for himself
as for her. After the debacle of his relationship with Brooke,
the idea of an engagement nearly gave him hives. "It's just
for the sake of appearances until the insanity dies down.
This way it won't look like you're all alone and ready to have
someone take advantage of you. If someone approaches
you, then they'll have to deal with me, too."

She frowned. "I'm stronger than I seem," she said.

"I know you're strong. After what you went through for
your mom and helping Emma to settle down, I know you're
strong. But it's gotta be damn tiring to feel like you've
always got to be on guard."

Coco sighed and her shoulders slumped. "You're right
about that." She met his gaze with a wince. "Are you sure
you don't mind doing this?"

"It's just for a little while," he said. "You mentioned that
a fiancé would fix things a few minutes ago. I had to run it
through my brain. It seems like the right thing to do."

She gave a slow nod and bit her lip. "Hmm. But it would cut into your dating time."

Benjamin laughed. "That's not a big focus at the moment."

"It would be a huge relief for me," she admitted. "If you're sure you don't mind. And we'll break it off the second you feel inconvenienced."

"No problem," he said. "I'll spread the word. Should be all over the county by lunchtime. No one can know the truth. That's the only way this will work."

Coco took a deep breath and closed her eyes as if preparing to take a jump into deep water. "Okay" she said, and opened her eyes. "Let's do it."

Will Coco be able to carry out the charade?

Find out in Leanne Banks's new novel—
A HOME FOR NOBODY'S PRINCESS.

Available October 2012 from Harlequin® Special Edition®

HARLEQUIN®

SPECIAL EDITION

Life, Love and Family

Sometimes love strikes in the most unexpected circumstances...

Soon-to-be single mom Antonia Wright isn't looking for romance, especially from a cowboy. But when rancher and single father Clayton Traub rents a room at Antonia's boardinghouse, Wright's Way, she isn't prepared for the attraction that instantly sizzles between them or the pain she sees in his big brown eyes. Can Clay and Antonia trust their hearts and build the family they've always dreamed of?

Don't miss

THE MAVERICK'S READY-MADE FAMILY

by Brenda Harlen

Available this October from Harlequin® Special Edition®

www.Harlequin.com

HSE65697

Another heartwarming installment of

⸺ TEXAS TWINS ⸺

Two sets of twins, torn apart by family secrets, find their way home

When big-city cop Grayson Wallace visits an elementary school for career day, he finds his heartstrings unexpectedly tugged by a six-year-old fatherless boy and his widowed mother, Elise Lopez. Now he can't get the struggling Lopezes off his mind. All he can think about is what family means—especially after discovering the identical twin brother he hadn't known he had in Grasslands. Maybe a trip to ranch country is just what he, Elise and little Cory need.

Look-Alike Lawman
by **Glynna Kaye**

Available October 2012
wherever books are sold.

www.LoveInspiredBooks.com

LI87770